Muffins and Mourning Tea

OXFORD TEAROOM MYSTERIES

BOOK FIVE

H.Y. HANNA

CONTENTS

CHAPTER ONE

May Day was always a big event in the Oxford calendar and this year it was extra special—after all, nothing makes a morning as memorable as when it ends in murder.

But even before I had any inkling of what was in store, I already regretted succumbing to my best friend Cassie's enthusiasm to "relive our student days" and join the May morning celebrations—in particular, the tradition of getting up at the crack of dawn to listen to the Magdalen College Choir sing from the top of their great bell tower. It was the kind of thing that seemed like a good idea after a couple of drinks at the pub, but now—as I stumbled around in the dark, struggling to get dressed, at 4:45 a.m.— I just wanted to kick myself for agreeing to the stupid suggestion.

I didn't know why I had been mad enough to agree. I suppose we all liked to secretly believe (especially when we were approaching the big 3-0!) that no matter what our age, we were still the same person inside—that we still had the same energy and zest of our youth. Sadly, I was rapidly discovering that what was "good fun" when you were nineteen, and a carefree student at university, was very different when you were heading into your thirties and running a tearoom business which kept you on your feet all day.

Yes, as I hopped around on one foot, looking for my other sock and cursing under my breath, I was more than happy to concede that I was older and wiser and... better at knowing when to conserve my energies (okay, I got tired a lot more easily). Still, I *had* promised my best friend and I knew that she would never forgive me if I didn't turn up now.

At least I had put my foot down when Cassie— buoyed by a wave of nostalgia—had suggested that we go the whole hog and *really* emulate our student days, including staying up the entire night before May morning. *Stay up the whole night?* I would be struggling to keep my eyes open today as it was. And it would be business as usual at the Little Stables Tearoom—I doubted the tourists who came from far and wide to sample my famous traditional English scones would appreciate me falling asleep in their teacups!

I fumbled my way to the bedroom door, biting off a yelp of pain as I smacked against the side of the dresser. *Ow!* I was going to have a nasty bruise there tomorrow. I really needed to get a lamp for my bedside table. In fact, I needed to get a lot of things for my new cottage but I hadn't had a spare moment since moving in last weekend. I'd barely managed to get the essentials unpacked and the place was still a mess of chaos and cardboard boxes. My fingers finally found the switch by the door and a dim light illuminated the bedroom.

"*Meorrw?*" came a sleepy little voice.

I looked back towards the bed where my grey tabby cat, Muesli, was curled up amongst the rumpled bedding. She blinked at me, gave a delicate yawn, showing the depths of her little pink mouth, then turned and snuggled deeper into the blankets.

I wished I could join her. Instead, I stooped down and found the missing sock and put it on. Then, pausing only long enough to throw on an extra woolly jumper, I left the room and groped my way down the rickety wooden staircase. Downstairs, there were more teetering piles of cardboard boxes threatening to ambush me, as well as random bits of furniture that hadn't found their proper parking spots yet. Somehow, I made it to the front door without stubbing any toes or toppling any boxes, and shrugged into my duffle coat. Then with a last look around, I stepped out into the chilly May morning.

May Day officially marked the first day of spring

in England but the morning was still cold enough that my breath formed clouds of condensation before me as I walked briskly up the towpath by the river. My cottage was situated by Folly Bridge, which spanned the River Thames at the south end of Oxford. I followed the road up from the bridge and turned right through the giant iron gates which led into Christ Church Meadow. This was a good shortcut to get to the High Street, the main boulevard which ran through the centre of Oxford and where most of the May Day celebrations would be concentrated.

The sky was still a hazy indigo blue, but already you could see the pale blush of pink on the eastern horizon. An early morning mist lay low on the ground and, through it, I could see the humped forms of the herd of English Longhorn cattle which grazed on the Meadow. Quickening my steps, I turned off the wide Broad Walk bordering the north side of the meadow and followed the footpath to join Dead Man's Walk—so called because it was the former coffin route to the Jewish cemetery in medieval times. Despite its ghoulish name and the fact that it was supposedly haunted, it was actually one of the prettiest pathways in Oxford, running alongside the ancient stone wall of Merton College, with its rambling roses and clumps of wild daisies bursting through the cracks, and the green of Christ Church Meadow stretching out in the distance.

It was getting lighter now. The faint sounds of

music and laughter drifted through the air, growing louder and clearer with every step I took, and in the distance, silhouetted sharply against the pale dawn sky, was the great bell tower of Magdalen, guarding the eastern entrance to the city. I reached the end of the walk and went through the kissing gates into Rose Lane and then, at last, burst out onto the High Street.

Normally, the wide boulevard would have been empty and silent at this time of the morning, but today there was a carnival atmosphere as crowds of people—tourists, students, and residents alike—milled past, talking and laughing excitedly. They were moving en masse towards the eastern end of the High Street where it joined Magdalen Bridge, just beneath the great tower of Magdalen College. Everybody wanted to find a prime spot at the base of the tower to listen to the choir sing.

I looked around, searching for a sign of Cassie. It was hard to make out faces in the crowd. Everyone was wrapped up in similar dark coats and anoraks, many with hoods or woolly hats to protect their ears against the cold. There seemed to be even more people than I remembered from my student days. The entire street was packed shoulder to shoulder with people shuffling along. I wondered suddenly if we should have come a bit earlier—at this rate, we'd never get a good spot under the tower...

"Gemma!"

I turned around and saw Cassie waving excitedly

as she pushed her way through the crowd towards me. She was looking disgustingly bright-eyed and cheerful for this ungodly hour of the morning. Her luxuriant dark hair was pulled back into a low ponytail and tucked into her hooded anorak, and she had a thick scarf wrapped warmly around her neck. She stopped in front of me and gave a little shiver.

"Brrr! It's chilly, isn't it? I don't remember it being this cold when we did this back in college."

"I don't remember it being this hard to get up at 4:30 a.m. either," I grumbled.

"Oh, you're not going to be a spoilsport, are you, Gemma? I should have known better than to ask you to come—you're such a grouch in the mornings." Cassie grinned.

"If Seth hadn't gone away to that research conference, I would have let him be dragged into this instead of me," I said.

Seth Browning was my other closest friend from college days. Shy, sweet, and studious, Seth had remained in academia and was now a Senior Research Fellow and a tutor at one of the Oxford colleges. Aside from the fact that he had a secret crush on Cassie and would have done anything for her, taking part in an ancient Oxford tradition like this would have been just another day in his life at the University.

"Well, instead, you can tell him all about it when he gets back," said Cassie cheerfully. "Come on! We've got to get going otherwise we'll never get a good spot under the tower!" She turned and plunged back into the crowd.

Hurriedly, I followed her. As I pushed my way through the bodies, trying to keep Cassie in view, I had to admit that I was actually beginning to enjoy myself. The carnival atmosphere and sense of gaiety were infectious, and it was hard not to respond to the exuberant smiles and eager faces around me. Several people had dressed up for the occasion—some obviously in costume for the traditional Morris dancing, which was to be performed in the streets later that morning—and others decked out with garlands of flowers and leaves, as walking trees and wood nymphs and other pagan figures.

I realised suddenly that I had been so busy gawking at the costumes, I had lost sight of Cassie. I peered ahead but couldn't see her in the mass of heads milling in front of me. I hesitated for a moment, then pushed on, deciding to just keep heading for Magdalen Bridge—I was sure I would catch up with her when I got there.

Magdalen Tower loomed up above, sitting at the juncture where the High Street merged onto Magdalen Bridge. The crowd was getting even thicker now, people jostling each other excitedly, talking and laughing, and gazing up avidly at the tower. I followed their gazes and saw movement at the very top—white-robed figures assembling behind the battlements: the choristers taking their places. It was almost 6 a.m. The choir would begin singing soon.

Already, a hushed sense of anticipation was descending upon the crowd.

I looked around for Cassie but couldn't see her. *Perhaps she's moved farther along, out onto the bridge?* I shuffled forwards, joining the crowds packing the width of the bridge, which had been closed to traffic for May morning. Still no sign of Cassie. In fact, I couldn't see much of anything, sandwiched here in the thick of the crowd. *This is a terrible spot*, I thought irritably. A sense of claustrophobia gripped me and I wanted suddenly to get out from the crush of bodies. I turned and spotted a gap next to a group of Japanese tourists and dived through. As I came out on the other side, I found myself at the edge of the crowd, up against the stone balustrade that ran along the side of Magdalen Bridge. There was a bit more space here and I breathed a sigh of relief.

A posh male voice with a deep, plummy accent said next to me: "D'you see Damian anywhere? Can't believe he didn't meet us. Lazy sod must have overslept..."

"It does not matter. We do not need him."

I turned my head to glance at the couple next to me. The boy looked like the typical cliché for an Oxford student, with his tailored Harris tweed blazer, designer jeans, and striped college scarf wrapped around his neck. The only thing that was slightly incongruous was the rainbow-coloured knitted beanie cap on his head, which would have looked more at home on Bob Marley's dreadlocks. I suppose—like many students—it was his "fashion quirk": something to make a statement and display his personality. Especially if you came from a conservative upper-middle-class background, you probably felt the need to assert your fashion individuality even more (I speak from experience here, having spent a large part of my student days in flannel red overalls from Oxfam).

It was the girl, however, who had drawn my attention when she spoke—mainly because of her deep husky voice and exotic accent: a sort of breathy, throaty intonation. I couldn't quite work out what it was—not German, not French... Russian? She certainly had a Slavic look about her, with her high cheek bones, defined jawline, and deep-set, almond-shaped eyes beneath dark arching eyebrows that contrasted sharply with her pale skin. Her hair was long and blonde, loosely plaited over one shoulder, with wisps escaping around her forehead, and her eyes were a clear grey, fringed by thick lashes. She was stunningly beautiful and could easily have graced any fashion show in Paris or Milan. The only thing which marred her looks was her bored, cynical expression and her air of weary contempt. I wondered why she had bothered to come this morning if she was so apathetic to it all.

Then I forgot everything else as above me, the bells in Magdalen Tower began to toll—rich, deep, sonorous—the sound clear and carrying in the bright morning air. We all waited, listening, enchanted, as the bells rang out above us.

Then they stopped. There was a beat of silence.

I was surprised at how quiet the crowd had gone. It seemed that even the birds had stopped singing as we all held our breaths, waiting.

Then, in that golden silence, came the sweet sound of voices raised in harmony, drifting down from the tower above. The Magdalen College Choir singing the Latin hymn, *Hymnus Eucharisticus*, as they had done every May morning for the last five hundred years, to herald the arrival of spring. Rich and pure, the voices of the choirboys and student choristers rose and swelled, filling the air and bringing unexpected goosebumps to my skin. Suddenly, I was very glad that I had agreed to come after all. It had been more than eleven years since I had last stood here, underneath this tower, but the magic was the same as that very first time.

The last verse was sung and the last voice died away. There was a soft sigh from the crowd—which burst suddenly into a roar as everyone yelled and whistled and clapped and cheered. People hugged impulsively, waved their arms, tossed things into the air, as a sense of exhilaration swept the crowd.

There was a commotion next to me—the crowd surging around the balustrade, people shouting excitedly as somebody lurched against the side of the stone railing and heaved up over the top. I turned swiftly, just in time to see a body roll over the ledge and go over the other side, followed by the resounding splash of water. I jumped forwards and leaned over the balustrade, smiling to myself as I looked down at the river below.

It seemed that another Oxford May Day tradition was still going strong: each year, students took great delight in jumping off Magdalen Bridge into the River Cherwell below, usually fully clothed—sometimes even in ball gowns and black tie! No matter how many pleas and warnings the authorities issued about the dangers of jumping into such a shallow river, high-spirited students persisted in following this thrilling ritual.

A cheer rose from the crowd now as everyone leaned eagerly over the side of the bridge to applaud the first jumper. I saw something break the surface of the water and recognised the Harris tweed blazer of the boy who had been standing next to me.

Then I frowned. Around me, the crowd began to fall silent as they too realised that something was wrong.

Instead of the usual head bobbing up and the student waving cheerily to the crowd above, the body floated silently, face down in the water.

There was a gasp from next to me and I turned to see the blonde girl with a hand to her mouth, her grey eyes wide and staring. She let out a strangled cry, then turned and pushed her way through the crowds until she reached the end of the bridge and ran down to the bank of the river below.

A man in a neon vest was already there—one of the posse of security guards deployed by the city council to keep the May morning crowds safe—and he was reaching out to pull the motionless body in. The girl thrust him aside, wading into the water to throw her arms around the boy and haul him onto the bank.

Then the air was split by a wrenching scream. Even from the top of the bridge, I could see the ominous red stain spreading across the boy's lower back.

The crowd had gone silent again, although this time it was the hush of foreboding. Into the silence came the girl's voice, choked and sobbing:

"*O bozhe moi!* He is dead! He is dead!"

CHAPTER TWO

"I love trying out your traditional English cakes and buns, and I think we've had all the famous ones, but I don't think I've come across banoffee pie yet—what's that?"

I smiled at the middle-aged American man and his wife. "Oh, it's one of the most popular British desserts. It's basically a sweet pie made with a crumbly biscuit base, covered with a layer of sticky toffee and sliced bananas, then topped with fresh whipped cream and, often, little curls of chocolate shavings on top. It's really decadent and heavenly, especially if you have a sweet tooth."

"Oh my, that sounds absolutely delicious!" exclaimed the American wife. "I think I've got to have a slice of that."

"It sounds a bit too rich for me," said the husband with a laugh. "I think I'll stick to the lemon meringue pie. That's always been one of my favourites."

"And would you like a pot of tea with that? We have a selection of premium loose leaf teas, from the traditional English breakfast to Earl Grey and..." I stifled a yawn and gave them an embarrassed smile. "I'm sorry, excuse me! I had a really early start this morning—"

"Oh! Did you go down to listen to the choir at Magdalen Tower?" asked the American wife. "We were there! Our hotel told us that we just *had* to get up to see it and we were so glad we did. It's apparently one of the biggest May Day celebrations in England."

"Yes, that's right," I agreed. "It's a really unique experience. I went the first time when I was still an undergraduate at Oxford, and my friend and I went back this morning to 'relive our student days'—and I have to say, it was just as special this time around."

"But so awful about that student falling off the bridge and getting killed," said the wife with a shudder. "We weren't close enough to see what happened—we didn't get a spot under the tower—but we heard everyone talking about it in the crowd afterwards and we saw the commotion up ahead. Was it an accident or something?"

I thought for a moment of that still body floating in the water and the ominous red stain spreading slowly across the boy's back. No, that had been no accident. But I didn't want to add to the gossip mill. Until the police released an official statement, the rumours would be spreading like wildfire already.

"Well, I heard that it *wasn't* an accident," said the American husband. "A couple of German tourists we met walking back told us that they were near the bridge and that the boy had jumped into the water himself. And that wasn't all! They said they were sure they saw blood. Seems like the boy could have been stabbed." He shook his head. "Shame we don't know anyone in the police force—could have got the inside scoop on things."

Well, actually—although I wasn't going to admit it out loud—I *did* have an inside track on things: my boyfriend, Devlin O'Connor, was a CID detective and one of the leading investigators in the Oxfordshire police force. I hadn't seen him arrive this morning— the uniformed constables had quickly moved me, along with the rest of the crowd, away from the bridge and closed off that section of the High Street—but I was sure that Devlin would have been the first to be called to the scene.

Aloud, I said, "I think the police are still investigating. They'll probably release a statement on the news this evening."

"Well, I have to say—it's very tragic for the poor boy but this is quite exciting in a way. I almost feel like I'm in one of those British crime dramas we love watching back in the States," said the wife with a laugh. "I half expect to see Inspector Morse or that nice detective from the *Midsomer Murders* walk into this tearoom and start questioning witnesses!"

And they'd have their job cut out for them, I thought dryly, as I completed the couple's order and started making my way back towards the counter. The whole tearoom was buzzing with talk of the boy's death. It seemed like every table was filled with tourists who had been out to the May morning celebrations and everyone was eagerly recounting what they had seen and heard. Snatches of conversation came to me as I walked between the tables and I had to hide a smile at the ludicrous accounts and theories being bandied about.

"He was shot. No doubt about it. Hmm...? No, I didn't hear a gunshot either but it was obviously done with a sniper rifle and a silencer. Probably from the top of the tower..."

"...and these secret college societies, you know, they make their members do the most *dangerous* things..."

"Suicide pact. Definitely suicide pact. Boy probably had depression. I knew a guy once..."

"...and I'm sure he was pushed! Didn't they say he went backwards over the side of the bridge? No? That's what I heard..."

"...I'm telling you, it must have been the girl! The blonde one! She's probably the girlfriend. Yeah, I know she was very upset, but people can fake it, you know..."

I paused by a table of Australian backpackers and

began clearing their empty plates as they talked excitedly around me.

"... I was standing so close to them—right next to the girl—when the choir was singing. I had no idea!" said one guy.

"Did you see him go over, mate?" his friend asked eagerly.

"No, it was only after I heard the cry—"

"Ah! Reckon he said something about his attacker?" a third guy said.

"Could be! I heard someone cry out—sounded like *'Bloody hell, why me?'* or somethin' like that—"

"No, you drongo, that was me," said his friend. "I stepped in some dog poo with my new shoes."

Loud guffaws. "Ha! Ha! Ha! I thought that was a weird thing to say—"

"Well, I heard a weird cry too—something like *'Aagh! NATO joy evict!'*" a fourth guy said.

"Huh? What's that mean?"

He shrugged. "Dunno. I'm just repeating what I heard: *NATO... joy... evict.*"

"Why would the boy say that?"

"It wasn't the boy—it was someone next to him. But it was just before he went over the bridge."

"Was it the blonde girl?" I spoke up.

They all turned to look at me in surprise, aware of my presence for the first time. I flushed slightly. "Sorry—I couldn't help overhearing."

"Hey, no worries," said the first guy with a grin as he lifted his empty plate. "When the grub is this good, you can overhear anything you like. Best blueberry cheesecake I've had in years."

My flush deepened, this time with pleasure. "Thank you—I'm glad you enjoyed it."

The others turned back to the fourth guy. "So he shouted out something to do with NATO, eh? Think it was a political crime?"

"I told you, it wasn't the boy himself. It was somebody next to him," said the fourth guy.

"Not the girl?" I asked again.

He shrugged. "Might have been her. It was a deeper voice, though."

I remembered the girl's husky tones and her throaty accent. That could easily have been mistaken for a masculine voice in the heat of the moment.

The first Australian leaned forwards, his eyes shining. "I reckon it was some kind of government conspiracy. Maybe the boy was a spy!"

I suppressed the urge to roll my eyes and headed back towards the counter, a stack of plates in my arms. When I got there, I found Cassie trying to load a tray with scones, jam, and clotted cream, while also fending off questions from four little old ladies who had just come into the tearoom. I smiled fondly as I saw them. Mabel Cooke, Glenda Bailey, Florence Doyle, and Ethel Webb. Known affectionately as the "Old Biddies", they were the reigning gossip monarchs of the little Cotswolds village of Meadowford-on-Smythe where my tearoom was situated. In particular, they prided themselves on knowing everything that went on—every morsel of rumour, every titbit of scandal—and they were very miffed at having missed out on one of the biggest news sensations of the day.

Mabel Cooke—a formidable woman in her early 80s with a helmet of woolly white hair, a booming voice, and a bossy manner—pursed her lips in annoyance. "If only we had known that there was going to be a murder there, we would have made sure to attend the May Day celebrations," she said, sounding like someone lamenting a missed show at the matinee.

"Yeah—shame they didn't announce it as part of the schedule of events," I said, hiding a smile.

"Cassie was just telling us that you were standing right next to the boy on the bridge!" said Florence Doyle, her plump figure quivering with excitement. "Did you hear him scream in agony, dear?"

"Was there a lot of blood?" asked Glenda Bailey, her pretty wrinkled face pink with excitement—as well as the rouge she applied so lavishly to her cheeks.

Ethel Webb, normally the quietest and gentlest of the group, piped up eagerly: "What about the weapon, dear? What was he stabbed with? I read a book once—when I was still working at the village library—about a lady who was stabbed by a knitting needle. Most creative! I didn't think one could kill anyone with a knitting needle... although I suppose if it was suitably sharpened..." She trailed off thoughtfully.

I looked at them in bewilderment. I could never understand how four little senior ladies, who looked so much like the stereotype of sweet old grannies, could have such a ghoulish appetite for mayhem and murder.

"I didn't really see or hear much of anything," I said. "There was just a commotion next to me and, the next thing I knew, I heard a splash and I realised that someone had gone over the bridge. I thought it was just one of the students following the jumping tradition—until I saw the body floating in the water..." I gave a shrug. "Anyway, we're not even sure if it's murder yet. The police haven't released an official statement."

"Oh, tosh—of course it was murder!" said Mabel, waving her hand impatiently. "When you next speak to that young man of yours, make sure you ask him everything about the case and then come back and tell us immediately!"

I certainly wasn't going to do anything of the kind. Devlin was exasperated enough with the Old Biddies' attempts to muscle in on police investigations in the past. He wouldn't take kindly to them trying to interfere again. Thankfully, the Old Biddies seemed happy to change the subject. They gathered around and beckoned me forwards eagerly.

"Now, dear," said Mabel, lifting up a plastic bag, "we must show you what we've got you for your new cottage."

"Oh, that's really sweet of you," I said, surprised and touched. "You know, you really didn't have to—"

"Well, we saw these at the weekend markets and we knew it would be absolutely *perfect* for your new home," Glenda gushed.

I smiled at her enthusiasm and watched as Florence reached a hand into the plastic bag and drew out something peach-coloured and knitted. My smile faltered.

"Er... that's... that's nice..." I said as I accepted the object into my hands. "Um... where are you supposed to put it?"

"In the toilet, of course!" boomed Mabel.

"Oh... uh... right..." I stared down at the hideous thing I was holding. One end of it was a plastic doll, which vaguely resembled a Barbie (Manic-Grinning Barbie) wearing some kind of lumpy knitted dress with a huge ruffled skirt, in a puke-worthy shade of peach. But what was particularly worrying was that where her legs should have been, there was a stumpy wooden rod instead.

"It's a crocheted doll toilet roll holder!" Ethel burst out proudly. "There, you see? You slide the toilet paper roll over the stick and then her dress comes down around it, to cover it discreetly." She demonstrated with a roll of toilet paper she had helpfully brought along as well.

"All the best toilets have them," declared Mabel.

"And look—you can move her arms too so you can

21

have her in different positions," said Florence helpfully, showing me the doll's full range of creepy poses.

"It's... er... it's lovely," I croaked.

"We were wondering whether to get you two, dear, but you only have one bathroom at the cottage, don't you? Although perhaps you'd like a second one just in case—"

"No, no, one is more than enough. Thank you," I said hastily. "It's very sweet of you all to go to the trouble—"

"We're not finished yet!" said Mabel, reaching into the plastic bag again.

I looked at her in horror, then relaxed slightly as she pulled out a cardboard box and I heard the clink of china. *It must be a set of mugs. Whew.* Okay, that wasn't too bad. After all, you could always do with more mugs around the house, right?

"These are a special limited edition." Ethel beamed. "The lady at the stall said they are so unique, each will be an investment piece."

I opened the box and looked at the lurid red, white, and blue mugs, my heart sinking. It was a set featuring the British Royal Family, with each member's head cut off by bad Photoshop and stuck crooked onto the side of the mug: the Queen, Prince Phillip, Prince Charles, Camilla, Prince William, and Prince Harry, all with their faces set in a rictus grin.

"A cup of tea with the picture of our dear Queen," said Mabel with satisfaction. "There is no better way to start the day!"

I groped for something to say. Now, don't get me wrong—I liked the Royal Family as much as the next person, and I had a great respect and admiration for the Queen—but mornings were hard enough for me without having to cope with her face grinning at me from my breakfast mug.

"These... um... these are really... uh... unique," I said. "In fact, they're so valuable... I'll... um... only save them for special occasions."

"Oh, don't worry, dear—the lady who makes them said she has many more in stock," said Glenda, patting my arm. "We can always get you another set. She even does teapots and milk jugs with them too. Oh, and soup tureens. Would you like one of those for Christmas?"

"NO!" I lowered my voice hastily. "No, thank you. That's really kind of you but... um... I'm all set for Royal Family crockery now."

CHAPTER THREE

It wasn't until well after two o'clock that the rush died down, and Cassie and I had a moment to catch our breaths. With just two tables occupied in the dining area—and both having been served—we grabbed the chance to sit down behind the counter and get a bite to eat.

"Got anything nice planned for this weekend?" asked Cassie with her mouth full as she tucked into a toasted buttered muffin.

"No… Devlin will probably be working late again."

Something in my voice caught her attention and she eyed me sharply. "Everything okay, Gemma?"

I avoided her eyes and looked down at the jam tart I was eating. "Yes, sure… why wouldn't it be?"

She put the muffin down. "Come on, Gemma—you

can't fob me off. Something is bothering you... something to do with Devlin? Have you guys had a fight or something?"

"No, no, nothing like that."

"Well, then?"

I hesitated, feeling a bit silly to voice it out loud. "I don't know... He just seems a bit... distant and preoccupied lately. Like, sometimes we'd be sitting together and he seems miles away... and if I ask him a question, I often have to repeat myself because he didn't hear it the first time. And when I ask him what's wrong, he always says it's nothing—that he's just a bit tired."

Cassie shrugged. "Maybe that *is* all it is. He does have a really tough job with crazy hours, you know."

"I know, I know that," I said quickly. "And I try to be understanding about it. I mean, I've lost count of how many missed dinners and last-minute cancellations I've had to put up with... and we still haven't even taken that weekend away that he promised!" I sighed with irritation. "But I get the feeling that this is about more than his workload—it's something else that he's not telling me."

"You don't think he's upset about you deciding not to live with him and moving into your own place instead?"

"I don't think so... I mean, we talked about it and he seemed fine with my decision. He seemed to understand that I needed my own space and was happy with that. At least, I thought so at the time." I frowned. "Maybe it bothered him more than he let on?"

"Have you tried asking him directly?"

"Yes, but like I said, he always just brushes it off. Says that he's preoccupied with work... if you can believe him."

Cassie raised an eyebrow. "What's that supposed to mean?"

Before I could answer, my phone beeped in my pocket. I pulled it out and glanced at the text message.

"Bad news?" asked Cassie, looking at my face.

I shrugged. "I was sort of expecting it. It's Devlin saying he's going to have to cancel dinner tonight because of the new murder case." I shoved the phone back into my pocket, muttering, "At least this time I know it's true..."

"What do you mean?"

"Nothing," I said, fiddling with my jam tart again.

Cassie gave me a severe look. "Wait a minute, Gemma—you can't make a loaded comment like that and then leave me hanging! What's going on?"

I sat up and said, trying to sound nonchalant, "Well, there are other distractions for a man besides work, aren't there? And you know with his looks, Devlin is very attractive to women."

Cassie's eyes widened. "You mean... you think there's someone else?"

I flinched slightly. Even though the insidious little thought had wormed its way into my mind, it was different hearing it voiced out loud by my friend.

"Wait... Wait..." Cassie caught my arm. "Are you saying you think Devlin might be... having an affair?"

"I don't know!" I burst out. "I just... There's something he's not telling me... and he's definitely not been himself the last couple of weeks."

"Have you seen anything suspicious? What gave you the idea?"

I shifted uncomfortably. "No, there hasn't been anything specific. It's just a feeling..."

"Did you check his phone? Look at his text messages?"

I recoiled from her. "Cass! I'm not going to be that kind of girlfriend, sneakily reading his text messages and stuff! I've always despised women like that!"

Cassie shrugged. "Well, it might put your mind at rest. Or... why don't you just ask him outright?"

I stared at her disbelievingly. "You're not seriously suggesting that I ask Devlin if he's cheating on me?"

"I thought the whole point of a good relationship was that you could talk about anything. If it's bothering you, then you should speak to Devlin about it."

"But I can't talk to him about this! I mean... He'd think I was... I can't! He'd probably get annoyed and think I was being ridiculous or paranoid or something—"

"Well, maybe you are," said Cassie.

I gritted my teeth, wishing now that I had never mentioned it to her. "I'm not imagining it, okay?

Devlin is hiding something. I can feel it. And I can't think why he would need to do that—unless it's another woman."

"I still think—"

My phone rang, cutting Cassie off. I dug it back out of my pocket and my heart skipped a beat as I saw Devlin's name on the screen. I went into the little shop area adjoining the tearoom for some privacy as I took the call.

"Hi, Gemma—did you get my text?"

"Yes, about dinner, you mean?"

"I'm sorry, sweetheart. It's been crazy here today. We had a homicide out at Blackbird Leys last night and then I got called in to the scene at Magdalen Bridge this morning... I'm going to be here all night."

"That's okay—I understand. What's happening with the Magdalen Bridge case?"

"Have the Old Biddies been putting you up to pump me for information again?" asked Devlin wryly.

I gave a sheepish laugh. "Well, yes, they have a bit—but this is just my own curiosity speaking. I was there this morning, you know."

"Yes, I know, and that's the reason I was calling— I wanted to get your account of what happened. You were standing on the bridge near the victim, right? You're a valuable witness."

"Oh." I felt a stab of disappointment. I had thought that Devlin was calling to apologise for having to cancel dinner and to check that I was okay, but this was strictly business, as usual. "Haven't you spoken to any of the other people on the scene?"

"It's been a nightmare, to tell you the truth. By the time they called us in, half the crowd had dispersed and no one had thought to hold them back as witnesses for questioning. I guess it's not really their fault—the security guards were mostly ex-Uniform branch, not CID, and they're not trained for this sort of thing. But it does mean our job is a lot harder now trying to get information."

"What about the boy's girlfriend? She was there, wasn't she?"

"Yes, but I haven't had a chance to speak to her yet. They had to sedate her and they've taken her to the Oxford Infirmary. I'm just about to head over there to question her, actually. There was another boy who rushed onto the riverbank a bit after the girl. Apparently he's the victim's roommate and was supposed to have met up with them earlier. That's what he told the security guard. But he did a runner just before I arrived and the constables are still looking for him."

"A runner? You mean he ran off? Doesn't that make him look guilty?"

"Maybe... although in my experience, people can panic and do stupid things sometimes. Especially if they've had a bad shock—and seeing your friend murdered in front of you would be enough to scare the hell out of anyone."

"So it's definitely murder?"

"Oh yeah." Devlin sounded grim. "No doubt about

that. The boy was stabbed in the back. I haven't had the full autopsy report yet but Jo reckons that the liver and spleen were probably punctured, and the inferior vena cava as well. Massive internal haemorrhage. He would have bled out in minutes."

I shivered. It was a pretty horrible thought. Once again, I wondered how Dr Jo Ling—the pretty Asian forensic pathologist who had just joined the CID team—could do her job. She looked like a fragile China doll and yet spent most of her days elbow-deep in bloody body cavities. It boggled the mind. And she did it all with such bubbly enthusiasm too.

"What was the murder weapon?" I asked.

"You're not going to believe this—it was a barbecue skewer."

"A *what*?"

"Yeah, a sixteen-inch kebab skewer shaped like a sword. You know, one of those novelty items that's often given as a gift. Although this one looked quite old—almost vintage. Very nice quality, with a fake jewelled handle. Sort of a Middle Eastern style. It might be part of a set."

"Do you have any idea where it's from?"

"I've got officers checking the shops around Oxford to see if anyone sells anything like it. But if this is really as old as it looks, it could have been bought somewhere else a long time ago."

"And no fingerprints?"

"No, it's been wiped clean and the killer must have worn gloves."

I shivered again. There was something horribly sinister about the thought of this innocuous kitchen tool being carefully wiped clean of fingerprints, before being used to kill someone.

"What about the victim? Have you found out anything about him? Was he an Oxford student?" I asked.

"Yes, his name was Charles Foxton and he was at Haverton College, just farther up the High Street from Magdalen. He was the son of The Rt. Hon. David Foxton, the financier, who was a bigwig up in the City and a Member of Parliament. Charles was an orphan, actually—his parents were killed in a car accident a few years ago, and he was the only child. He inherited the whole estate. It was being managed by trustees but he was essentially a very rich boy."

"And was he involved in anything? Drugs? Gangs?" I said the last doubtfully, thinking back to the boy I remembered seeing that morning. Somehow, I couldn't imagine a guy who looked so preppy upper-class being involved in gangs and other "rough stuff". He looked more like the stereotype of the British elite, spending his time in posh drinking clubs or going down to Wimbledon or Ascot to watch proceedings from a private box—when his family home wasn't being featured in *Hello* magazine. Still, appearances could be deceptive. And besides, wasn't it well known that the rich often got bored with their privileged lifestyles and craved a bit of risk and excitement?

I realised that Devlin was speaking and hurriedly pulled my mind back to the present.

"It's early days," Devlin was saying. "But so far, nothing's turned up. I've spoken to his college. He seems a pretty typical student. A few loud parties in his room which got shut down by the college porters but that's nothing unusual. Quite a nice chap, actually. Well liked. No disciplinary measures from the college. Second-year linguist, and, according to his tutor, was expected to do quite well in his final exams."

"So basically no enemies, huh?" I shook my head in puzzlement. "The whole thing is bizarre. Why would anyone want to kill him—and in such a public place?"

"Well, that's why I was hoping your account might give me some leads."

"Okay, what do you want to ask me?"

"Just tell me everything from the beginning— everything you can remember—from when you arrived at the bridge and first noticed Foxton and his girlfriend."

I did as he asked, trying to give as many details as I could. I could hear Devlin making notes at the other end.

"Did you hear anything they said?" he asked when I'd finished.

"A couple of words here and there—they seemed to be waiting for someone and complaining about him not showing up. I think they called him

Damian."

"That's the roommate who's done the runner," said Devlin. "Interesting... So they were supposed to meet up with him and he didn't show, eh? I wonder where he was..."

"He could have just got lost in the crowd. It was really packed and very easy to get separated from your friends by mistake—that's what happened to me. I was trying to follow Cassie and I lost sight of her, which is how I ended up on the bridge by myself. This Damian chap can't have been far if he arrived on the riverbank soon after the girl."

"Yes, it would help if we had more eyewitness accounts." Devlin sounded frustrated. "If only we could speak to one of the tourists nearby who might have seen something—"

I gave a chuckle. "Well, if you want helpful tourists, just come down to my tearoom. According to the conversation at every table this morning, everyone saw something or heard something—and you should listen to some of their theories!"

Devlin groaned. "That's what I'm afraid of. People are so suggestible and everyone wants their fifteen minutes of fame. We put out a request for help from the public earlier today and we've been fielding calls ever since from people claiming to have seen everything from a drone shooting a laser beam at the boy to a mermaid stabbing him with a spear in the river. I'm not kidding."

I choked back a laugh.

"Of course, the people who actually saw or heard anything important will probably not come forward and those are the ones we really need to speak to." Devlin sighed. "Anyway, thanks for that, Gemma. I'd better get on now."

I spoke hurriedly, "I know we're not doing dinner but will I see you later? Maybe you could come over after you're finished at the station and we could have drink or a late night snack—"

"Sorry, Gemma, but I'd better not promise anything. I could be here until midnight the way this case is going—I'd hate for you to wait up for me for nothing."

He was right, of course. It all made perfect sense. And yet I couldn't help the niggling sense of unease.

"Devlin... um... You're not upset about me moving into my own place, are you?"

"Upset? No, why should I be?" He sounded genuinely surprised.

"Well, I just thought... maybe..." I trailed off, not quite sure how to continue. I felt so silly even saying the words: "*You've been so distant lately.*" It sounded like something out of a bad daytime TV soap opera!

"I'm really happy you found that cottage," Devlin assured me. "Especially given what a hard time you had looking for somewhere to rent. I think it's practically a miracle finding a place in central Oxford at that price—and it allows pets too! No, it was a real find and you were right to snap it up." He hesitated, then added, "And I totally understand about needing your own space. In fact, I... well, I think you were right about us not moving in together."

"Really? I thought you were really keen for us to live together."

There was a little pause, then Devlin said, "Yes, well... maybe I didn't think things through properly. I think you're right and it's good for us to each have our own space. Living together would probably have been rushing things."

The prickle of unease grew. This was a change of tune! Devlin had been so keen for me to move into his place. It was really at his urging that I had done it and he had seemed genuinely happy to make room for me and Muesli in his home—and his life. Now it felt like he was suddenly trying to put more distance between us again. What had changed?

I remembered what Cassie had said earlier and took a deep breath to ask Devlin directly, but before I could say anything, he cut in:

"Listen, Gemma, I'm sorry but I've got to go. I've got someone waiting for me in the interview room and I've still got to get down to the Oxford Infirmary to interview Foxton's girlfriend."

"Oh, sure... no problems," I stammered. "I... um... I guess I'll see you when I see you."

"I'll give you a call tomorrow," Devlin promised. "Have a good evening and give Muesli a pat for me."

He rang off and I stood staring at my phone. Devlin wasn't the mushy type to indulge in telephone kisses and sugary endearments, but still... I couldn't help feeling that the abrupt goodbye had sounded more like a distant colleague than a loving boyfriend...

CHAPTER FOUR

I was just about to close the tearoom late that afternoon when the front door opened and a middle-aged woman stepped in. She was probably in her late fifties but looked much older, with a thin, careworn face and dark circles under her eyes. Her greying brown hair was tucked into a low bun and she wore no make-up. The only thing glamorous about her was the beautiful handbag she carried, its surface covered in a mosaic pattern of beads and sequins which reminded me of the designs seen on Arabian mosques and palaces. There was something faintly familiar about her and yet I was sure I hadn't met her before.

She came forwards and said hesitantly, "Excuse me... I was wondering—is Dora around?"

I gave her a smile. "Are you a friend of hers? She's in the kitchen. Here, let me take you through."

The woman glanced around the tearoom. "Oh, I didn't want to disturb you..."

"No, it's fine. I'm just closing up for the day, actually."

I flipped the "OPEN" sign to "CLOSED", then ushered the woman through the swinging baize door into the tearoom kitchen: a large comfortable space dominated by a huge wooden table with a faded, scrubbed surface that was usually covered in trays of freshly baked scones and buns. My baking chef, Dora Kempton, was standing at the far end, industriously pushing a rolling pin across a large slab of dough. The late afternoon light that slanted through the kitchen windows highlighted the curve of her cheeks and I was pleased to see that she looked like she had put on some weight.

When I had met Dora, she had been down on her luck and practically fainting from hunger—mainly because of her own stubborn pride and unwillingness to admit that she needed help. It had taken a bit of persuasion for her to accept the position of baker here at the tearoom but it was an arrangement that was working out great so far. Dora's baking was absolutely divine and helped my tearoom maintain its reputation as having the best scones in Oxfordshire. And I quickly learned that beneath her stiff, prickly exterior was a kind and warm-hearted soul— although she was still *very* proud and sensitive to anything that she considered "charity" from anyone.

Now her eyes lit up as she glanced over and saw her friend standing in the kitchen doorway.

"Miriam, how nice to see you!" Dora hurried over, pushing back a wisp of grey hair and leaving a smear of flour on her temple. She turned to me and said with a smile, "This is Miriam Hopkins. She and I used to work as scouts together at Wadsworth College."

I realised why Miriam Hopkins had seemed familiar. I had seen a framed photo on Dora's hall table, showing the two friends in pinafore aprons, standing together in the front quadrangle of Wadsworth College. It must have been taken several years ago when they had been scouts there together.

"Are you still working at Wadsworth?" I asked her.

She shook her head. "No, I transferred to Haverton College a few years ago. But I'm coming up to my retirement soon."

"Well, don't just stand there—sit down," said Dora briskly, waving her friend over to the table. "I've just got to finish this off but I won't be long."

"Would you like a cup of tea?" I asked.

"Oh, please don't bother on my account," said Miriam quickly. "I only came by to ask Dora if she would be free to come with me to see my mother. Mum's in a home, you see," she explained to me. "She's got advanced dementia and... well, they're having some trouble coping with her."

"They don't *want* the trouble, you mean," said

Dora darkly. "That place is a disgrace! They neglect their residents dreadfully and just do the minimum possible."

Miriam looked distressed. "Yes, they don't seem to make much effort. I know Mum can be difficult and she really needs specialised care, but they don't seem to try at all..."

"Is there nowhere else that she could stay?" I asked.

Miriam sighed. "Not really. There *is* one other place—a private home which specialises in seniors with dementia—but it's so expensive and I... well, I just can't afford it."

"Oh... I'm sorry..." I murmured, embarrassed to have asked.

Dora gave a disapproving sniff. "It doesn't help that that son of yours keeps siphoning off money every chance he can."

Miriam stiffened. "It's not Jeremy's fault that he ends up in those scrapes," she said quickly. "He just got mixed up with some people who weren't very good for him and they took advantage of him. He only borrows the money to tide him over—he always promises that he'll pay me back soon."

"And has he yet?" demanded Dora.

Miriam flushed. "Well, not yet... but I know he means to, as soon as he can. He's got a new job over in Ireland."

"In Ireland?" said Dora. "What's he doing there?"

"Some kind of investment scheme," said Miriam

vaguely. "Jeremy didn't really explain. But he said it was a great opportunity and that he stood to make a lot of money from it. Then he could pay me back several times over." She gave a hopeful smile.

Dora snorted. "That's not going to help you with your mother now."

Miriam sighed. "Yes... in fact, the reason I'm going in this evening is because the Matron rang and said she needed to discuss my mother with me. She sounded a bit irritable on the phone." She gave us an agonised look. "I'm worried now that they'll say they can't look after Mum anymore and ask me to move her elsewhere. I don't know what I would do! I can't have her at home—and there's nowhere else nearby that can take her. I've just been worrying about it all day...!"

Her voice broke and she hastily fished in her handbag for a tissue and blew her nose. I looked away, embarrassed, while Dora patted her friend's hand in a gruff fashion.

There was an awkward pause, then I said hastily, "That's a beautiful bag, Miriam. I was admiring it when you came in. Where did you get it?"

"Oh, this..." Miriam looked grateful for the diversion. She patted the handbag and smiled. "I got it at a flea market in London. It's by a Moroccan designer. I love things with a Middle Eastern theme and I collect them whenever I can."

"You should see her house—it looks a bit like something out of the *Arabian Nights*," said Dora with a chuckle. "Sequined cushions, genie lamps, sheer veiled curtains, fake Persian carpets... I told her she could make a fortune hiring it out to movie producers for film sets"

"Maybe I should consider that. If this Home decides that they can't keep Mum anymore, I'm going to have to do something drastic to raise the money for the other place," said Miriam, her face crumpling again.

Dora glanced at me, then said, obviously trying to change the subject, "That student who jumped off Magdalen Bridge this morning—I heard that he was at Haverton?"

Miriam nodded, a flash of grief crossing her face. "Yes, I knew him very well actually. He was one of mine."

"One of yours?" I looked at Miriam in confusion.

Dora gave a small laugh. "One of the students on the staircases Miriam looks after as a scout," she explained to me. "We like to call them 'our' students... and we had our favourites of course. The ones we didn't mind doing a little bit extra for."

I looked at Dora sceptically. Scouts—or "bedders" as they were called at Cambridge—were part of a unique tradition that still remained in place at Oxford and Cambridge Universities. They were basically a sort of housekeeper who looked after the student rooms and kept a motherly eye over the undergraduates. Each scout was in charge of several staircases and would clean each student room, as well as the communal bathrooms and toilets on the staircase. It might seem weird in modern times—and to students at other universities—to think that there was someone who would come daily to empty your bins and once a week to vacuum, dust, and tidy your room (and even, I've heard in some cases, wash up your dirty mugs and help with your laundry!)—but I suppose it was all part of the eccentricities of the Oxford experience.

Scouts also performed an important unofficial role in many cases, providing a nurturing presence for the students—especially the Freshers who might be away from home for the first time in their lives, and feeling lonely and bewildered in their new surroundings. Having a caring, older presence nearby could really help with homesickness. Still, I had a bit of a hard time imagining Dora in a soft, motherly role. I imagined that her students would have been too terrified to leave a speck of dust anywhere for her to find! Miriam Hopkins, on the other hand, looked just the sort of gentle, comforting type to provide a substitute mother figure.

"So the boy who was killed this morning lived on one of your staircases?" I said to Miriam.

She nodded, her face clouding. "He was a lovely boy. Charlie was his name. Charlie Foxton."

"It was Charlie?" Dora looked at her friend in dismay. "Oh, I'm sorry, Miriam—I didn't realise. I know how fond you were of him."

Miriam sighed. "I just can't believe that he's dead.

Such a stupid thing to do—jumping off the bridge like that! I know the students do it on May Day every year but I thought Charlie would have had more sense. The police are always warning students how shallow the water is in the Cherwell and how easy it is to hurt yourself. Oh, it's such a waste! Such a waste!"

I looked at her in surprise. It didn't sound like Miriam realised that Charlie had been murdered. It was strange how gossip worked, some people getting all the information and others remaining completely ignorant. Still, I would have thought that with Miriam working at the same college, she would have heard most of the rumours going around.

"Have the police been to the college?" I asked carefully. "Did they give any more information on exactly what happened?"

"I'm not sure. I had a day off today so I haven't actually been into the college at all. I just happened to hear about the death on the radio as I was driving up to Meadowford this afternoon and I was shocked when I heard Charlie's name."

Ah, that explained it. I hesitated, wondering if I should enlighten her. She was so upset already, I didn't want to share more unpleasant news. Besides, so far, the statements released by the police only mentioned that "a student had died in an incident involving a fall from Magdalen Bridge on May morning". There had been no mention of stabbing or murder. I decided that it was better if I kept the information to myself for now.

Dora made an exasperated noise. "These Oxford students... they're supposed to be the brightest in the land and many of them seem to have no common sense at all! Last year, there was one silly chap who decided to do a backflip as he jumped off the bridge and he struck his head against the side of the balustrade as he was going down. Ended up in Emergency and was lucky he didn't lose his life. The problem with them is that they've had too good a life and think nothing can touch them. It's the arrogance that comes from having too much, too young. They're rich, they're good-looking, they're in one of the world's best universities—"

"Oh, no, Charlie wasn't like that," said Miriam quickly. "I mean, he did come from a very wealthy background—and yes, he did dress like a bit of a fop sometimes—but underneath it all, he was a really nice lad. He was always so polite and treated me so nicely. Sometimes, after I'd finished cleaning his room, he would ask me if I'd like a cup of tea and get me to sit down and have some biscuits with him..." She gave an embarrassed laugh. "I think maybe he was just lonely, although he would never say it. You know he was an orphan—he lost his parents in a car crash a few years ago. I think he felt comfortable with me and didn't have to put on an act, like in front of his friends. I imagine that he might have been worried about being teased by his friends if he'd admitted that he was missing his mother or something like that."

She gave a sad smile. "Charlie was so sweet: he always gave me these little presents at the end of each term—luxury chocolates and perfumes and silk scarves... and last year, he even bought me a bouquet of flowers for Mother's Day! I was too embarrassed to accept, but he said he had no one else to give them to..." Her voice choked up for a moment and she swallowed quickly.

"Charlie had a girlfriend, didn't he?" I asked gently.

Miriam's face darkened. "Yes, a Russian girl, Tanya. She's a student at Haverton as well— although not on one of my staircases. Thank goodness," she added acidly. She glanced at Dora. "Now, *she* would fit your stereotype perfectly. An absolute spoilt princess, that one is. And never a smile on her face! I just don't know what Charlie saw in her. Plenty of nice English girls about."

"Had they been together long?" I asked.

"Well, I'm not sure when they became 'official', as it were, but I think they've been together for nearly a year? At least six months, anyway. It was hard to tell because they seemed to have the most dreadful rows—I used to hear them sometimes when I came to clean Charlie's room. Terrible screaming matches. Well, usually it was the girl screaming at Charlie, saying that they were finished and it was over. But then they would seem to make up again a few days later and the next time I saw them, she'd be sitting on his lap and all over him."

"Some relationships are like that, I guess," I said. "The couple enjoy the drama of fighting and making up."

Miriam compressed her lips. "Well, I don't think it was good for Charlie at all. He really needed some peace and stability in his life, especially with his mother gone, not all them hysterics! I think the girl was a bad influence on him—her and that dreadful Damian."

"Damian?"

"Charlie's roommate. Damian Heath. He and Charlie shared one of the larger suite rooms at the top of the staircase. They each have a bedroom and share a sitting room." Miriam made a face. "Damian is a bad sort. Always getting into trouble. He never looks you in the eye and there's always something a bit... well, *dishonest* about him. I really don't understand why Charlie was friends with him—and they seemed to be such good friends too! Apparently, they met as Freshers in First Week and got on so well that they asked to room together in the second year. But Damian was always getting Charlie involved in some trouble or other. Like the wild parties they had—I'm sure they were all Damian's doing!—and their rooms would be in an absolute state the day afterwards... The cleaning up I had to do..." She shook her head with remembered annoyance, then her expression hardened. "I wouldn't be surprised if Damian had egged Charlie to jump off Magdalen Bridge. It's just the sort of fool thing that boy would do."

Miriam glanced down at her watch suddenly and sprang up with a cry. "Oh! Dora, we'd better get going…"

"I'm done," said Dora, wiping the table. "I just need to wash up—"

"You two go on—I'll clear up here," I said.

"Thank you, dear," said Dora gratefully, taking off her apron. "I'll see you tomorrow then." She gave me a stern look. "And I hope you haven't got any plans for tonight, young lady. You look completely done in. You should go home to rest."

I stifled a yawn. "Oh, don't worry, Dora—I'm going straight home after this and just having an early night. Getting up at dawn this morning has really taken it out of me." I gave a rueful laugh. "I guess I'm not as young as I used to be and just haven't got the stamina anymore. It's sad how much I'm looking forward to getting into bed!"

CHAPTER FIVE

Muesli was waiting at the door for me when I finally got back to my cottage and proceeded to tell me—in loud plaintive *meorrws*—how long she had been waiting, how hungry her little tummy was, and how inconsiderate I was to be so late.

"All right, all right... it's coming," I said as I hurried into the kitchen to prepare her dinner.

The little cat scampered after me and twined herself around my legs as I got her food ready, adding an impatient "*Meorrw!*" every so often to hurry me up. Finally, I set it down and she crouched next to the bowl to eat. The kitchen was soon filled with the sound of dainty munching, coupled with a loud, contented purring.

I stood and watched Muesli for a minute, a smile

on my face, then I wandered out into the sitting room and collapsed on the sagging old couch in the corner. It was a faded, floral two-piece that had come with the cottage and felt like it was missing most of its springs, but honestly, I was so tired at that moment, I could have happily sat down on a fakir's bed of nails.

Tilting my head back, I closed my eyes and gave a huge sigh. Then I opened them again and looked around with appreciation. Yes, the place was an absolute mess with cardboard boxes piled haphazardly everywhere, not to mention the threadbare curtains, cracked walls, and crooked windows... *But it's mine*, I thought with a little thrill of pleasure. This was my very own space, where I could do what I liked, have things my own way, and not have to worry about sharing or fitting in with the whims of others.

And not having my mother popping up constantly, meddling in my life, either, I thought with satisfaction.

The sound of the front doorbell interrupted my thoughts. *Who could that be?* I wasn't expecting visitors. I heaved myself off the couch and went to the door. It swung open and I wondered if I was seeing things. There seemed to be an enormous—and I mean *enormous*—palm tree standing on my doorstep, its spiky fronds splaying in every direction. A minute later, I was sure I was hallucinating because the palm tree spoke with my mother's voice:

"Darling—look what I got for your new home! Isn't it marvellous?"

"Mother?" I said uncertainly.

My mother's head popped out from behind the tree. I realised that it was so big, it obscured most of her body.

"Such a bargain, darling! I just got it at the garden centre this afternoon—they're having a 'Burst Into Spring Sale' at the moment and, as soon as I saw this, I knew it would be perfect for you!"

I stood back in bemusement as my mother marched into the cottage, propelling the enormous potted palm on a portable trolley in front of her.

"Mother, I don't have space for that..." I protested as I shut the door and followed her into the sitting room.

"Oh, once this goes into a corner, you'll hardly notice it. Now... where would be a good spot? Ah! By the window would be perfect."

I watched helplessly as she shoved the gigantic palm tree into a spot by the windows, where it blocked half the light coming into the room.

"What on earth is it?"

My mother turned to me and said enthusiastically, "It's a sago palm, darling, and it's a wonderful houseplant; so easy to care for! It's from an ancient botanical family, you know—dating back to prehistoric times!"

Yeah, and this one looked like it had come straight out of the Jurassic era as well. I'm not joking—it was practically the size of a dinosaur and was bristling all over with spiky leaves, like a giant green porcupine.

"Mother, I wasn't really planning on having any indoor plants," I said. "You know, I was going for a more... uh... minimalist sort of style—"

"Oh, nonsense, darling! Everyone knows that a house isn't a home until you have some indoor plants. They clean the air and absorb all sorts of toxins—and they help to maintain the humidity, so your skin doesn't get too dry. *And* they make you feel happier too! Did you know, I read a report that said researchers at Kansas State University found that patients in hospitals who had plants in their rooms recovered so much faster and needed far less pain medication than those without any indoor greenery. Fancy that!"

"Well, couldn't I have something smaller... like... like a miniature bonsai tree?" I said desperately.

"But that wouldn't be enough to purify the air! They say you need one large plant per 100 square feet." She looked around the cottage. "This is quite a small place but you could probably do with a few more—you can't have too many, anyway. Take a deep breath, darling, breathe, breathe..." my mother instructed me, inhaling and exhaling noisily and waving her arms like a conductor directing an orchestra. "There! Can't you feel how much fresher the air is in here already?"

What I felt like was a pounding headache coming on. Still, I obediently took a few sniffs and agreed that the air seemed refreshed already. My mother nodded her satisfaction and then began going around the cottage, peering into cupboards and running a finger over surfaces to check for dust.

"Really... this place is so dreadfully shabby, Gemma. I can't understand why you would want to move here when you have a perfectly lovely room back home with us in North Oxford."

I sighed. How could you explain that while you were grateful your parents welcomed you back into the bosom of the family home, living in such close quarters with them (especially with someone like my mother) was enough to drive you bananas?

"It'll look a lot better once I've unpacked and tidied the place up, Mother," I assured her. "And I might get some new curtains and a couple of pieces of furniture from the weekend markets in Meadowford. It'll be a really cosy little cottage. You'll see."

"Hmm..." My mother didn't look convinced. Then she brightened. "Oh, I almost forgot—I brought you some soup, darling."

As she took out a thermos flask from a plastic bag and proceeded to pour some home-made chicken soup into a bowl, I realised suddenly that I was starving. Aside from a couple of hastily eaten jam tarts with Cassie earlier that afternoon, I hadn't eaten anything all day. I sat down gratefully in front of the steaming bowl of hot soup and felt much more charitable towards my mother.

"Now, don't forget about the dinner on Wednesday

night," my mother said as she cut up a stick of crusty French bread that she had brought.

"Dinner?" I said, reaching for a chunk of bread.

"Yes, darling, don't you remember? I told you about it last week. Professor Obruchev—he's the world expert on the History of the Russian State. He's published a twelve-volume definitive account of the early nineteenth-century national history of Russia. Such a learned man," my mother gushed. "Your father has been corresponding with him for years and they've even co-authored a few journal articles together. Well, he's coming to visit Oxford for the first time—in fact, he's arriving tomorrow—and I've invited him to dinner on Wednesday. I know he'd love to meet you."

My father, Professor Philip Rose, was an Oxford professor and, ever since I could remember, there had been a steady stream of scholars who came to visit from overseas and were entertained at my parents' house. This promised to be another of those evenings of dry academic conversations at the dining table. Still, I had been so busy lately that I hadn't seen much of my parents and I felt a bit guilty about that.

"Sure, I'll be there," I said. "I might be a bit late, though, as I'll have to come back here first to feed Muesli."

"Oh! Muesli—that reminds me!" My mother got up and went to her handbag. "You haven't forgotten that her first therapy visit is on Monday have you? It's at the Magnolia Court Nursing Home, just on the other side of Magdalen Bridge."

I groaned inwardly. I *had* forgotten about the therapy visit. To be honest, I still wasn't convinced that enrolling Muesli in the Therapy Cats programme was a good idea. Most of the time, my mischievous little feline seemed to do things which *raised* my blood pressure, not soothed it. I was really dreading our first visit and wondered what mayhem Muesli was likely to cause. Still, my mother had been so enthusiastic about volunteering for the programme that I had gone along with things. I did feel a little peeved though. Monday was my one day off a week and it would have been nice just to spend the morning lazing about my new cottage...

"Would you like me to come along with you, dear?"

"Oh, no," I said quickly. "No, I'll be fine. Thanks, Mother." Wrangling my cat was hard enough—I didn't need to add my mother into the mix.

To my relief, she didn't argue and left soon afterwards, wheeling the trolley behind her.

***

I was woken up the next morning by the distant sound of tolling bells, followed by a much closer sound: Muesli scratching at the bedroom door and meowing to be let out. I threw on a dressing gown and followed her downstairs and out to the garden, where I stood, breathing deeply of the fresh morning air. It looked like it was going to be a beautiful day with the sky already a brilliant blue, marred only by a few wisps of white clouds.

On an impulse, I decided to go for a walk before breakfast. The tearoom didn't officially open until 10:30 a.m. and I still had plenty of time. Quickly getting dressed, I left the house and started down the towpath beside the river. Unconsciously, I found myself following the same route as I had done yesterday morning: the wide path along the north side of Christ Church Meadow, up Dead Man's Walk, into Rose Lane, and then finally out onto the High Street. From there, I wandered slowly towards Magdalen Bridge.

As one of the main roads leading into Oxford, Madgalen Bridge and the High Street had been quickly re-opened yesterday, and now everything looked back to normal. Well, almost normal. There were certainly more people than usual congregating around the balustrade where Charlie Foxton had gone off the bridge into the water: tourists and locals coming to gawk and gossip about what had happened. The police had finally given a press conference last night and there was no doubt now that they were treating this case as murder.

Still, you can't really blame people for their curiosity, I thought as I watched the tourists leaning over the side of the bridge and staring at the river below. After all, what was *I* doing here? Why had I come back?

I wandered over to the side of the stone balustrade and peered in my turn over the edge at the murky green water below. The Cherwell was a small tributary which ran under Magdalen Bridge, down past Christ Church Meadow, to join the Thames at the south end of the city. The surface of the river was calm and serene now, but I couldn't help seeing again, in my mind's eye, that body floating lifelessly in the water. Hastily, I jerked my eyes back up and found my gaze drifting to the opposite bank, where several neat blocks of housing lined the side of the river. One of these was a large purpose-built block, with symmetrical balconies and windows, several with pretty window boxes bursting with spring blooms.

Something on the top level caught my eye. I squinted into the distance. There seemed to be some kind of winking, flashing light... After a moment, I gave up trying to work out what it was and turned away. I cast another troubled glance around the bridge, then turned and started walking back up the High Street. If there were any clues as to what had really happened yesterday morning, they were not to be found here.

A couple of hours later, I was cycling down the main street in Meadowford-on-Smythe and pulled up in front of the Little Stables Tearoom.

"Morning!" I said as I breezed into the kitchen and deposited my things on the side table.

Dora looked up anxiously from the large wooden

table. "Oh, Gemma—I've been waiting for you to come in!"

I paused and looked at her in surprise. Her face was strained and her eyes wide with worry.

"Is something the matter?" I asked.

"It's Miriam," Dora said. "The police are arresting her for the May morning murder!"

CHAPTER SIX

"What? Why?" I looked at her in puzzlement.

Dora plucked at her apron nervously. "The police came for her last night. We'd got back from seeing her mum at the nursing home and were just about to have a cup of tea when the detective sergeant turned up on her doorstep. He said they wanted her for questioning—"

"Oh, that's nothing to worry about," I said soothingly. "I'm sure they're questioning everyone who might be connected to the victim. Since Miriam was his scout, it's only natural that the police should want to speak to her."

Dora shook her head vehemently. "No, you don't understand, Gemma—this wasn't just 'helping with enquiries'. I could tell from the way the sergeant was speaking to her. They're treating her as a suspect, not as a witness!"

"But why would they do that? They must have a good reason."

Dora shifted uncomfortably. "They do. The barbecue skewer used to kill Charlie belonged to Miriam."

I stared at her. "What? How can that be?"

Dora threw her hands up. "I don't know! Miriam doesn't know either! That's what we told the sergeant but he just kept badgering her... and we were so shocked to find out that Charlie had been murdered... *Murdered!* Did you know that he had been murdered?" she demanded.

"Y-yes, I did, actually," I admitted. "But I wasn't sure whether to say anything yesterday. The police hadn't announced it officially yet and I didn't want to upset Miriam any more than—"

"We thought it was an accident! Poor Miriam was beside herself... and then she realised it must have been for that party Charlie and Damian were having... although it was really for Tanya's costume and she had given it to the Russian girl and that's when she had last seen it... that's what she told the sergeant—"

"Whoa... whoa..." I held my hand up. "I'm sorry— I'm hopelessly lost now. Can you start from the beginning?"

Dora took a deep breath. "The police questioned Tanya yesterday afternoon and she identified the weapon that was used to stab Charlie as a barbecue skewer that belonged to Miriam."

"But how could she know that?" I asked.

"Because—it's a bit of a long story—Charlie and Tanya decided last week to have a party on Thursday night; that was the night before May morning. It was a fancy dress party and Tanya said she wanted to go as a warrior princess—someone called Xena or something like that—and she wanted a sword to go with her costume. Well, Charlie remembered when he was chatting to Miriam before that she had mentioned collecting things with a Middle Eastern theme, so he asked her if she had anything that Tanya could use as a prop. And Miriam said, yes, she had a set of barbecue skewers she had bought years ago which were designed to look like Arabian swords, with jewelled handles. So she took one into college earlier in the week for Tanya to borrow."

"Okay... so wouldn't Tanya be the last person who had the weapon?"

"Yes, but Tanya says that she changed her mind and decided to not to go as a warrior princess after all. So she didn't need the sword-skewer prop anymore and she left it in Charlie and Damian's sitting room, to return to Miriam. She says she never saw it again after that."

"And Miriam hadn't picked it up?"

"No. Miriam said when she went into Charlie and Damian's room on Thursday morning, she didn't see the skewer there. Both the boys were out so she didn't see them—and in any case, she wouldn't have thought to ask for it, since she didn't know that Tanya had changed her mind about her costume. She just assumed that it was still with Tanya."

"So… it's Tanya's word against hers, really," I said. "The problem is, nobody knows what happened to the skewer after Tanya left it in the boys' room and the police will say that they only have Miriam's word that she didn't take it back. She could have picked it up on Thursday and taken it away—but claimed that she never saw it." Then I had another thought. "How are they sure it's Miriam's? I mean, couldn't it be a skewer that looks like hers?"

"I suppose it could," said Dora doubtfully. "But they're fairly unique. They're vintage. And anyway, the sergeant showed Miriam a picture of the weapon and she agreed that it looked like one of her skewers. He asked to see the rest of the set and she gave them to him—he's taking them back to the station for Forensics to compare to the weapon, but he's pretty sure that they'll match."

I bit my lip. I didn't want to say it to Dora but it didn't look good for her friend. Being linked to the murder weapon was always a bad thing. Still, I dredged up a smile and said as cheerfully as I could:

"Well, there must be a… a misunderstanding or something. I'm sure the police will get to the bottom of it—"

"We can't just wait for the police," said Dora fiercely. "That detective sergeant was *awful* to

Miriam! Treated her like a common criminal! He's never going to give her a fair hearing! And Haverton College have suspended Miriam from her duties in the meantime and there's even a possibility that she might lose her job, as well as her retirement benefits. Oh God, as if poor Miriam isn't having enough troubles already with her son and her mum... This is the worst thing that could happen to her now!" Dora took a step towards me and reached out a hand. "Gemma, I was thinking... Maybe you could help?"

"Me?" I said in surprise. "I don't understand..."

"You could help to find the real killer and prove Miriam's innocence."

I raised my hands, palms up. "Whoa, Dora... I think you're getting confused. That's a job for the police. Or at least a private investigator. I'm not a professional. What you need is a detective—"

"But you're good at getting to the bottom of things," insisted Dora. "In fact, I think you've got an advantage, not being a professional detective. You're just the young woman who runs the local tearoom. People talk to you—they trust you and they let their guard down. Plus, you've got access to the Oxford colleges—you know the world of the University really well and have connections the police don't have."

"That's not really true," I said. "You know Devlin— Detective Inspector O'Connor—used to be at Oxford with me. We were at the same college together. So he has a foot in the door of the University too."

"Yes, but he's a policeman! People are always

suspicious of policemen. They get nervous around them. They won't talk to them the same way they talk to you. Besides, this isn't the first time you've helped with a murder case," Dora added earnestly. "You've done it before. Several times, in fact! The villagers are always talking about it: how you solved that American tourist's murder here in the tearoom... and that girl who was poisoned at the art gallery... and then the murder of Professor Barrow from my old college... and even at the recent village fete, you were the one who found out the truth about Dame Clare's murder at the cat show!"

"Well, I... okay, yes, I did get involved in those cases and dig up some answers, but... but a lot of it was probably luck," I said lamely. "And it wasn't just me. I had a lot of help from—"

"Us!" came four eager old voices.

I turned to see the Old Biddies sticking their heads through the half-open kitchen doorway. I wondered how long they had been there, listening to our conversation.

"Oh yes, Gemma could never have solved all those cases without our help," said Mabel smugly, coming into the kitchen, followed by Glenda, Florence, and Ethel.

I gave them an exasperated look. Actually, I had been going to say that I had a lot of help from the *police,* and from Devlin in particular. The Old Biddies had certainly *tried* to help, but half the time, their efforts just seemed to land me in the worst predicaments—and then abandon me there!

"Of course we'll help your friend clear her name," Mabel said to Dora, rolling her sleeves up briskly. "It's obvious that she has nothing to do with this murder but the police have no idea what they're doing—as usual! We will start an investigation—"

"Wait, hang on," I cut in hastily. "This isn't a game. This is a real murder we're talking about. And the police are the ones who are in the best position to investigate—"

"Pooh! What do the police know?" said Mabel with a contemptuous wave. "I've met that detective sergeant and he is as useless as a chocolate teapot. He couldn't find a pair of knickers in a lingerie store!"

I winced. I didn't particularly like Devlin's cocky young sergeant either but that seemed a bit harsh.

Dora put a hand on my arm and said quietly, "Gemma, I... I wouldn't be asking if it wasn't important. Miriam is my closest friend, and right now she needs someone on her side. I really believe you can help her. Will you at least think about it— please?"

I was moved by Dora's plea. Knowing how proud she was, and how much she hated asking anyone for anything, I realised suddenly how much it cost her to swallow her pride and ask for help like this.

I squeezed her hand. "All right, Dora, I'll try my best. But I don't want to get your hopes up—"

"All we need to do is go to Haverton College and speak to the other students," said Mabel loftily. "They all live together in those dormitory staircases—I'm sure they'll know all the secrets and scandals."

"You can't just walk into a college and start interrogating people," I protested. "That's what I mean. We're not CID and we don't have the authority to question people. We'll be lucky if the college porters don't throw us out!"

"Who said anything about *questioning* people, dear?" said Mabel. "We are just going to have a little chat with them. People love chatting, especially if you ask them about themselves. And they're much more likely to give something away or reveal a clue when you are just chatting with them, than when police are questioning them in a serious manner."

Well, maybe she was right. As I went about my duties for the rest of the morning, I mulled over what Mabel had said. Perhaps it wouldn't hurt to visit Haverton College and try to speak to some of the students there. I was unlikely to get any time today, though—the tearoom seemed to be even busier than usual. I rushed around with Cassie, serving large groups of tourists, many of whom had been enticed by the beautiful spring weather out into the Cotswolds countryside.

Meadowford-on-Smythe, with its winding cobbled lanes and pretty thatched-roof cottages, was one of the most popular destinations for visitors to the area, especially given its proximity to Oxford. It was a short bus ride from the University city centre and, for the foreigners, it was the perfect postcard English village, with its historic pub, lovely village green, and the charming old church with its elegant steeple silhouetted against the rolling Cotswolds hills in the distance. Tourists loved ambling down the village high street, peering into the windows of the antique and craft shops, and then rounding it off with some delicious baking and traditional English tea at my quaint little tearoom.

My business had only been going for about six months, but already the Little Stables Tearoom was building quite a reputation for itself in the area. There had been so many times when I had wondered if I had done the right thing: going against all advice by giving up my high-flying executive job in Sydney to come back to England and start this venture. And as if risking my career and my savings weren't bad enough, I had to deal with a lot of social disapproval as well. As my mother had put it so succinctly at the time: "You didn't go to Oxford University just to become a tea lady!"

Still, I was really pleased to see that my mother had changed her tune since and even seemed proud of what I had achieved. And looking around the dining room now, with its happy hubbub of laughter and conversation, and the contented smiles on people's faces as they tucked into the delicious cakes and scones, I felt a wonderful glow of pride that I had never felt back in my corporate career.

"Don't forget—you're delivering that catering order to the college in Oxford," said Cassie as she came up to me at the counter.

"Oh, my God, I'd completely forgot!" I smacked my forehead.

This was a great coup—our first catering order from an Oxford University institution. The college was holding a special High Tea for their alumni and I had been delighted when the Little Stables Tearoom had been contacted and asked to provide the food. It seemed that word was really spreading about my tearoom and its delectable baking.

"Thank goodness you reminded me. I'll go and load up the car now," I said to Cassie.

"I'd come and give you a hand, but I'd better not leave the dining room," said Cassie, eyeing the full tables around the room.

"Don't worry—I'm sure I'll manage."

I had stopped off in North Oxford on the way into the tearoom that morning and swapped my bicycle for my mother's car, and I loaded it carefully now with trays and boxes of cakes, buns, and delicate finger sandwiches, trying to jostle the food as little as possible. The toasted teacakes with apricot compote smelled absolutely heavenly and the Victoria sponge with luscious fresh strawberries looked so delicious that I had to restrain myself from dabbing a finger into the soft whipped cream to steal a taste.

Parking in central Oxford was always a bit of a nightmare and my heart sank at the thought of finding anywhere near the High Street, but thankfully the college had a few parking spaces reserved for "Trade", off the lane running along the side of the college grounds. A lovely old gentleman, who was the Steward at the college, came and helped me unload the food, then showed me the beautiful Georgian dining room where the High Tea would be served. He had even rustled up several multi-tiered cake platters to display my scones, cakes, and finger sandwiches, and brought out the college's prize silver tea service.

"My goodness, this looks amazing!" I commented, staring in admiration and thinking that it made my offerings at the tearoom look rather drab in comparison.

"Well, people do love the old-fashioned etiquette and traditions, don't they?" said the Steward. "It's part of the charm of the English way of life. And in a place like Oxford, we excel at keeping the old traditions alive!" He beamed at me.

After thanking him for his help, I made my way back out of the college and headed for my car. However, just as I was about to get in, a loud creaking caught my attention. I glanced up. On the opposite side of the lane ran a long stone wall and I realised belatedly that it marked the boundary of the next adjoining college. *That must be Haverton College*, I realised, as I remembered where I was on the High Street. Like many Oxford colleges, Haverton had a main gate leading into the front quadrangle of the college, but also one or more smaller gates leading out of the back or side. The creaking had come from one of these side gates: a heavy wooden door embedded in the stone wall, obviously leading into the back of the college.

It swung open now to reveal a slim figure: a tall blonde girl with exotic good looks and a Louis Vuitton bag slung over her shoulder. Tanya. She stepped through the door, followed by an older bearded man in a tweed jacket and shabby corduroy trousers. As I watched, Tanya said something carelessly to him, then the two of them began walking down the lane, away from me.

I hesitated for a second, then, on an impulse, slammed the car door and darted down the lane after the girl.

CHAPTER SEVEN

"Tanya?"

She swung around. "Yes?"

It was the same deep, husky voice I remembered from the bridge yesterday morning. She was looking at me with surprise, obviously wondering who I was and why I was calling her. I realised belatedly that I hadn't planned this properly. I had no idea what to say, no ready excuse to give.

"Yes?" she said again, impatiently.

The older man rushed forwards. "If you are from newspaper, you will go! She will not speak to you!"

He glowered at me from beneath bushy eyebrows, looking like an angry terrier protecting its mistress. He had a heavy Russian accent—oh yes, there was no doubting *his* accent: he sounded exactly like the

Russian gangsters in all the Hollywood movies—and he was dressed in a dark brown tweed jacket, a matching waistcoat, olive green corduroys, and a faded silk neckcloth tucked into his lapel. He looked slightly ridiculous, almost as if he had stepped out of the pages of a book about nineteenth-century Russian scholars, and I half expected him to pull out a pocket watch to consult the time.

"It is okay, Mikhail," said Tanya, waving her hand. She looked at me curiously. "What do you want?"

"I'm not from the press," I said quickly. "I... I just wanted to say I'm sorry. About your boyfriend, Charlie. I was... um... on the bridge next to you yesterday morning. It must have been... uh... terrible for you."

Her eyes softened for a moment, then the impression disappeared, replaced by a mask of cool indifference. Whatever she might have felt about her boyfriend, she certainly didn't intend to show it in public.

"It was not nice. I do not want to talk about it," she said shortly.

"She does not want to talk about it!" barked Mikhail, still glaring at me.

"Oh, of course, I'm sorry." I hesitated, casting around for another way to continue the conversation. Just as I was thinking I might have to accept defeat and slink away, the Russian girl surprised me by speaking up.

"You say you were on bridge next to us?"

I nodded. "I was standing right beside you and Charlie when the choir was singing, although I got pushed aside afterwards when everyone was cheering and jumping about."

"The same for me also," said the girl. "When they start to cheer, people move around and hug each other, and I was pushed away from Charlie."

I hesitated, then said gently, "I didn't see him go over the side of the bridge. The crowd got so rowdy, I didn't notice anything until I heard the splash. Did you... did you see what happened?"

"No," she said. "It is same for me. The crowd was excited, they push me aside... and then I hear splash. I run to side of bridge and I look down and see his body..." Her mouth twisted at the memory.

"Had he been planning to jump? I know it's a tradition for students to jump off the bridge on May morning so maybe—"

"No, it was not his plan."

"Then why do you think—"

"I do not know!" she burst out. "The police—they ask me same thing! Why? How? What happened? I say, I do not know! I did not see! There is nothing... except that barbecue skewer. The weapon that killed him. Yes, that I can answer. That I know—it is same one that was from Charlie's scout. I tell police: it is to *her* that they must ask questions."

"But Charlie's scout said that she lent the skewer to *you*, for your costume, and it hadn't been returned to her. So you were the last one who—"

She gave me a contemptuous look. "That old woman. She does not tell truth. Charlie is her *malysh*—her baby—and she does not like me. I know, she does not think I am good enough girl for him. And now she wants to put blame on me."

I was slightly taken aback. This was a new slant on Miriam Hopkins that I hadn't considered.

"Have you told the police this?" I asked.

"Yes, I speak to that detective. The handsome one with blue eyes. Detective Inspector O'Connor." She gave a ghost of a smile. "A very interesting man, no? He is not what I expect from English police."

"He is imbecile, like all other English police," growled Mikhail. "They should not be questioning you. They should be speaking to that boy, the roommate. Without a doubt, he is *lzhets*—a dirty liar."

"Damian?" I said quickly. "Do you think he's involved?"

"Of course he is involved," Tanya spat. "He is weasel. He should not have been Charlie's friend."

"They are both same," said Mikhail. "Even Charlie—he was just stupid English boy. I do not understand why you stay with him."

Tanya gave a bitter smile. She seemed to treat the older man like some kind of overprotective guard dog, to be tolerated for his amusing devotion.

"Mikhail does not understand," she said to me. "He is too old and serious; he cares only for his books and his thesis. He does not know what it is like to be young and in love."

The older man bristled. "I know about Romance. We Russians—we have great novels about love. There is no love story greater than Tolstoy's *Anna Karenina*. It is classic! It is pinnacle in history of literature!"

Tanya's eyes were bleak. "Yes, and it also ends in death."

***

My conversation with Tanya and Mikhail had given me a lot to think about but I wasn't sure it was a good idea to share it with Dora, so when I got back to the tearoom, I kept quiet about the chance meeting. In any case, things were busy enough that I soon put aside the mystery of Charlie Foxton's murder and concentrated on serving customers.

But as I was shutting up for the day, the memory of the conversation came back to me and I decided to ring Devlin and see what he thought. As I picked up my phone, I frowned. I hadn't heard from him all day and hadn't he said last night that he would ring? Wasn't that a bit odd? Then I chided myself. We weren't the kind of couple that lived in each other's pockets and I certainly didn't expect Devlin to make a "duty call" every day. Besides, he had probably been stuck in the interview room all day, interrogating witnesses, and hadn't had a moment free to himself. Still, I'd give him a ring and, if he was unavailable, I could just leave him a message.

I couldn't get through on his phone so I tried Oxfordshire CID but to my surprise, when I was put through to Devlin's sergeant, he told me that his senior officer had left already.

"Oh..." I said. "I thought he might be working late on this new murder case—"

"Yeah, that's right—he's got a bunch of reports and statements to go over. But he said he was going to take 'em home and do it back at his place."

"That's strange—I just tried his mobile and there was no answer."

"Like as not, he's switched his phone off," said the sergeant. "He does that sometimes when he's working, otherwise it would be going non-stop."

"Oh, right... I guess that must be it."

I hung up, vaguely unsettled, but tried to ignore the feeling. Instead, I finished closing up and set off home. I arrived back at the cottage to find something waiting for me on the front doorstep: a big plastic pot with a strange spindly tree growing out of it, its large, broad leaves spread out in a circle, almost like a parasol. There was a note attached to the base of the stem and I picked it up gingerly. I recognised my mother's elegant handwriting:

Darling,
Saw this and thought it would be perfect for your cottage! It's a Taiwanese dwarf umbrella tree and it can grow up to 6 metres! Perfect for any size house and evergreen too. Don't forget to water regularly—but

not too wet. And make sure you find a good spot to put it. The ideal setting is directly in front of an east-, west-, or south-facing window with a sheer curtain to diffuse the direct sunlight.

I sighed and unlocked the door, then slowly pushed the pot inside. Muesli came trotting up to greet me, then froze in her tracks, staring at the potted tree. The tip of her tail twitched as she stretched her neck forwards and sniffed one of the leaves suspiciously.

"Say hello to our new housemate, Muesli," I said wryly. "A Taiwanese dwarf umbrella tree."

I dumped my bag and coat on a nearby chair and looked around in exasperation. Where was I going to put this new plant? It would have to go in the corner by the window, next to that monstrous sago palm thing. At the rate my mother was going, the cottage was going to look like a miniature botanic garden soon.

I had to move a few boxes aside to have enough room to push the pot through, and by the time I was finished installing my new umbrella tree in the right position, I was panting and sweating and covered in dust. *A hot shower,* I thought, *and then I'll rustle up some dinner and have a nice relaxing evening with a book...*

However, when I finally wandered into the kitchen an hour later and pulled out a microwave meal from the freezer, I looked at it without much enthusiasm.

Suddenly, the evening seemed to stretch out in front of me and the prospect of spending it curled up in the middle of a mountain of cardboard boxes didn't really appeal.

Then I had an idea. Why was I sitting here having my dinner alone, when I could spend it with my boyfriend? I glanced at the clock. It was nearly eight o'clock—even if he was working, surely Devlin would appreciate a break for dinner? *I'll pop over and surprise him*, I thought with a smile. He always kept his kitchen well stocked. I could rustle up something there for both of us, then we could spend the rest of the night curled up in front of his nice flat-screen TV.

Delighted with my idea, I bundled Muesli into her cat carrier, then hopped into the car, pleased that I hadn't returned it to my parents yet. The drive to Devlin's place was fairly quick, although twilight was drawing in by the time I got there. With summer around the corner, the days were getting longer now and the sun wasn't setting until nearly eight-thirty. I pulled up in front of Devlin's house—a converted barn set in a quiet country lane—then felt my happy anticipation drain away.

The house looked empty, the windows dark.

I got out of the car and walked over to the front windows, peering in to see if there was a light on at the back of the house—perhaps Devlin was working in the kitchen or something. But no, the place looked empty, and when I tried the doorbell a moment later, it rang hollowly, with no answer.

I stepped back from the front door, frowning. Had Devlin gone out again?

But surely if he had come home and then gone out again, he would have put on the lights and drawn the curtains? A typical policeman, Devlin was paranoid about security and was always careful about leaving lights on in advance if he planned to be out after dark. Besides, the curtains weren't even drawn. It looked like no one had been back to this house since Devlin had left this morning. And yet his sergeant had sounded so sure that Devlin was coming straight home from the station...

I tried his number again and, once again, got no answer. Walking slowly back to the car, I stared out into the gathering darkness.

Where was he?

CHAPTER EIGHT

As if in answer to my question, headlights swung suddenly around the corner of the road and caught me in their glare. I raised a hand to shield my eyes as a black Jaguar XK pulled into the driveway. It was Devlin's car. The driver's door swung open and he got out. As he strode towards me, the streetlights caught his handsome profile and glinted on his wavy dark hair. I noted that he was wearing a sharply tailored Italian suit—his usual workwear—instead of something more casual... so I was right in thinking that he hadn't come home from work and then gone out again.

"Gemma!" There was surprise and something else in his voice. A note of dismay?

"Hi... I thought I'd come over and surprise you," I

said.

He bent to give me a swift kiss. "Have you been waiting long?"

"No, I just arrived..." I hesitated, then added casually, "Your sergeant said you were coming straight back here from the station to do some paperwork at home."

Devlin gave a nonchalant laugh. "Yes, I did plan to do that—but then I had a few leads to follow up."

"About the May morning murder?"

His blue eyes slid away from mine. "No... it's another thing I'm working on..."

"Oh? Another murder case?"

"You know I can't always talk about my cases, Gemma," he said, turning quickly away and busying himself opening the front door.

I didn't reply but, as I followed him into the house, I couldn't help thinking that Devlin had never minded sharing details with me before. I knew he trusted my discretion, and in the past he had even brainstormed problems with me. Why was this any different? An uneasy thought entered my head. Maybe Devlin was lying and his reason for not coming home was nothing to do with work...

I pushed the thought away and hurriedly let Muesli out of her cat carrier. She scampered around in delight, re-acquainting herself with Devlin's place, rubbing her chin against the corners of his couch and the edges of his bookshelves. I followed Devlin into the kitchen and watched as he poured us both a drink. He looked tired, his dark hair slightly ruffled and a hint of stubble showing along his jawline. He had taken off his suit jacket and his tie, and undone the top few buttons, so that the tanned, muscular column of his chest showed starkly against the crisp white cotton of his shirt.

For a moment, I flashed back to when we had been students at college together and how Devlin had looked just like this after an all-nighter to complete an essay before a tutorial. Except that he hadn't looked so pre-occupied then and there hadn't been that strange, distant expression in his piercing blue eyes.

I cleared my throat. "Um... so how is it going with the May morning murder? Did you speak to Charlie Foxton's girlfriend yesterday afternoon? What's she like?"

Devlin shrugged. "On the face of it, she seems like any other spoilt little rich girl. Her father's Vladimir Ivanovich Koskov, one of the richest men in Russia. The girl's name is Tatiana—Tatiana Vladimirovna Koskov."

"Wow, talk about impressive name."

"Actually, one of our police constables is of Russian descent and he was explaining Russian naming traditions to us. Apparently everyone has three names: their first name, their last name, and then a special kind of middle name which is actually a patronymic—it's made up of your father's name and a suffix, like *–ich* if you're male or *–ovna* if you're female. So your name, if you were Russian, would be Gemma Philipovna Rose. Tanya is called Tatiana Vladimirovna—after her father, Vladimir. He, in his turn, is called Vladimir Ivanovich, after *his* father, Ivan."

I laughed. "People don't seriously go around using such long names? They're such a mouthful!"

"I think they get used to it. Most Russians never use the full name except on legal documents. In the workplace and in formal situations you always call someone by their first name and the patronymic. Well, unless you're their boss, then you can use just their first name. So, for example, I could call my sergeant by his first name alone but he would have to call me by my first name plus the patronymic. Confused yet?" Devlin grinned at me. "And just to make it even more complicated, when Russians are with close friends and family, they don't even use first names—they use a 'short' version of their name, like a sort of nickname."

"Oh... like Tanya instead of Tatiana."

"Yes, although I think Tanya has decided to simplify things while she's here in England and just call herself Tanya Koskov."

"Thank goodness for that! So did you get anything out of her?"

"Mm... Yes, she had some interesting things to say—including identifying the murder weapon as belonging to Foxton's scout and suggesting that *she* might have something to do with the murder."

"That's ridiculous!" I said hotly. "Miriam can't have murdered anyone!"

Devlin eyed me sharply. "Miriam? You know her?"

I flushed slightly, ruing my unguarded tongue. "Yes, actually, she's Dora's friend—she came over to the tearoom yesterday afternoon. They used to work as scouts together at Wadsworth College, before Dora retired. Miriam has transferred over to Haverton College now. Anyway, you know all this. Dora told me that your sergeant questioned Miriam last night."

"Yes, and I spoke to her again this morning."

"Oh?" I looked at Devlin warily. I knew he wouldn't have made the effort to question Miriam again unless she was a strong suspect. "Surely you don't really consider her a suspect?"

"She has no alibi for the time of the murder. She told us that she wasn't anywhere near Magdalen Bridge on May morning, and yet when my sergeant spoke to her neighbour—a Mrs Fisk—her neighbour says that she saw Miriam Hopkins leave her house at around 4:30 a.m. that morning."

"What was the neighbour doing up at that time?" I asked sceptically.

"Mrs Fisk suffers from insomnia. She couldn't sleep so she got up to make a milky drink. Her kitchen window faces out the front and she distinctly saw Miriam leaving her house before dawn. She noticed because it seemed unusual. In fact, she wondered if Miriam was going to join the May morning celebrations."

"Did you ask Miriam about it?"

"Yes, *she* says she couldn't sleep either and got up early to go for a walk at the local park. Of course, she saw nobody there so there's no one to corroborate her statement."

I shrugged. "She could just be telling the truth, couldn't she?"

"Yes, she could... but what I find interesting is that she was so vague about the actual route of her walk, and yet she was adamant that she wasn't near Magdalen Bridge."

"What's so strange about that? I mean, it's easier to know for certain that you *weren't* somewhere. It's like, you might not be sure which is your favourite cake but you know for sure you don't like carrot cake."

"Perhaps..." Devlin conceded. "But I've had a lot of experience interviewing people now and I can tell you something: Miriam Hopkins was lying about where she went that morning."

I shifted uncomfortably. The thought of Miriam being dishonest made me uneasy. But I knew that Devlin was a shrewd detective and I trusted his instincts. If he said Miriam was lying, then he was probably right.

"She's not your only suspect though, is she?" I said. "I mean, what about Tanya? Maybe she's trying to make Miriam the scapegoat."

Devlin raised his eyebrows. "You think the girl did it herself?"

"Well, she would have been in the best position to do it—she was standing right next to the victim."

"Yes, but that would have been a bit of a stupid thing to do, wouldn't it? Stab your boyfriend in public in broad daylight? Surely, if she wanted to get rid of him, there were other more discreet ways she could have done it?"

"Yes, but you weren't there that morning—you don't know what it was like, Devlin. You say 'in public' but actually it would have been the easiest thing to stab someone in that crowd. We were all jammed together like sardines and the whole street was crammed head-to-head with people. We were standing so close together that you couldn't see where people's hands were or anything—all you could see was a sea of heads in front of you, behind you, and around you. And everyone was jostling and shuffling and moving around. So if someone stabbed you from behind, then turned and slipped away through the crowd, nobody would even notice until it was too late."

I paused and thought for a moment, then added, "And besides, it might actually be very clever on Tanya's part. Sort of like... a double bluff? Like, she would know that that's how the police would think— that they would discount her as a serious suspect because no one would believe that she would take a risk in public like that. And then it would also give her the best chance of creating a public scene—all the screaming down by the river. Everyone would see how upset she was and, again, nobody would think that she was likely to kill her boyfriend and then cause a scene like that, to draw attention to herself... when, in fact, she was essentially making everyone in the crowd her alibi. I think there's a lot more going on beneath that cool manner and pretty face than you do, and it's just the sort of convoluted plan that Tanya Koskov would be clever enough to come up with."

Devlin looked at me speculatively. "You sound like you know her very well and yet you haven't even spoken to her."

I flushed and looked down. "Well, actually... I... I have."

"What do you mean?"

Reluctantly, I told him about my "chance meeting" with Tanya and Mikhail that afternoon.

Devlin looked annoyed. "What did you think you were doing, questioning her like that?"

"I wasn't questioning her—I was just making conversation," I said. "Besides, I promised Dora—" I broke off.

Devlin's brows drew together. "Promised Dora what?"

"I said I'd... I'd find out a bit more about the case."

"You mean you promised to help her friend clear her name."

I flushed. Devlin had always been too sharp for his own good.

"Gemma." His voice was stern. "This is a real

murder investigation. It's no place for amateurs."

"I'm not such an amateur anymore!" I said indignantly, thinking back to Dora's praise and echoing it unconsciously. "In those last murder cases I was involved with, I uncovered things that the police never even would have thought of."

Devlin made an impatient gesture. "You might have got lucky once or twice, Gemma, but that's not the same as doing serious detective work. I'm sure I don't need to remind you that your snooping in the past almost got you very badly hurt, even nearly killed."

"Well, there's no danger to me here. I mean, this is nothing to do with me personally and—"

"There's always danger when there's a murderer on the loose," Devlin said grimly. "Don't forget, this person has killed someone in cold blood once already *and* managed to do it in broad daylight, in a crowd full of people. This is not a simple domestic murder we're talking about. This is a ruthless person who knows exactly what he's doing."

Something in the way Devlin said that made me look at him sharply. "What do you mean, 'knows exactly what he's doing'?"

Devlin hesitated, as if debating whether to tell me, then sighed and said, "I spoke to Jo Ling this afternoon after she sent me the post-mortem report. She mentioned something very interesting: Charlie Foxton was killed by a stab wound in his lower back, but that's actually not an easy way to kill someone.

You have to know exactly where to stab, to aim for the liver and spleen, and the inferior vena cava—the major artery running down your lower back—in order to cause enough damage to kill quickly. So the murderer is someone who is very familiar with human anatomy."

"You mean like a doctor?"

Devlin nodded.

"What about a medical student?" I asked.

Devlin gave me a look of grudging admiration. "You're very quick. Yes, a medical student would have the knowledge to do it. And before you ask me, yes, Tanya Koskov is studying Medicine at Oxford. I checked with her tutors: all medical students dissect a corpse in their first year, so they would all have a very detailed knowledge of human anatomy. But..." He leaned forwards. "By that token, Miriam Hopkins would be just as much in the frame. She used to be a hospital nurse in her younger days before she started working as a scout, so she would also have an excellent working knowledge of human anatomy and know exactly where to stab to inflict a fatal injury."

I digested this in silence, then said, "What about the roommate? Damian—?"

"Damian Heath. Yes, he finally came back to his college room last night. We had a constable stationed there. I spoke to him this morning: he claims that Tanya Koskov told him the wrong time to meet—on purpose!—and that's why he was late on May morning."

"Wait... I thought he shared a room with Charlie, so wouldn't he have got up with his friend?"

"Charlie spent the night in Tanya's room. It seems she had a fancy dress party there the night before—it's common for students to have big parties on the eve of May Day, you know that—and Charlie had had quite a lot to drink, so he decided to just crash in Tanya's room instead of going back to his own room. Damian went back, however, and so he was alone in the boys' place on May morning. He says that as he was leaving the party the night before, Tanya told him to meet her and Charlie at the front gate at 5:30 a.m. to walk to the bridge together—but when he got there, they were nowhere to be seen. He hung around for ten minutes, waiting, then when they didn't show up, he decided that they must have started without him—so he hurried off after them. Of course, by then, it was so late and the High Street was so crowded that he didn't manage to push his way close enough to the bridge and the tower. He had to wait until the singing was over before he could make his way there."

"And he arrived to find that his friend had been murdered," I said. "So why did he run off?"

"He says he lost his head. He just wanted to get away from the crowds and everything."

I frowned, thinking back over what Devlin had just told me. "But... why would Tanya Koskov tell him the wrong time to meet?"

Devlin's blue eyes met mine. "Damian says it was so she could get Charlie alone..."

I took a sharp intake of breath. "So he suspects Tanya too? Do you believe him?"

"I don't believe anyone yet," said Devlin evenly. "Right now, it just seems to be a big game of 'he said—she said'. We need solid evidence if we're to have any chance of uncovering the truth."

CHAPTER NINE

We had a simple meal of mushroom risotto accompanied by a glass of red wine, and afterwards washed up in the kitchen together. Devlin seemed to be in a playful mood, teasing me and coming up behind me to slide an arm around my waist and steal a kiss as I stood at the sink. There was a lovely cosy domestic atmosphere and it felt just like it used to when I had been living here. I felt ashamed of my earlier suspicions and chided myself for my silly paranoia.

But when I flopped down on the living room couch and said, reaching for the TV remote, "I wonder if there are any good movies on..."—Devlin made a grimace.

He rubbed the back of his neck and said, "Better

not get too comfy, Gemma—I've got a really early start tomorrow morning."

"Oh, okay." I gave him a loaded smile. "I don't mind an early night. I've got my overnight bag with me. I'll just go and get it from the car—"

I started to get up from the couch but Devlin put out a hand to stop me.

"No, actually, Gemma..." He paused awkwardly. "That's probably not such a good idea. As I said, I've got to get up really early—"

"Don't worry, you won't disturb me. You know what I'm like in the mornings. You practically need to dig me out of bed." I laughed.

Devlin looked uncomfortable, his blue eyes not meeting mine. "Yes... but you probably don't sleep as well here as back in your own bed. Besides, you'd have to get up even earlier than usual to go back to your place to drop off Muesli and change for work. And especially after waking up so early for May morning yesterday and then having to work in the tearoom... you're probably knackered. It'll be good for you to stay at your own place where you can relax and catch up on sleep properly. In any case, I... I probably won't be very good company anyway. I'm so tired—I think I'm just going to crash."

I stared at him as it suddenly dawned on me that Devlin didn't want me to stay the night. I felt a chill of doubt. Why didn't he want me here? True, we were both tired and probably a bit sleep-deprived—and we both had a long day of work ahead of us tomorrow—

but that never stopped him wanting me to spend the night before.

"Okay..." I said slowly. "I suppose you're right. I need to drop the car back at my parents' house anyway and pick up my bike, which I left there. It'll be a lot easier to do that tomorrow morning on my way out of Oxford from my cottage."

"Yes," said Devlin, looking relieved. "And you've got Muesli too."

He was right. I knew there were good practical reasons for me not staying the night. And yet...

I tried not to think about it. Instead, I collected my things and got ready to leave. Muesli, however, was not pleased to be disturbed from her comfy position on the couch. She was lying on her back, with her little front paws tucked against her chest and her belly exposed. Her eyes were shut, her chin tilted up, and she looked the picture of relaxed contentment. I saw Devlin wince slightly as he reached over and gently touched her head to wake her.

"*Mmm...meorrw?*" She stirred sleepily and opened one green eye to look at us.

"Come on, Muesli, time to go home..." Devlin said.

"*Meorrw!*" Muesli sat up and yawned, looking peeved.

Devlin reached gently to pick her up but she gave an irritated *chirrup* and jumped off the couch, trotting away. She hopped up on the entertainment unit and climbed onto the top shelf, turning around and presenting her bum to us.

Devlin looked embarrassed, and I had to admit I was secretly pleased that Muesli was giving him a hard time. At least she was getting a bit of payback for me! I stood back and hid a smile as I watched Devlin try to explain to Muesli why she couldn't spend the night curled up in her favourite position on his couch.

"Muesli, come down now... come on, sweetie," Devlin pleaded.

The little cat ignored him.

Devlin tried to reach for her but she was too high up.

"*Muesli!* Come down here!" said Devlin, trying to sound stern and commanding.

Hardened criminals had cringed at that tone of voice from Detective Inspector Devlin O'Connor, but my little cat just twitched the fur on her back, like flicking away an annoying fly, and didn't even turn her head around to look at him.

Devlin heaved an exasperated sigh, then grabbed one of the dining chairs and climbed up to get her. I thought Muesli might wait until he was almost level with her before jumping nimbly to the next shelf—it was just the kind of devious thing she enjoyed doing—but Devlin's reflexes were too quick for her. He caught her, squirming, just as she tried to dart away, and brought her back down.

"*Meorrw!*" she cried petulantly as she was lowered gently into the cat carrier.

"Sorry, sweetie," said Devlin, putting a finger

through the bars of the carrier and trying to scratch her chin.

Muesli sniffed and turned her face away, flattening her ears against her head. She was not forgiving him that easily.

Devlin looked embarrassed again and stood back, clearing his throat. "Uh... well, drive back carefully, Gemma... and sleep well."

I said nothing as I picked up the cat carrier and marched to the front door. Devlin followed me out to the car and gave me a quick kiss before I got in. As I drove away, I thought about that kiss. I couldn't remember the last time Devlin had given me a proper kiss—one that made the world spin and my toes curl. That peck on the lips had been just like everything else Devlin had done lately: quick, hurried, and preoccupied—like his mind was somewhere else.

Or... I thought uncomfortably, *his mind was with someone else.*

***

"It's all a pack of lies!"

I stared at Dora in astonishment. I had just walked into the tearoom kitchen the next morning and found her pummelling a slab of dough on the wooden table with so much force that I was surprised the table hadn't cracked.

"What's the matter?" I said.

She gave me an angry look. "Those village gossips!

Nothing better to do with their time than tell nasty stories about other people! How dare they say that about Miriam! They don't know anything about her and yet they're spreading such malicious rumours—"

"What are they saying?"

"They're saying that Miriam killed Charlie Foxton for money."

"What? But that makes no sense—why would she gain any money from his death?"

Dora looked slightly uncomfortable. "Well, apparently Charlie left her some money in his will. Quite a lot of money."

"Oh." I was surprised. "That's a bit... unusual, isn't it?"

She shrugged. "Well, it was his money to do what he likes with. He was over eighteen. And he saw Miriam as a second mother, I think. He knew that she wasn't well-off so he wanted to make sure that she was provided for. I think it's a beautiful sentiment—there's no need to put an ugly slant on it!"

"No, no, of course not," I said hastily. "But you have to admit, it does give her a motive to murder him, especially as Miriam was in financial difficulties, wasn't she? I mean, she sounded quite desperate that evening when I saw her... and with her son asking for money... and her mother needing to be in a special nursing home..." I gave Dora a sideways look. "Having a sudden windfall now would mean that Miriam could move her mother into that private home which specialises in care for patients with dementia, right?"

"Yes," Dora admitted. "And the nursing home that Miriam's mum is currently in has said that they can't keep her there anymore. That was the reason they called her in on Friday evening. The Matron said Miriam had to find another place for her mother." She scowled. "But that doesn't mean Miriam would murder Charlie just to get the money!"

"Dora..." I cleared my throat. "Er... are you absolutely sure that Miriam is telling you the truth about everything?"

"Of course I'm sure!" she snapped. "Miriam wouldn't lie to me!"

"Well, it's just that... I spoke to Devlin about the case last night and he told me that he had questioned Miriam about her movements on May morning."

"So?" Dora looked at me belligerently. "Miriam said she wasn't anywhere near Magdalen Bridge."

"Yes, except that Devlin is sure she was lying."

"Based on what?"

"Well... based on his instincts and experience as a detective, I guess."

"His instincts are wrong!" Dora snapped. "I know Miriam. She has been my friend for over twenty years now and you couldn't find a more decent, honest, kind woman than Miriam Hopkins. To think that she has to be dragged through this now because of some unfortunate coincidences—"

"But that's just it, Dora," I protested. "There seem to be *too many* coincidences. I mean, it's her barbecue skewer that was used as the murder weapon. And now it seems that she has a very strong motive... and she can't really explain why she left her home so early on May morning or prove where she went."

"She went for a walk. That's not a crime, is it?" snapped Dora.

"No, but, you must admit, it does make things look very suspicious. You can't blame the police for treating her as a suspect," I said gently.

Dora set her mouth in a mutinous line. "I don't care what it looks like—I know Miriam can't have murdered anyone. Especially not the boy that she was fond of and practically treated like a second son." She picked up the rolling pin and waved it threateningly. "It's ludicrous to even think that she could harm him!"

"Okay, okay..." I held up my hands in a placating fashion. "I'm just trying to see things from every angle here. We can only help Miriam if we know what she's up against."

Dora's face softened and she looked contrite. "I'm sorry, Gemma—it was unfair of me to take it out on you. But you've got to believe me: Miriam is innocent! And with everyone against her now, you're the only one who can help her. You've *got* to find the real killer and help to clear her name!"

CHAPTER TEN

When I finally left the kitchen, I felt troubled and uneasy. Dora seemed to think that I could fix everything for her friend, but I had no idea how to do that. And even if I did, I was uncomfortably aware of Devlin's warning last night not to get involved in the murder investigation. I didn't want to let Dora—and Miriam—down, but I didn't want to antagonise Devlin either. *Aaargh!* I felt like I was stuck between the proverbial rock and the hard place.

It was a busy morning again and I was grateful to the Old Biddies for coming in to help out. We had worked out an unofficial arrangement a few months ago when Mabel and her friends discovered that they loved the chance to gossip with—er, I mean, serve—the customers in the tearoom and so they had decided to help out on a regular basis. They flatly refused any payment for their time, so I repaid them the best I could by offering them free access to the tearoom's menu and, of course, the use of the tearoom itself as a sort of Seniors HQ and meeting place with their friends.

So far, the arrangement was working out better than I could have ever imagined. Mabel delighted in treating the place as "her" tearoom, showing it off to her friends in the village and bossing everybody around, and the tourists seemed to think that being served by four little white-haired old ladies was part of the tearoom's charm.

"I took a phone call from a College Steward about the catering order you delivered yesterday," said Cassie during a brief lull mid-morning. "He said that the High Tea was a raving success and everyone was asking where the food had come from. Next time, you should leave some business cards for people to take away."

I groaned. "That's a great idea. Why didn't I think of that?"

"Don't worry, I'm sure this will be the first of many catering jobs, if the Steward's comments were anything to go by," said Cassie with a grin.

"Oh, I hope so," I said fervently.

"Seriously, though, Gemma, if things keep up, you might even need to think about hiring another waitress," said Cassie. "I mean, if the Old Biddies weren't helping, we'd be totally swamped—especially if you had to start popping out to deliver catering orders all the time."

"Mmm, you're right... I've been lucky so far with the Old Biddies always providing an extra pair of hands, but I suppose I shouldn't get used to relying on them."

"Still, I don't think they're going anywhere soon," said Cassie with a laugh. "Not unless Oxfordshire CID offered them a job! You should have heard Mabel this morning—she was in full stride just before you arrived, acting like she was giving a press conference on the May Day murder."

I made a face. "I suppose she heard the village gossip about Miriam Hopkins benefiting from Charlie Foxton's will?"

Cassie nodded. "She was the one who told Dora. She heard everyone talking about it at the village post shop this morning and rushed here to tell us."

"I don't suppose there's any doubt that it's true?"

"Well, I guess you'd better double-check with Devlin just to be sure. There were some other wild theories being bandied about, so perhaps this is just a rumour too... but I got the impression that this was real."

"What other theories?" I asked.

Cassie laughed. "Oh, some pretty silly stuff. The most outlandish one was that Miriam Hopkins is a member of the MI5 Secret Service and that she assassinated Charlie as part of a political assignment!"

I shook my head in disbelief. "Where do people get these ideas from?" Then I sobered. "Still, I wonder if there *could* be a political motive?"

Cassie stopped laughing and stared at me. "You're not taking that suggestion seriously?"

"No, no, not about Miriam being an assassin—of course not! But there was something..." I frowned in an effort to remember. "That morning, after the May Day celebrations, everybody was discussing the murder here in the tearoom and I overheard a group of Aussie backpackers talking about it. One of them had apparently been standing on the bridge next to Charlie Foxton, and he said he heard someone cry out just before Charlie went over the bridge."

Cassie looked at me, puzzled. "So?"

"So... what if it was the *murderer* he had heard crying out?"

"Saying what? 'Die, you victim!' as he stuck the knife into Charlie?" asked Cassie, chortling.

I gave her a reproachful look. "No, but it *was* something weird."

"What did he hear?"

I closed my eyes briefly, then recited slowly: "'*NATO joy evict*'... Yes, that's what he said he heard. A cry like 'Aagh!' and then '*NATO joy evict*'."

"*NATO joy evict*?" Cassie furrowed her brow. "You think he was talking about NATO? As in the North Atlantic Treaty Organisation—the alliance of countries that are against using nuclear activity in war?"

"Yes, that's what I thought it was—which is why I wondered if there might be some kind of political motive."

"Did Charlie Foxton have any political leanings?" asked Cassie sceptically.

"I don't think so. I'll have to check with Devlin but he didn't mention anything. I'm sure the police would have checked that angle as part of the general background on the victim, and if Charlie had been involved with any radical political groups, Devlin would have mentioned it. Still—"

We were interrupted by the tinkling of the bells attached to the front door and we both looked over to see three people enter the tearoom. My eyes widened in surprise as I recognised my parents. They were accompanied by an elderly man with bushy beard and eyebrows.

"Darling!" My mother hurried forwards. I realised as she came towards me that she was holding something and my heart sank as I saw what it was. Yes, you guessed it: another weird-looking plant. This one had long green leaves shaped like sword blades and a strange spiky orange thing in the centre that looked like a skinny pineapple.

"What on earth is *that*?" I demanded.

"It's a bromeliad, darling!" said my mother, beaming. "It's marvellous at maintaining the humidity indoors. And—unlike other indoor plants— it actually *releases* oxygen during the night. So this way, combined with the other plants in the cottage, you will have round-the-clock air purification!"

At this rate, I was also going to have round-the-clock nightmares from all the creepy plants I was living with. Still, I accepted the spiky bromeliad with as much good grace as I could muster and stowed it hastily behind the counter. Then I turned to look at their guest questioningly.

My mother waved an airy hand. "This is Professor Obruchev, darling—remember I told you that he was coming to visit? We've been taking him for a little drive around the Cotswolds and thought that we just *had* to stop at your tearoom for some morning tea!"

The elderly man came forwards with both hands outstretched, his face beaming beneath his whiskers. "Ah! It is great pleasure to meet beautiful daughter of my colleague!"

I stifled a laugh at his old-fashioned, gallant manner. He was a stoop-shouldered man with twinkling brown eyes beneath thick eyebrows and a bushy beard that obscured half his face. He was dressed like he had stepped out of a period drama, in a three-piece suit of faded brown, with a spotted neckcloth and vintage brogues. And he had a thick Russian accent to match. In fact, he reminded me of another Russian scholar that I had met recently: Tanya's friend, the pompous, belligerent Mikhail. Professor Obruchev was a lot older, though, and more than that, he had a happy, smiling manner that couldn't have been more different from the other grumpy Russian scholar.

He clapped his hands now as he looked around the tearoom and said with enthusiasm, "Your parents tell me that you serve full traditional English tea. I have had some tea at my hotel but they assure me that this will be very different experience!"

I grinned. His ebullience was infectious and seemed to lift the mood of the whole tearoom. I saw Cassie chuckling from behind the counter and several customers look over and smile as I led him and my parents to a table by the windows. They sat down and Professor Obruchev scanned the menu with great interest, making little exclamations as he went down the list.

"Ah! The scones! I have heard much about them... and the crumpets also... yes, yes... and Victoria sponge cake—this is English cake made for the Queen, no? Ah, and I know cheesecake—in Russia, I eat cheesecake also but it is different. It is called *zapekanka*. They make it with Farmer's Cheese and raisins and we eat for breakfast."

"Cheesecake for breakfast? My goodness!" said my mother.

"It is very healthy, I assure you!" said Professor Obruchev. Then he adjusted his spectacles and peered at the menu. "But this... I do not understand... *finger* sandwiches? It cannot be! I have not heard that the English—they eat the fingers?"

I laughed. "That's just the name—because the sandwiches are cut up into small rectangular segments called 'fingers'. They are very dainty.

They're supposed to be a light snack eaten with afternoon tea and they usually have things like cucumber and butter, or egg and cress, or smoked salmon and cream cheese inside. But no fingers, don't worry!"

"And you have them for afternoon tea?"

"Well, yes, traditionally these foods were eaten around four o'clock in the afternoon. But as you can see from the menu, we offer them all day now. People don't just have 'tea' in the afternoons now, anyway— morning tea is also very popular. That's usually around ten-thirty, eleven o'clock. In fact, some people call it 'elevenses'. It's when people usually stop work and have a little break between breakfast and lunch."

"It is delightful tradition! But I think I will let *madam* order for me," said Professor Obruchev, making a little bow towards my mother. "I cannot choose! It is all delicious, I think. You know, we in Russia—we also love the tea and we have many cakes and biscuits, also."

"You make your tea slightly differently, don't you?" I said. "In a samovar?"

He beamed at me. "Yes! That is right—in samovar; this is metal container which boils water for tea. We have ones of bronze and copper, with beautiful engravings—they are antiques, yes! The samovar—it is very important because, you see, we make our tea in different way. We have two steps: first we make tea with dry leaves in small teapot, then each person will take some of this into a cup and add hot water to dilute for his satisfaction."

"That's actually a very good idea," I said. "That way everyone can get their tea to the strength they like and you never have to worry about it being too strong or too weak."

He nodded enthusiastically. "Yes! Yes! That is exactly so! But now, I am delighted to try this English way of tea."

"It's a shame you didn't arrive a few days earlier, Professor Obruchev," said my mother. "Otherwise you could have taken part in another old English tradition: celebrating May morning."

"Ah! I have heard this—it is great event in Oxford every year, is it not? But there was a problem this year, no?" asked the elderly Russian professor, frowning. "They speak about it at my hotel. The death of student... the accident from bridge?"

"Not an accident," my father spoke up. "It was murder."

"*Murder?*" The professor stared at him. "*O bozhe!* Really? But why? Who would want to do this?"

"The newspapers have put forth several theories," said my father. "The police are conducting an investigation and they do have several suspects. The roommate of the victim... his scout at the college..."

"And his girlfriend," said my mother. "Although I saw a photograph of her in one of the papers and, I must say, I just can't believe that she could be a murderer! Such a pretty girl! And she comes from a very good family too: daughter of the Russian billionaire, Vladimir Ivanovich Koskov, I believe, and—"

"Excuse me," Professor Obruchev interrupted her. "Did you say Vladimir Ivanovich Koskov? But I know him! We were at same university. He is younger than me, you understand, but we were doing graduate studies together and we spend much time, drinking, talking in student bars."

"I didn't realise you were friends with Mr Koskov," said my mother, looking impressed.

The professor made a self-deprecating gesture. "Ah, perhaps not friends like you think. We are not in same social circle, me and Vladimir. He goes in very different direction, since time of our student days, and he is very important man now. But yes, we keep in touch still and from time to time, when he needs to talk and somebody to listen, he comes to me and we go drink together again."

"Have you met his daughter?" I asked.

"Little Tatiana? Yes, many times. I watch her grow up. She is beautiful, like her mother. Yulia was one of top models in Russia, but—*Oy*—she die young. She had cancer in breast." Professor Obruchev shook his head sadly.

"Has Mr Koskov married again?" asked my mother.

Professor Obruchev shook his head. "There are lady friends, of course, but they do not stay long. Vladimir—his heart was only with Yulia. Now, his heart is all in his business and in Tatiana. She is only child, you see, and she is his great treasure. Whatever she wants, she will have! There is nothing that her *papa* will not do for her." He smiled. "Ah, but I did not realise that she comes to Oxford! Indeed, I have not spoken to Vladimir for long time—over one year ago now. But I am very happy to hear that Tatiana is here—she has brains, that one. Always very clever, even as little girl. She could always—how you say—turn her *papa* around her little finger?"

"Twist him around her little finger," my mother corrected. She laughed. "Tanya Koskov sounds like quite a young lady."

The professor nodded eagerly. "Like her *mama*, she is. Ah, even same temper! She is tigress! One does not want to anger her; once, when she was younger and she was thinking of following mother's footsteps, she went to audition for modelling. And there was another girl... and there was trouble... and little Tatiana—*Oy!*—she was very angry! She attacked other girl with knife!"

I stared. "She attacked the other girl?"

The professor shrugged. "It was with provocation, I think. Other girl made unpleasant comments about Yulia, Tatiana's *mama*... so Tatiana took knife from cheeseboard and she stabbed girl."

"Oh my goodness!" exclaimed my mother. "What happened?"

Professor Obruchev shrugged again. "The girl, they took to hospital—it was bad cut. But she did not lose her life. Her parents were angry but what can you do? It is Vladimir Ivanovich Koskov's daughter. He gave them money and... they did not call police. After a while, it is forgotten."

"Well, I think that's completely reprehensible!" said my mother disapprovingly.

"Ah, but you do not realise what Vladimir will do for his Tatiana, how he will protect her..." The professor sighed. "It is unfortunate, perhaps. It has made her a *printsessa*—a princess, I think you say also in English. Always, Tatiana has her own way."

"Well, the British police certainly won't be giving her special treatment," said my mother firmly. "In this country, she will be treated just like everyone else!"

"The rich are always treated differently, my dear, no matter what the country," said my father with gentle cynicism.

Talk returned to the subject of afternoon tea and I finally left their table with an *enormous* order (in spite of his declaration to leave all the ordering in my mother's hands, Professor Obruchev couldn't resist adding several items himself from the menu). As I walked slowly back to the counter to put the order through, I mulled over what I had learned. So Tanya Koskov had a history of aggression and assault... Very interesting...

CHAPTER ELEVEN

Cassie glanced over as I joined her at the counter and her eyes bulged when she saw the order in my hands.

"Bloody hell! Is that an order for a huge birthday party or something?"

"No, just a huge appetite," I said with a laugh. "It's for my parents and their guest, a Russian professor who's visiting Oxford." I indicated the table by the window. "He's never had a proper 'English afternoon tea' before and he wanted to try everything."

"Brilliant," said Cassie. "All we need is a customer like him every morning and you'd make enough to take the rest of the day off!" She paused thoughtfully, then said, "You know what you ought to do, Gemma? Play up to the whole 'English afternoon tea' thing. I mean, tourists come here because they want the genuine experience, right? So you should offer them a set menu package: a full tea service with a variety of cakes and scones, and charge a price for the whole set. That way, you get a big order and the tourists love it too. I mean, half of them are always asking me what to order from the menu. They're unfamiliar with a lot of British baking and confused about the differences between a Bakewell tart and a Bakewell pudding, or how our muffins aren't really muffins at all—or what they think of as cupcakes—but a type of flat, round, toasted bread... I'm sure they'd love it if somebody just ordered a selection for them and matched the tea as well. You could even create different sets—like a 'Cream Tea' menu of just scones with jam and clotted cream, or a 'Savoury & Sweet' menu, which could include some finger sandwiches, as well as cakes and buns..."

I felt a smile coming to my face as I listened to Cassie's suggestions. "That's a fantastic idea, Cass. You know, when I dropped off the catering order at that college, I was admiring the way the Steward had got all these lovely three-tier cake stands for the food—it made it seem so much more 'special' and gave it a sense of occasion, somehow."

"Yes, that's exactly what I mean!" said Cassie, getting even more enthusiastic. "Play up the whole image of the English afternoon tea experience. It isn't hard—it's just a few props—but the tourists would love it and I'll bet you could charge a premium for those packages too."

"But wait... what about the village residents?" I said. "They're always saying how they like the simple, rustic style of my tearoom. They're not going to take kindly to having their cakes and scones presented on a multi-tiered silver platter—they'll think that's a lot of poncy nonsense for tourists in London hotels!"

"Well, you can offer both! If the locals just want to come in and have their cuppa with a slice of cake on an old chipped plate, you can do that," said Cassie with a grin. "But there's nothing to stop you offering the full experience for tourists, complete with all the fancy trimmings. Trust me, Gemma, it'll work out great! And I could design special menu cards for the packages," said Cassie, her eyes lighting up. "I'll do a couple of watercolours of a teapot and cups, maybe some cakes and flowers—we can print these in the bottom corner... and then the name of the package in lovely, old-fashioned calligraphy across the top... and then a list of all the foods included in that set menu, together with the choice of teas. And we can have a version online... I've been telling you to sort out the tearoom website, Gemma—have you done anything about that?"

I gave her a sheepish look. "No, sorry—it's on my To-Do list but I've just been too busy."

Cassie heaved an exasperated sigh. "Gemma! How can you expect to do business in the twenty-first century without a website? People need to know where to find us, our opening hours, what sorts of things we serve, the history of the place... You could get some great artistic shots of the tearoom and put them in a gallery on the website." She gestured around the room, indicating the inglenook fireplace and the picturesque dark wood beams across the ceiling. "This place! It's the perfect chocolate-box setting for Olde World English charm. You know how much foreign tourists love these kind of things! You've *got* to milk it more."

"Yes, I know—you're right. I'm sorry, I'll get onto it... I promise."

"No, you won't," said Cassie cynically. "Listen, I'll tell you what: *I'll* do it. If you don't mind leaving it in my hands—I'll set up a website and design the pages... and I'll get my brother, Liam, to come and take some photos of the tearoom. He's getting quite good with his camera, actually, and I know he'd love the project. It would be great for building his portfolio."

I gave her an impulsive hug. "Thank you so much, Cassie! Yes, I'll hand everything over to you, but... on one condition."

"What's that?"

"I want to pay you a fee."

Cassie frowned. "Don't be silly, Gemma—"

"No, I mean it," I insisted. "If I hire a professional website designer, I'd be paying a huge fee anyway. Think of it as a commission, Cassie. If someone asked you to paint them a portrait, you wouldn't do it for free, would you? This will be taking up your spare time—so I want to pay for it."

"Well, all right..." said Cassie reluctantly.

I had a feeling that when it came to it, she would probably insist on only charging me "discounted rates"—that was the kind of generous friend Cassie was—but at least this was a start.

"A website would make all the catering orders a lot easier too," Cassie continued enthusiastically. "I could set up an online form that people can fill in with their requirements so that we get all the necessary information when the request comes in, rather than all this back-and-forth calling and taking messages at the moment. It'll free up a lot more time for us *and* look more professional *and* be a way to promote any monthly specials we might have running—"

"You sure you want to be an artist?" I said to Cassie jokingly. "I think you'd have a brilliant career as a marketing manager in a top executive company."

Cassie made a face. "Me? Work in the corporate rat race? No way!"

***

I had just flipped the sign on the tearoom door from "OPEN" to "CLOSED" and was tidying up the counter when the Old Biddies marched up to me, an expectant look on their faces.

"Are you ready, dear?" asked Mabel.

I looked at her blankly. "Ready? For what?"

"To go to Haverton College, of course!" she said. "We're going to speak to the students there."

"For the murder investigation," added Glenda, her eyes sparkling. She held up a plastic carrier bag. "And we've got disguises!"

"Disguises?" I gaped at her.

As I watched in bemusement, Glenda reached in and pulled out four frilly pinafore aprons from the bag, whilst Ethel said, with a little bounce of excitement:

"We're going to wear these and pretend to be scouts!"

"Er... don't you think you look too... um... well, *mature* to be scouts?" I asked.

"I don't think I look a day over sixty-nine," said Glenda, tossing her head and patting her hair. She had obviously just had a particularly powerful blue rinse and her hair looked almost aqua.

"Don't worry—nobody will suspect, especially since we have props!" said Florence, pulling more things out of the bag. She brandished a plastic spray bottle and an enormous rainbow-coloured feather duster in my face.

I sneezed violently. "Uh... I don't think this is going to work," I said, rubbing my nose.

"Nonsense! Young people nowadays... you have no imagination!" said Mabel, pursing her lips.

"Don't worry, Gemma dear, we haven't left you out. We went to the second-hand charity shop in Oxford and these are for you. You'll be disguised as

117

a student."

I looked down with dismay at the pile of clothes that Ethel had thrust into my hands. There was a pair of faded drainpipe jeans with rips at the knees, a baggy T-shirt, and some kind of strange top that looked like a cross between a poncho and a shower curtain. I suppressed a shudder. Did I really have such bad fashion sense when I was a student?

"And I got you a pair of glasses as well, dear," added Ethel, holding up a pair of thick horn-rimmed glasses which would have made Velma from *Scooby-Doo* proud.

"You'll need to do something about your face, though," said Mabel, examining me critically. "We need you looking different from your normal self! Put some colour on your cheeks, so you look young and blooming."

Thanks, I thought. *Obviously my normal self looks pale, old, and haggard.*

"Would you like me to help you with that, dear?" said Glenda eagerly, taking a compact out of her handbag. "I've got some blusher here. I can apply a bit of a rosy hue to your cheeks—"

"Uh... no, no thanks," I said hastily, taking a step back. Judging by the bright pink glow on her own cheeks, Glenda's idea of "a bit of a rosy hue" would probably leave me looking like a feverish clown.

"Well, hurry up and change, dear—we haven't got all day," said Mabel, making a shooing motion with her hands.

I hesitated. It was on the tip of my tongue to say that this was a ridiculous idea and I wasn't going to allow them to do it—and to repeat the lecture that Devlin had given me the other night about amateurs meddling in murder investigations. But to my surprise, what came out of my mouth instead was:

"All right—give me five minutes."

As I struggled to change in the tearoom toilet, I asked myself why I was going along with the Old Biddies' ludicrous plan. Okay, so I had to admit—maybe I *did* want to go to Haverton College to snoop around a bit, and the Old Biddies had given me a convenient excuse. As for Devlin... well, it wasn't as if we were doing anything really *illegal*, was it? I mean, as a member of the University alumni, I was allowed to visit any of the colleges any time I liked. And as for the Old Biddies—well, there wasn't any law against wearing pinafore aprons, was there? It wasn't their fault if people mistook them for scouts.

I was still trying to reassure myself with these excuses some forty minutes later as we stood outside the imposing eighteenth-century baroque façade of Haverton College and surveyed the giant iron-studded double doors which guarded the entrance to the college. They were still open, thank goodness. Like many colleges, Haverton didn't close its main gate until twilight. We just had to figure out a way to get through the gate and across the wide expanse of the Front Quadrangle without catching the eye of the college porters.

"This is the tricky bit," Mabel hissed. "Once we're past the Front Quad and into the Rear Quad, we'll be fine. Ethel—you go first. You are the smallest and people are least likely to notice you. Just keep to the right side of the quad, in the shadow of the cloisters, and keep walking very purposefully. The key is to look like you belong there and then no one will question you. Go through the archway on the far side of the quad and wait for us there."

We all held our breaths and watched as Ethel tottered through the main gate, past the door of the Porter' Lodge. So far, so good. No one seemed to have noticed her. She turned right and followed the wide flagstone path, which ran around the outer edge of the pristine square of grass in the centre of the quadrangle. Finally, she reached the far corner where a large archway led the way through to the Rear Quad and disappeared.

"She made it!" said Mabel. "Right, you next, Florence."

"Perhaps I ought to pause halfway and pretend I'm dusting the side of the quad?" said Florence, holding up her rainbow duster hopefully.

"No! Keep that duster down and by your side. I told you to buy the dark blue one, Flo—rainbow attracts too much attention."

"I think rainbow is a lovely colour," Florence protested. "And besides, I thought once we're finished here, Gemma could have it for her cotta—"

"NO!" I said hastily. I made an effort to lower my

voice. "Uh... thanks, that's really sweet of you, Florence but I don't need a duster." *Especially not one that looks like a giant psychedelic caterpillar.*

"Oh, but of course you do. Every household—"

"Go *on*, Florence, before a porter comes out!" said Mabel, giving her friend a shove towards the main gate.

Florence turned back and glared at us, then straightened her pinafore apron, tucked the feather duster under her arm, and marched through the gate. She began ambling across the quad. Unlike Ethel, who had followed the path around the outer edge of the grass, however, Florence had somehow ended up on the pathway that cut through the centre of the lawn. She stopped suddenly as she realised her mistake and hesitated. But she was already nearly halfway across, and to get to the outer path (without walking across the grass—which was one of the biggest taboos in Oxford) she would have to turn around and come all the way back to the front gate.

"Keep going!" hissed Mabel loudly.

Florence squared her shoulders, then turned and kept going. I watched her nervously. Suddenly, two students entered the quad from the archway at the other end and began walking down the centre path towards Florence. I saw them slow down as they approached her and one of them pointed to the rainbow feather duster, but to my relief, all she did was nudge her friend and the two of them burst into giggles as they passed Florence. A minute later

Florence gained the other side of the quad and disappeared in her turn through the archway.

Two down, two to go, I thought, looking at Mabel and Glenda.

"We'll go together," said Mabel to her friend. "Keep your head down and nod as if you're listening to what I have to say. If we look very busy and important, and walk briskly like we're heading somewhere, nobody will stop us. In fact, take that little address book out of your handbag, Glenda, and flip the pages as you are walking—and I'll pretend to point to something in it as I'm talking."

I watched in awe as the two of them set off, each enacting their part perfectly. Mabel should have been in the Secret Service—how did she stay so cool and where did she come up with all these ideas? Then my heart lurched as I saw a black-suited figure step out of the Porter's Lodge. It was one of the college porters. He paused and looked at the two elderly ladies trundling across the quad in their pinafore aprons. I saw his forehead crease in a frown and he took a step forwards as if about to say something. Then he stopped. Somehow, Mabel's air of brisk importance must have convinced him. He stood and watched them walk to the other side of the quad, then gave a barely perceptible shrug and went back into the Lodge.

I let out the breath I had been holding. Okay, that was the Old Biddies through. Now it was my turn.

CHAPTER TWELVE

I took a deep breath and tried to channel "carefree uni student". I adjusted my posture, letting my shoulders slouch backwards and my face relax into a vacant, naïve smile. Shoving my hands into my pockets, I strolled through the gate. To be honest, I didn't really have anything to fear—I could always whip out my university alumni card if I really got stuck—but it would have been better if I didn't have to explain myself to the college porters.

It was a relief when I gained the safety of the archway on the other side of the quad and found the Old Biddies huddled there. They were grouped around a large bulletin board covered with flyers and posters about university clubs and college events. There was an open doorway next to the bulletin board with the letters "J.C.R." engraved across its top: the Junior Common Room—where undergraduates congregated to socialise, watch TV, eat, drink, and play pool or other recreational games.

"You go in there, Gemma," said Mabel, jerking her head towards the J.C.R doorway. "Get chatting with some of the students, dear, and see if you hear any gossip about Charlie or his girlfriend or roommate."

"Where are *you* going?" I asked, looking at the four little old ladies in front of me.

"Investigating," said Mabel cryptically.

On second thoughts, I decided that it was probably better if I didn't know what the Old Biddies were getting up to. I left them huddled whispering outside and went into the J.C.R. It was fairly empty at this time of the day and, for a moment, I wondered if I wouldn't be able to find anyone to "chat" with. There were a couple of boys around the pool table and a girl curled up in an armchair in the far corner, engrossed in a book, but neither group looked very open to a stranger coming up and starting a conversation. As I was hovering just inside the doorway, wondering what to do, someone else came into the common room and nearly bumped into me.

"Oh! I'm sorry!"

I turned around and found myself facing a pretty, plump girl with frizzy yellow hair.

"No, it's my fault," I said quickly, smiling at her. "I shouldn't have stood so close to the door."

She returned my smile in a friendly fashion and I

seized the opportunity. I pointed to her feet.

"I love your shoes! Where did you get them from?"

She beamed. "Oh, this little shop in the Covered Market. They do loads of vintage stuff. These are actually second-hand—can you believe it?"

I gave an appropriate gasp of appreciation. "Really? I would never have guessed. What a fantastic find. But then, you've got really good taste," I said shamelessly.

She flushed with pleasure. "Well, I do love poking around vintage stores—it's sort of like treasure hunting—and I guess you get a knack. The shoes aren't very comfy though," she admitted with a grimace. She hobbled over to a couple of chairs by the TV and sat down with a sigh. She took off one shoe and wriggled her toes. "I think I'm getting a blister..."

I sat down next to her and she looked at me enquiringly. "Are you a student here? I don't think I've seen you around the college."

"Um... I'm at a different college," I said, telling myself that it wasn't really a lie. I *had* been at a different college... eight years ago. Quickly, I changed the subject. "Do you like being at Haverton?" I asked chattily. "I've always wondered what it was like being in a college right on the High Street—like with the May Day celebrations and all the crowds..."

"Oh, it isn't that bad," she said. "I mean, the student rooms are set back from the street so it isn't too noisy if you want to sleep in. Anyway, it's only once a year and it's kind of nice to be practically on the doorstep of the celebrations." She gave a sudden shiver. "Well, except it wasn't so nice this year—that awful thing that happened on the bridge..."

"Did you know the boy who died?" I asked. "I heard that he was at Haverton."

She nodded. "Yes, he lived on my staircase! He and Damian had the room on the top level." She opened her eyes very wide. "They're saying that Charlie was murdered. Can you believe that? It's just too unreal to even think about."

"Was he the type to have enemies?" I asked.

"Charlie Foxton?" She gave me an incredulous look. "No, he was the nicest chap! Everyone liked him. I can't imagine anyone who would want to harm him."

"Did you know him well?"

"No... I mean, I knew him to say hello to and we'd stop to have a natter sometimes if we met on the staircase, but I wasn't really in his crowd. He did invite me to his parties though—he was always really nice like that. Whenever he and Damian had a party, he'd always come round and invite everyone on the staircase."

I gave her a conspiratorial smile. "Were they good parties?"

"They were really popular," said the girl. "The college porters had to come shut them down a few times."

"Oh, was there trouble at the parties?"

"No, not really. No more than usual. They just got a bit loud and wild sometimes, you know, if people drank a bit too much." She saw my questioning look and added, "Not Charlie. He wasn't the aggressive type when he got drunk. Damian, though, is a different story. He can be a nasty piece of work when he's had one too many. He's nothing like Charlie, actually—I used to wonder sometimes why they were friends. Charlie was so nice, whereas I wouldn't trust Damian as far as I could throw him. And Charlie was so generous too; Damian's a bit of a leech, always trying to scrounge money off you."

"Was Damian hard up?"

"No, I don't think so. But I think he liked to live the rich life and, you know, being around Charlie... well, I suppose he felt like he had to keep up with his friend."

A dark-haired girl with a Mediterranean look walked into the J.C.R. and my companion looked up with a smile, "Hey, Nicola! You're back late."

"Hi, Kate..." The dark-haired girl flopped onto the couch next to us and blew out a breath. She was not exactly pretty but there was something very attractive about her thin, clever face with her large brown eyes and olive complexion, set off beautifully by the orange sweater she wore. "I had to hang around after the lecture to ask the prof something." She glanced at me curiously, obviously wondering who I was.

"We were talking about Charlie," said Kate. "I just

can't believe that he was murdered—can you?"

I chipped in and said in a gossipy tone, "Yeah, it seems like he was such a nice guy—he wouldn't have any enemies."

The dark-haired girl gave a cynical smile. "Well, you know what they say: 'with friends like these, who needs enemies?' Or in this case, maybe it should be— with *girlfriends* like these, who needs enemies..."

I raised my eyebrows. "You think his girlfriend had something to do with it?"

Nicola gave a shrug. "Wouldn't surprise me."

"Didn't... didn't they get along?" I asked.

Nicola gave me a sharp look. I shifted uncomfortably. This girl wasn't as naïvely trusting as Kate with her cheerful chatter; I would have to be careful with her. I was just wondering how to answer if Nicola asked me why I was so interested when Kate rushed into the silence with:

"Oh, they used to fight all the time! I could hear it even two levels down from my room. Well, to be fair, it wasn't really Charlie fighting—it was mostly just Tanya screaming at him. My goodness, she could really sound like a fishwife! They were having a flaming row only the day before he got killed. I was trying to do my essay and it was impossible with all the screaming." Kate shook her head sadly. "I wonder if she's feeling guilty about that now, having said all those nasty things to him—and now he's dead."

Nicola snorted.

"Well, she *does* seem very upset," insisted Kate.

"I've seen her a few times since May Day and she looks really miserable."

"You mean more than usual?" scoffed Nicola. "I've never seen that girl look happy—and you'd think someone who has everything would be able to dredge up a smile sometimes."

"Well, she hasn't got everything now, has she?" said Kate softly. "She's lost her boyfriend. And I know she used to be horrible to him at times but I think she really loved him. So she must be feeling terrible now about their fight just before he died."

"What were they fighting about?" I asked.

Nicola rolled her eyes. "The usual, I'll bet. Tanya accusing Charlie of cheating on her..." She glanced at her friend. "Am I right?"

Kate nodded. "Yes, Tanya kept screaming and saying that Charlie was seeing someone else behind her back and that she wouldn't stand for it... or something like that."

Nicola gave a humourless laugh. "You'd think someone who looks like Tanya Koskov wouldn't be so bloody insecure! I mean come on, she could be a supermodel! But she was always watching Charlie all the time and getting worked up if he spoke to another girl and flying into a jealous rage... And my God, has she got an absolutely foul temper! I was at dinner in Hall once, sitting at the same table, and she got into an argument with one of the Freshers and she suddenly sprang up and slapped him across the face!"

"She did apologise afterwards," said Kate. "And the college authorities did have words with her."

"I'll bet she didn't get any disciplinary measures though—Daddy Koskov probably got on the phone from Russia and 'exerted his influence', as they say, to protect his little Tanya," Nicola said. "In fact, I'm surprised he hasn't hopped on his private jet and come over immediately since Charlie's murder, to protect his daughter from 'police abuse'."

"I heard Tanya say that her father's in hospital, recovering from surgery," said Kate.

"Well, then I'm surprised he hasn't sent a bodyguard to watch over his precious princess," said Nicola sarcastically.

"Had Tanya and Charlie been together for a long time?" I asked.

Nicola shrugged. "On and off. They seemed to have one of those weird relationships—you know, always fighting and breaking up, and then making up again. Still, I don't know why Charlie didn't just chuck her, the way she treated him sometimes."

Kate gave an exclamation as she looked down at her watch. "Oh, we're going to be late for dinner! And it's Formal Hall tonight. I have to dash back to my room to change and grab my gown."

"I'd better go too," I said quickly, getting up. I saw Nicola look at me searchingly again and wanted to get away before she started asking me what I was doing in the college. "Nice to chat with you. I'll see you around!"

Giving them a cheery wave, I hurried from the J.C.R.

***

I thought I would have trouble finding the Old Biddies again but they were waiting for me just around the corner from the archway.

"Gemma! Over here!" Mabel hissed, beckoning to me from the shadows by the college chapel.

I went over to join them. Quickly, I told them what I had learned.

"Hmm... that's all very interesting," mused Mabel. "But I still think we need to examine the boy's room."

"The police would have done that," I protested.

Mabel gave a sniff. "The police? What do they know?"

"They would have sent the SOCO team over and—"

"SOCO my foot! Those Scene Of Crime Officers are only interested in silly things like fingerprints and DNA... they don't know how to look for *real* clues."

I gave her an exasperated look. "If fingerprints and DNA aren't real clues, then what are?"

"The boy's belongings. The state of his room. His clothes. His diary—"

"I'm sure the police would have confiscated that," I said.

Mabel waved a hand. "There will be other things they won't have thought of. The point is, we need to find out more about the victim and his life, his relationships, his personality, to really understand why he was murdered. As Poirot says, the answer lies in the nature of the victim and in the psychology of the murder—all the stories that people around him tell, all the extra details which don't seem important..."

I sighed. I should have known this was coming. The Old Biddies had an unhealthy devotion to Agatha Christie novels and seemed to spend half their time thinking they could enact the storylines in the books.

"That's a detective story," I said impatiently. "It's all very well in a mystery novel but people don't solve crimes in real life by relying on personality observations. Not when you've got advanced science and forensics! And besides, even if there are clues to be found... well, you can't just go snooping around in student rooms—"

"Who said anything about snooping?" said Mabel indignantly. She pointed to their pinafore aprons. "We're simply doing our job as scouts and making sure that the room is cleaned properly. After all, Miriam Hopkins hasn't been able to come and fulfil her duties, has she, since she's been suspended? I'm sure the boys' room could do with a thorough clean and tidy-up."

Before I could answer, Mabel turned and began marching towards the far corner of the Rear Quad, the other Old Biddies trotting behind her.

"Wait, wait..." I said, hurrying to catch up with

her. "You don't even know where Charlie's room is—"

"Of course I do. It's on the top level of Staircase 5—there, in that corner." Mabel nodded in the direction she was heading.

Grrr. Why did Mabel always have an answer for everything?

I followed them and watched helplessly as they keyed in the combination for the staircase door (I didn't even want to ask how they got that information!). With a stealthy look around, they darted inside one by one. I hesitated, then hurriedly followed. As they began creeping up the staircase, I reflected with a sense of resignation that, somehow, I always seemed to end up skulking in Oxford college staircases with the Old Biddies.

It was slow going, with Mabel and her friends needing several rest stops at each landing, and I was terrified that a student might come out of their room at any minute and see us on the staircase. Then I remembered what Kate had said about being late for Formal Hall and I glanced at my watch. It was dinnertime and probably all the students would be in the dining hall. We couldn't have timed it better, in fact. We'd have at least twenty minutes before even the fastest eaters would begin to return.

We reached the top landing at last and looked around. Most of the landings we'd passed on the way up had two doors, one on either side, but this one only had one, which no doubt led into the two-bedroom suite that Charlie and Damian had been sharing. In fact, I could see the name badges on the door, with "C. FOXTON" and "D. HEATH" side by side.

"How are you going to get in?" I asked. "Don't tell me you've managed to get the key—"

Mabel reached out and turned the doorknob, and, as if by magic, the door swung open.

I gaped at her. She smiled complacently.

"Did you think we'd been twiddling our thumbs while you were in the J.C.R.?" she said. "We found out that the boys were known for never locking their doors—Charlie, especially, was very gregarious and always happy for people to drop in any time and help themselves to things, even if he wasn't around. Apparently, there were often impromptu parties in their room."

She slipped inside the room and we followed, shutting the door quietly behind us. I relaxed slightly. We were safe, for now.

"Hurry—we don't have much time," Mabel urged the others.

The Old Biddies began bustling around the main sitting room, opening drawers, looking under rugs, examining the motley assortment of food and drink in the fridge, flipping through stacks of books... I stood in the centre of the room and looked around slowly. It was a spacious living area, with dark panelled walls, high ceilings, and wide sash windows overlooking the quad below. There was a three-seater sofa upholstered in a faded chevron fabric and two non-matching armchairs. There was also a modern-looking beanbag (probably the boys' own addition), a wooden sideboard resting along one wall, littered with empty bottles, glasses, paper plates, and other party paraphernalia, and an old-fashioned desk on the opposite side, covered with piles of books, papers, stationery, computer cables, and an open laptop. Two doors faced each other on opposite sides of the sitting room, obviously leading to the boys' individual bedrooms.

Nothing jumped out at me. It looked like numerous other Oxford student rooms that I'd been in. Turning, I headed towards the door on the right wall, which I guessed to be Charlie's bedroom from the crime-scene tape stretched across the doorway. I hesitated a moment, then gingerly turned the doorknob and eased the door open. I knew that the police forensic team would have already done a sweep and taken anything that looked suspicious. Anyway, I wasn't planning to go in—I just wanted to have a look from the doorway. Perhaps Mabel was right—perhaps getting a better sense of who Charlie Foxton was would help to solve his murder.

I ducked my head under the crime-scene tape, leaned into the room, and flicked on the light. It was disappointingly normal. In fact, there was something very sad about how "everyday" it looked—almost as if its owner had just stepped out and would return any moment. I scanned the room, trying to see if there was something that could explain the mystery of the boy's murder, but if the clues were there, I couldn't see them. It looked just like a typical boy's room: there were shoes kicked off on the floor, posters of football players on the wall, rumpled clothes piled in an untidy heap at the foot of his bed, various game consoles and some expensive Bose speakers on the bedside shelf, a dark grey hoodie with the letters "OKMC" slung over the chair by the desk, which held a pile of books and what looked like a half-finished essay. There were also a couple of stained mugs and a plate with some congealed food on the windowsill.

A sound behind me made me jerk my head around. My eyes widened as I heard steps outside on the landing and saw the doorknob in the main room turning.

Blast! Someone's coming in!

I yanked the door to Charlie's bedroom shut and ran into the centre of the sitting room, looking desperately around for a hiding place. But it was too late. The door swung open and I froze in horror as I saw Damian Heath standing in the doorway.

CHAPTER THIRTEEN

Instantly, the Old Biddies went into an orgy of dusting and spraying and wiping and cleaning. Damian stared at them in astonishment.

"What...? You...? Uh...?" he stammered.

Mabel turned around and gave him a casual look. "Ah, Mr Heath! We're just finishing up here," she said, flicking her cloth with a flourish across the side of the coffee table. "There. That should do it. So dreadfully dusty, this place! We'll be back to empty the bin tomorrow morning. In the meantime, try not to get any biscuit crumbs on the floor."

"But... you..." Damian spluttered, looking completely befuddled as Mabel marched past him, clutching her cloth and spray bottle, followed by Ethel, Glenda, and Florence. The last couldn't resist giving the bookshelf another flick with her rainbow feather duster before she went out the door. It shut behind them with a resolute *click*.

I stared at the closed door in dismay. *Aaaarrgghh!* I couldn't believe it—they were doing it again! Leaving me to face the music alone! I gritted my teeth. I was going to kill the Old Biddies when I next saw them!

Damian's expression was changing from bewildered to suspicious. He was no fool and he must have begun to realise that there was something very odd going on. Scouts normally came in the mornings, not at dinnertime.

"What are you doing here?" he demanded, turning to me.

"Oh, I... uh..." I floundered, groping for something to say. Then I remembered that sometimes the best form of defence was attack. I lifted my chin.

"I came to see you, actually, Damian. I wanted to talk to you—about your friend's murder."

His eyes widened and I saw him turn pale.

"I didn't do it!" he blurted out. He licked his lips nervously and said, "I told you! I wasn't even near the bridge when it happened. I answered all those questions at the police station—what else do you need to ask me?"

I realised suddenly that he thought I was a member of the CID, perhaps one of Devlin's sergeants. After all, all the detectives wore plainclothes. My bold manner must have fooled him. I decided to press my advantage.

"I'd like to go over a few details. I understand that you were supposed to meet Charlie and his girlfriend on May morning to watch the celebrations together. Why weren't you with them?"

"I told you—they'd gone ahead without me and I couldn't find them. And it was too close to 6 a.m. by then; everything stopped when the choir began to sing." He swallowed. "And then the next thing I knew, there was all this screaming and when I finally pushed my way through to the bridge, there... there was Charlie's body in the water."

"Had you arranged to meet at a certain time?"

"Yes, and I was there at exactly the time that bloody Tanya Koskov told me, but they weren't there!" said Damian. "She told me 5:30 a.m. I'm sure of it. But now she's telling the police that she told me 5:20 a.m. I think she gave me the wrong time on purpose, so that she could get Charlie alone."

"Why would she do that?"

His face turned ugly. "Because she was the one who wanted to kill Charlie, not me!"

I raised my eyebrows. "That's a serious accusation. Tanya was Charlie's girlfriend. She loved him. Why would she want to kill him?"

Damian gave a sarcastic laugh. "Loved him? That bloody witch just wanted to control him and have him around her like a little pet. And if she thought he wasn't giving her enough attention, she'd throw a tantrum."

"It still doesn't seem like she would have a motive

to murder him."

"She would if she thought he was cheating on her!" Damian retorted. "They had a huge fight the day before May Day. I was in my bedroom and I heard everything. She stormed in here on Thursday morning and accused Charlie of seeing another girl behind her back. Charlie tried to reason with her, but she wouldn't listen—kept screaming about how she would get revenge for his treachery, that she would kill him for betraying her. Talk about drama queen! If you ask me, she could have murdered him simply out of spite—"

"You are telling stories about me, Damian?" came a silky voice.

We spun around to see Tanya Koskov standing in the open doorway. She had her arms up, hands braced on either side of the doorjamb, and her hip tilted to one side, like the model poses often seen in magazines. A mocking smile played on the corners of her lips. I had to admit, it was a pretty dramatic entrance.

Damian gave her a dirty look. "I'm not saying anything that isn't true. I heard you threaten Charlie that day—the day before he was murdered! You said you'd kill him for cheating on you and got all jealous and hysterical over nothing—"

"It was not nothing! I know Charlie was cheating on me!" Tanya hissed. "There are signs. When a man is with you but always, his mind is somewhere else. He will not answer properly when you ask him what he is thinking or where he has been, and he finds reasons for why he cannot see you... I know these signs, I am not wrong. I know Charlie was doing things behind my back. And I will not allow anyone to make a fool of me! Not I, Tanya Vladimirovna Koskov—I will not accept it." She tossed her head back, her nostrils flaring and her eyes flashing.

I had to admit, she looked pretty magnificent and I was impressed, in spite of myself, by her sheer ego and arrogance.

"Yeah, well, Charlie's dead now," said Damian bluntly. "And you're not welcome here anymore."

"I come to get my scarf. I left it in Charlie's room," said Tanya loftily, turning away from us and sauntering over to Charlie's bedroom. She opened the door, ducked under the crime scene tape, and went in. A moment later, she emerged with a cashmere scarf in her hands.

"Er... are you sure you should be removing that from the room?" I asked. "It's an ongoing murder investigation and the police might need to—"

She gave me an insolent stare. "It is mine, not Charlie's. The police have no right to my things."

Damian was looking at me strangely and I realised that he must have been wondering why I was being so diffident with Tanya. If I was really a CID officer, I wouldn't have let her remove anything from the room.

"Aren't you from the police?" he asked.

I flushed. "No. But I... er... I work with them

sometimes."

"You mean, like a private investigator?"

"Er... well, not really... but sort of... in a way..." I stammered. "Um... anyway, I've got to get going. See you later!"

Leaving the two of them staring after me, I practically ran to the door and escaped from the room.

CHAPTER FOURTEEN

I was exhausted when I finally got back home that night. It had been a full day at the tearoom and then the tension of snooping around Haverton College and being caught by Damian Heath had absolutely drained me. Still, I was eager to call Devlin and tell him everything I'd learned.

"Gemma—I was just about to ring you," he said when he picked up his phone.

"How's your day been?"

"Manic. It's just been really bad timing with these two homicide cases coming in practically at the same time."

"Is your case in Blackbird Leys a murder as well?"

"At the moment, it's looking like aggravated assault which resulted in death—the man died in hospital—but we'll have to conduct a full investigation. And then there was a potential kidnapping reported in Summertown." He sighed. "It's just been one of those days..."

Devlin sounded tired and harassed. I felt suddenly sorry for him.

"I won't keep you if you're busy—"

"No, it's great to hear from you, Gemma," he said, his voice warming. "So tell me what you've been up to. It'll be a nice break from all these forensic reports and witness statements. Things busy at the tearoom today?"

"Very. And in particular, I had a customer who shed some light on your May Day murder case."

"Really?"

"Yes, my father has a colleague visiting: a Russian history professor. It's his first time in Oxford and my parents brought him to my tearoom because he was keen to experience a traditional English afternoon tea."

"Well, he went to the right place," said Devlin with a smile in his voice. "I have to say, Gemma, I was daydreaming about your tearoom this afternoon when I was sitting in one of the dreary interviews. I was almost ready to commit murder myself for a decent cup of tea—not the black sludge they brew here in the station cafeteria—and one of your delicious scones."

I laughed. "Well, you know there's one with your name on it waiting for you any time." I sobered and returned to the subject. "Anyway, I got talking to this Professor Obruchev and d'you know what he told me? Tanya Koskov assaulted another girl during a modelling audition and stabbed her with a cheese knife."

Devlin whistled. "When did this happen?"

"A few years ago back in Russia. In her teens."

"It's interesting we didn't pick that up. We ran a background check on her, of course, and I'm still waiting for more information from Interpol, but the preliminary search didn't find any records of assault or other criminal conviction."

"I'm not surprised," I said. "Tanya's father is such a powerful man back in Russia. Professor Obruchev is an old friend of his from university days and he says Vladimir Koskov will do anything to protect his only child. In that instance, he paid off the injured girl's parents so they wouldn't report the incident to the police and he managed to hush the whole thing up."

"Yes, Mr Koskov has been harassing my Superintendent as well. The upshot was that I got called in today and told that I had to tread carefully where Tanya Koskov is concerned. It's why I've been holding off on questioning her again until I've gathered more evidence. Besides the fact that we're not allowed to speak to her anymore unless a lawyer is present, I get the feeling that it would take very little to trigger a complaint all the way up the chain to the Chief Constable. We've already had Mikhail

Petrovsky making noises about police harassment."

"Oh him!" I cried. "He's such a pompous git, isn't he? Who is he anyway?"

"Graduate student at Haverton College, doing a DPhil in Russian philosophy. A complete Slavophile—don't get him started on the subject of great Mother Russia! As you say, a bit of a pompous old bag. Seems to have taken it upon himself to protect a fellow countryman: he was outraged that we would dare to suspect a Russian of murder and kept lecturing us about how we should be treating Vladimir Ivanovich Koskov's daughter," said Devlin irritably. "I'd love to get him for obstruction of justice. I don't know how Tanya stands having him around."

"She probably enjoys it and finds it very amusing," I said. "I get the impression that Tanya likes being the centre of attention and having people fuss over her. It would suit her to have a self-righteous prat hovering around her and defending her honour. But surely with what I just told you about her history of aggression and assault, you'll have enough ammunition now to use on her?"

Devlin didn't sound as enthusiastic I thought he would be. "Perhaps. However, people often do things in their wild youth that they grow out of later on. It's well known that the teenage years are a difficult time, and while some people may have trouble controlling their impulses then, with maturity they become very different people. You can't hold something against Tanya that happened nearly ten years ago. That's what a good lawyer will argue and I know that Koskov will be getting the best solicitor for his daughter. I need a stronger case than this. Right now, what we really need is a motive."

"I can give you a motive," I said. "I heard that Tanya is incredibly jealous and possessive. There are witnesses who overheard an argument between her and Charlie the day before May Day. She was screaming at him and accusing him of cheating on her and threatening to make him regret it."

"Where did you hear this?"

I hesitated. I had been hoping that I wouldn't have to tell Devlin about my evening's activities with the Old Biddies. "Um, well... I sort of got talking with some students at Haverton College."

Devlin sounded annoyed. "Gemma, have you been snooping around again where you shouldn't? I told you not to meddle with the investigation."

"I wasn't meddling—I was just being social. What does it matter if I chat to a couple of the students at Haverton, if we can get valuable information for the case? People don't always like talking to the police but they're happy to have a bit of a gossip."

"Gemma!" Devlin made an exasperated noise. "You know it's not as simple as that. I can't have you going around speaking to witnesses and possibly confusing the issue with leading suggestions. If we then questioned them later, they might say something just because you put the idea into their heads."

"I wouldn't give them leading suggestions!" I said indignantly. "I know better than that! I'm very careful about what I say and I try to let them do most of the talking."

Devlin sighed. "All right... what else did you find out?"

"Well, mostly I was chatting to two girls in the college J.C.R.—one of them happens to live on the same staircase as Charlie and Damian. She was the one who told me she overheard the fight between Tanya and Charlie the day before he was murdered; she also said that Damian is totally different from Charlie—that he could get 'nasty' if he had a bit too much to drink. I got the impression that Damian Heath isn't very well liked and that he's been trying a bit too hard to 'keep up' with his richer roommate."

"Hmm... well, right now he's definitely one of our top suspects. He certainly had the easiest access to the murder weapon, if it's true what Tanya Koskov said about leaving the skewer in the boys' sitting room. Damian could easily have taken it and used it."

I frowned. "It seems a bit stupid, though, don't you think? I mean, he must know that the skewer would be traced back to their room and he'd immediately be flagged as one of the people with access to it. Why use such an incriminating murder weapon?"

I remembered something else and added, "You know, Damian told me that he thinks Tanya gave him the wrong time to meet on purpose."

"Did you talk to Damian too?" Devlin asked sharply.

"Yes, I... um... sort of bumped into him near his room..."

I swallowed nervously. This was now straying out of white lie territory and I hated having to deceive Devlin. But there was no way I was going to tell him about the Old Biddies' stunt impersonating college scouts and sneaking into the boys' room uninvited. In fact, I was suddenly glad that we were having this conversation on the phone because Devlin had always had an uncanny ability to read me, and if we were talking face-to-face, he'd see through my lies in a second.

As it was, he already sounded suspicious as he said, "That was a convenient coincidence, meeting him like that."

"Yes, wasn't it?" I said, as airily as possible. Quickly, I rushed on. "Damian thinks that Tanya had engineered the whole thing so that she could get Charlie alone on May morning. He said that he heard her threaten to kill Charlie during their fight the day before and that she was likely to do it in a jealous rage."

"Now that's very interesting that he told you that..." Devlin's voice was sarcastic.

"Why?"

"Because he conveniently didn't bother to mention that *he himself* had a big fight with Charlie the day before the murder as well."

I drew in a breath. "He did?"

"Uh-huh. My sergeant spoke to some students at Haverton this morning and they said that they overheard Charlie and Damian having a huge bust-up down by the college boathouse the evening before May Day."

"What were they fighting about?"

"That's what I'd like to know," said Devlin. "According to these students, it was something to do with Tanya Koskov—one boy reported hearing Charlie say that it was 'disgusting' and that Damian was 'taking advantage of a vulnerable girl'. Then Charlie said Damian had gone too far this time and threatened to report him to the police."

"Wow..." I said, my mind spinning.

"And what's even more interesting is that these students said Damian stormed away just as they arrived on the scene and that he looked 'murderously angry'—those were the words they used."

"We've got to find out what the two boys were fighting about."

"Don't worry, I'm going to be questioning Damian Heath again at the first opportunity and ask him about this. But Gemma..." Devlin's voice became stern. "I'm telling you again: this is a complicated case and no place for amateurs. I appreciate what you have done but you've got to leave this in the hands of the police now."

I sighed. "All right. I was just trying to help."

Devlin's tone softened. "I know you are. And I do appreciate it, sweetheart."

"Are you almost done for the night?"

"Yes, just about; I've got a couple more reports to read through."

"Why don't you come over when you're done? I can rustle up a late dinner if you—"

"It's okay, I've eaten already. My sergeant got me a sandwich earlier in the evening."

"Oh. Well, I've brought a couple of things back from the tearoom—some Chelsea buns and some delicious chocolate fudge...?"

There was a moment's hesitation, then Devlin said, "Thanks, Gemma. I would have liked to but I've had a really long day and I'm exhausted. I think it's best if I just go home and get an early night. I've got another early start again tomorrow morning."

"Okay. How about lunch tomorrow then? You know it's my day off. I can meet you anywhere you like."

Again, there was hesitation on the other end of the line, then Devlin said, sounding regretful, "I'm sorry, Gemma—with the way these cases are going, I'll probably end up eating lunch at my desk again."

I tried to keep my voice light. "So... I suppose I won't be seeing you tomorrow?"

"I'll try to pop by after work but I can't promise anything. I'll definitely give you a ring tomorrow evening and we'll talk then, okay?"

Devlin's deep voice sounded genuinely contrite

and I felt slightly mollified. Still, when I finally ended the call, the memory of Tanya's bitter words came suddenly back to me:

"There are signs. When a man is with you but always, his mind is somewhere else. He will not answer properly when you ask him what he is thinking or where he has been, and he finds reasons for why he cannot see you... "

CHAPTER FIFTEEN

The next day was the day of Muesli's first therapy visit and I got up early to give her a bath, then groomed her and put her harness on, ready for her special appearance. I was still in two minds about whether this whole "Therapy Cat" thing was a good idea. It was really my mother's enthusiastic prompting that had got me to enrol Muesli but now I wondered whether I had made a terrible mistake.

Oh, Muesli certainly had the right temperament for a therapy cat: she was confident, friendly, and great with strangers, and enjoyed going to new places, regarding everything with a cheeky curiosity. The problem was, she was a bit *too* confident, really, and not inclined to follow orders.

Since it was our first visit, Jane Banks, the

program coordinator, had offered to accompany us with her own cat, a lovely placid Ragdoll, to show us the ropes. She met us outside the nursing home, a small establishment just on the other side of Magdalen Bridge, situated on the banks of the river. In fact, I thought the residents must have a great view of Oxford city when they looked out of their windows.

"Everyone is very excited to meet Muesli," Jane said to me as we went in. "The Matron has organised for us to start in the lounge area as she thought this might be easier. You won't have to take Muesli from room to room—you can just meet several of the residents in one place. And then Muesli can relax in one environment and get comfortable."

I looked down at my little tabby. Muesli seemed to be having no problems getting comfortable already. She was squirming eagerly in my arms, eyeing everything with great interest, as we walked through the reception area. We were shown into the comfortable lounge room, furnished with plump sofas upholstered with floral covers and a thick pink carpet underfoot. Several of the residents were already waiting and their faces lit up as we entered.

"Oh! I want to hold the new kitty!" cried one lady, stretching out her gnarled hands.

Jane gave me a nod and I unclipped Muesli's leash from her harness, then leaned forwards to place her gently on the old lady's lap. But no sooner had I let go of the little cat than she sprang off and jumped onto the back of the sofa.

"Oh!" cried the lady in surprise.

I flushed. "Sorry!" I exclaimed. "It's Muesli's first visit today so she's not... um—"

"I think she likes *me* better!" said a second lady sitting at the other end of the couch, as Muesli began making her way along the back of the sofa towards her.

She reached the other lady and sniffed her inquisitively. "*Meorrw?*"

"Hello sweetie..." The second old lady beamed, putting out a hand to stroke her.

Muesli perched by the second lady's shoulder and sniffed her ear. I began to relax slightly. *Okay, maybe Muesli just needs a bit of time, but she'll soon be cuddling in the woman's lap...*

My hope was short lived. Muesli gave the second lady a thorough sniffing-over, then continued her way to the next couch, jumping and hopping across laps and shoulders and eliciting a series of startled gasps and *Oh!*'s as she went. I glanced over at Jane and squirmed with embarrassment. *Great.* Her cat was sitting placidly in the lap of an elderly gentleman, purring gently. My cat was being an absolute terror, climbing around the room, using the senior residents as a jungle gym.

"I'm so sorry," I said again. "She's not normally like this..."

Who am I kidding? This was exactly what Muesli was normally like. Never in her life has she sedately done what she was told or sat where she was supposed to. What on earth had possessed me to think that she could be a good therapy cat?

"Oh, be careful!" cried the Matron, putting up her hands in alarm as Muesli leapt from the back of an armchair onto the shelf above the mantelpiece.

Several ornaments had been arranged along the shelf—little china dolls and dainty glass animals—as well as a large vase of flowers. My heart lurched as Muesli began walking along the shelf, lifting her paws up deftly and stepping over the ornaments.

"Muesli! Get down!" I cried, running over towards her. I didn't dare grab her in case it might startle her into swiping one of the ornaments off the shelf, so instead I hovered anxiously next to the shelf, watching in agony as she carefully picked her way across.

"*Meorrw?*" she said as she reached the other side, giving me an innocent look.

"What are you doing, you little minx?" I hissed under my breath. "You're supposed to be cuddling with the residents and providing soothing comfort, not causing havoc!"

"*Meorrw!*" Muesli gave me a cheeky look and jumped off the shelf, onto the floor. I made a dive for her but she evaded my grasp, trotting across the room. I heard a tinkle of laughter and looked up to see an old lady in a wheelchair leaning forwards, her eyes sparkling.

"Your cat is a funny one!" she quavered. "I don't

think we've had this much excitement in years!"

I smiled weakly. Then I heard a startled cry and turned quickly, my eyes widening with horror. Muesli had finally decided on the one person she was happy to settle down on—the only problem was, the person she had chosen was a large elderly gentleman and the place she had chosen to curl up was on top of his bald head!

I ran across the room, gasping, "Oh! My God, I'm so sorry! I—"

"No, no, it's all right. Leave her," said the elderly gentleman, his voice muffled from behind Muesli's fluffy tail, which was hanging down over his face. He looked like he was wearing a bizarre Russian *ushanka* fur cap. I didn't know whether to laugh or cry.

His faded blue eye twinkled at me. "I like cats. She seems to be comfortable."

Yeah, Muesli certainly seemed to be comfortable. She perched happily on top of the gentleman's bald head for the next ten minutes while I sat next to him in mortification and tried to make conversation. The other residents were delighted, pointing and giggling at him, and several got up to hover around the armchair and fuss over Muesli on his head.

The elderly gentleman gave me a wink. "Haven't had this much attention from the ladies in years," he said with a chuckle. "I think I shall have to hire your cat as my headpiece on a regular basis."

I laughed in spite of myself. "I really am very sorry.

She is just so naughty."

"Ah, but the naughty ones always have the most personality," he said with a smile.

Finally, Muesli deigned to come down off the man's head and make herself comfortable on his lap. He stroked her and chatted to her for a few moments, then I managed to get hold of her and snap her leash back onto her halter. I had expected the nursing home to cut short our visit and hustle us out after that disastrous episode but, to my surprise, when I turned around, I found the Matron standing next to me, smiling.

"Everyone in the Home is talking about Muesli now and some of the residents who are still in their rooms are desperate to meet her. Would you mind taking her around to visit some of them?"

"Uh... sure, of course," I said, dumbfounded.

With Jane giving me a wave and a smile of encouragement, I left her and her Ragdoll entertaining the residents in the lounge and followed the Matron to the lift. We went into several different rooms on each level and I was relieved that, on the whole, Muesli behaved herself.

The last room we visited was on the top floor and belonged to an elderly man with a military bearing who held himself very erect, despite needing a cane to walk. He patted Muesli perfunctorily but I quickly realised that he wasn't that interested in cats—he was just keen to have company and someone to talk to. I listened politely as he told me about his career in the British Royal Navy and dutifully admired the tiny model ships encased in glass bottles that were displayed along his windowsill.

"You've got a fantastic view from here, Captain Thomas," I commented, looking out through the window. His room was one that faced the river and had a view of the famous Oxford skyline, with Magdalen College and its great bell tower in the forefront. In fact, they looked so close, I wondered if one could hear the choir singing from here on May mornings.

As if reading my thoughts, Captain Thomas said, "Yes, I asked for a top-floor room. Like to be up where I can see things—keep an eye out for what's going on. Got a great view a few days ago of the May morning hoo-ha."

I glanced down again and suddenly noticed something at the far end of the windowsill, tucked behind the curtains. A pair of binoculars. Something jogged in my memory: that morning—the morning after the murder—when I had gone for an early walk and come to Magdalen Bridge, I had seen what looked like a strange winking, flashing light from one of the windows on a building on this side of the river. Now I suddenly realised what that was. Not a flashing light, but sunlight reflecting off glass—like the lens on a pair of binoculars.

"Do you often use your binoculars to look out, Captain Thomas?" I asked, reaching over to pick them up.

The old man gave a start and looked slightly shifty. "Ah! Er... yes, those are for birdwatching. Bit of a hobby of mine, you know... there are many interesting species of... um... ducks and... and birds down by the river."

I turned away, hiding a smile. *Birdwatching my foot!* as Mabel would say. The captain was obviously a nosy old fellow who enjoyed using the binoculars to spy on the pedestrians in the streets below. In fact, from this angle, he could see clearly across Magdalen Bridge, past Magdalen Tower, and halfway up the High Street into Oxford city itself. He'd be able to amuse himself watching the tourists, students, and local residents going about their daily business. For an elderly person who was alone a lot of the time, it was probably a very good hobby.

And maybe even a very helpful one, I thought suddenly.

"Did you happen to use your binoculars on May morning?" I asked casually. "You know, when the choir was singing?"

"Always watch it every year," he said.

I turned eagerly. "So you saw the boy go off the bridge?"

"Saw the whole thing. Not the first time that sort of thing's happened, of course—silly buggers are always at it every year, despite all the police warnings about how shallow the river is. Students have no sense! Of course, they're usually fine—although there were several bad injuries a few years ago.

Ambulances there for hours afterwards. But I have to say, I'd never seen one go down like this year. Gave me a bit of a shock when I saw the body float up like that. The stupid boy must have hit his head on the side of the bridge going down or something. Poor chap. Nasty accident..." He shook his head.

I stared at him. "It wasn't an accident, Captain Thomas. In fact, the police think it might have been murder."

His eyebrows shot up. "Murder?"

"Yes, it's been in all the papers."

"Don't read the papers," he snapped. "Full of nonsense these days. Don't print anything worth reading."

"Oh... well, the police are very keen to speak to anyone who might have information about the incident. I'm sure they'd be interested in what you saw."

He frowned. "Didn't see anything like murder. Just saw the boy go off the side of the bridge."

"But right before that? Did you see anything—perhaps in the crowd—right before the boy went over?"

He frowned even harder. "No, just the usual. People throwing things in the air and waving their arms and cheering. Lots of moving about, of course—people embracing and all that. Then I saw a body—the boy—lurching over the top of the balustrade, then rolling over and going into the water. And the crowd rushing to the side of the bridge after him. I thought at first that there would be more jumpers getting up on the balustrade, but then I saw the body floating and the crowd going quiet."

I shivered again at the memory that his words brought back. It had been an awful moment: that horrified, eerie stillness after all the cheering and elation.

"And that's all?" I asked. "Nothing else you noticed?"

He shook his head. I tried to hide my disappointment. Oh well, it would have been too good to be true. It was only in books and movies that witnesses conveniently see the murderer when they look out the window.

I gave him a smile. "Well, I'm sure the police would still like to speak to you. Would you mind if I—"

"There was that odd bloke running away," he said suddenly.

"What do you mean?

"Well, it was after the boy went over. I told you the crowd all rushed towards the side of the bridge— except that I noticed one chap going in the opposite direction. It caught my attention because I've got the view from above and I could see him pushing his way through the crowd, *away* from the side of the bridge, rather than towards it. I thought that was a bit odd because most people were rushing to see what had happened, whereas he was rushing away from it."

"Did you see his face?"

"No, had his back to me."

"How did you know it was a man then?

"Hmm... I suppose it could have been a woman. Wasn't very tall. But I thought the way he moved— seemed like a man."

"What about hair colour?"

"Oh, he was wearing one of those things that young people like to wear nowadays. A sort of cotton jumper with a hood."

"A hoodie? What colour was it?"

"Dark grey, I think. Or a sort of faded black. It had some letters across the back."

"What letters?" I asked eagerly.

He furrowed his brow in an effort to remember. "My memory isn't what it used to be... Think it was O...E...M...C? Or maybe O...K...? It definitely had an O at the beginning and a C at the end." He shrugged. "Sorry I can't be more help."

I gave him an understanding smile. "That's okay. I think that's still really valuable information that the police would want. Would you be happy to speak to them?"

His chest swelled with importance. "Naturally, naturally. Delighted to help."

"Great. I'll let them know." I turned around, suddenly remembering Muesli. She had been very quiet and now I realised why. She had curled up on Captain Thomas's pillow and gone to sleep! It had been a big morning for the little tabby and even her boundless energy had run low. I went over and gently scooped her up. She was a warm, floppy bundle in my arms.

"*Me...orrw?*" she said sleepily.

"Come on, Muesli—time to go home, I think," I said with a grin.

I thanked Captain Thomas again, then returned to the ground floor with my sleepy cat. Jane was waiting for us in the reception with her Ragdoll already back in his cat carrier. She was chatting to the Matron and looked up with a smile as I stepped out of the lift.

"I was just about to come and find you," she said.

"Sorry, I got a bit side-tracked chatting to one of the residents," I said.

"Poor Muesli—she looks worn out!" said the Matron, putting out a hand to stroke my little tabby as I placed her gently back into her carrier.

I laughed. "Oh, I think it's good for her. She really enjoyed herself this morning."

"And we've really enjoyed having her—no, I mean that," said the Matron with a smile as she saw my expression. "She's really livened up the place. I can't tell you how much the residents have perked up. They'll be talking about her antics for days, I'm sure! We're all eagerly looking forward to her next visit."

"Oh... thank you," I said, flushing with surprise and pleasure.

A few of the residents had congregated in the reception area to say goodbye to the cats and finally, with a smile and wave, Muesli and I bade goodbye to her new fan club and left the nursing home.

CHAPTER SIXTEEN

I cycled home and deposited Muesli in her favourite spot on the sagging old couch, then rang Devlin. His mobile was engaged, so I tried the CID office. His sergeant answered.

"The guv'nor? He's just gone out for lunch."

"For lunch? But I thought... He told me he was having a working lunch in the office today. Was it a last-minute thing?"

"Dunno. Just told me that he was planning to go out for lunch. Had a meeting, he said."

"Something in connection with one of your cases?"

"Maybe. He didn't give any details. Plays his cards close to his chest sometimes, the inspector does."

Yes, he certainly does.

"Um... Well, when he comes back, can you ask

him to give me a ring? I've got some information for him, about the May Day murder case."

"You could speak to me," the sergeant said importantly. "I'm interviewing a lot of the witnesses on that case, as the inspector's so tied up with the Blackbird Leys homicide."

"I think I'd rather speak to Devlin directly. I'll try him again on his mobile but, just in case, can you give him the message too?"

"Yeah, sure. But it might be a while before he gets back—he only left about ten minutes ago."

I hung up and stood in my living room, undecided. It was ironic—Monday was the one day I had off each week and I usually looked forward to it with great anticipation. It was wonderful having a day where I could sleep in, laze around the house, catch up on chores and other things, curl up with a book, watch a movie... but today, the hours seemed to suddenly stretch in front of me, with no work or events to take my mind off things. Instead, I was struggling not to let my imagination run away with itself, conjuring up images of Devlin having secret assignations with leggy blondes...

I heaved an exasperated sigh. *This is ridiculous!* I decided I would go out for lunch myself, and then maybe have a little wander through town, do some window-shopping. That would stop me sitting at home, brooding over Devlin's whereabouts. I grabbed my coat and keys once more and left the cottage.

As I turned onto the towpath by the river and

began walking towards town, I felt a sense of delight again at having found such a great place to live. Oxford was probably one of the most expensive cities to live in the U.K.: it had easy access to London and a beautiful location near the Cotswolds, not to mention its own spectacular architecture, vibrant cultural scene and shopping. I had searched in vain for somewhere I could afford and I had almost given up hope—when I had found this cottage. It was perfect, situated at the south end of the city, in a secluded close on the banks of the River Thames. Yes, it was old and rundown, but the bones were solid and I knew it was perfect for me and Muesli.

I had been expecting—given its brilliant central location—that the rent would be astronomical. But to my surprise, I found that the cottage had been sitting empty for so long that the owners were happy to accept a heavily discounted rent. *It was almost as if it was meant to be*, I thought with a smile as I walked slowly up St Aldate's Street, heading towards Carfax, the main crossroads at the centre of Oxford.

My steps faltered as I suddenly saw a man coming down the other side of St Aldate's, towards me. It was Devlin! There was no mistaking his tall handsome figure. I started to raise a hand to wave and catch his attention, but then something stopped me. He was walking in a hurried manner, casting an occasional look over his shoulder, and I suddenly remembered his mysterious lunch appointment.

Was he on his way to meet somebody?

I ducked behind a tall red Royal Mail post box and watched Devlin as he continued past me on the other side of the street. He paused on the corner of a small winding lane that led off from St Aldate's, gave a last quick look around, then ducked into the lane and disappeared. I hesitated for a second, then, with a hasty look both ways to make sure that no car was coming, I ran across the street and arrived at the mouth of the lane myself.

I peered cautiously around the corner. Devlin was already quite a long way down the lane, walking at a brisk pace. I darted after him. The lane slowly widened into an open area with some shops on the left side, and then a series of wooden tables arranged beside an old building with whitewashed walls and black framed windows. I came around the curve and into the open area just in time to see Devlin's tall figure disappear into the doorway of the old building.

I recognised it: it was the Bear Inn, a thirteenth-century town pub and one of the oldest in Oxford. Tucked down this back lane, away from the hustle and bustle of the city, it was a bit of a hidden gem that most tourists didn't know about. It hadn't been one of my "regular" pubs as a student but I had come here a few times and I was familiar with the layout. My heart sank. The Bear Inn was charming partly because of its tiny, cosy interior, with the low ceilings and dark wood panelled walls of an old historic pub. If Devlin was standing by the bar, it would be practically impossible to enter the pub without being seen, and there would certainly be nowhere to hide.

But luck was with me. As I was debating what to do, I saw Devlin step out again, carrying two pints of beer, and make his way to one of the wooden tables that made up the Bear Inn's outdoor beer garden.

I dropped quickly behind a low wall with an ornamental hedge and held my breath. Had he seen me? I edged to the side of the wall and looked around. No, Devlin was sitting at one of the tables very close to me but his back was turned. He was facing the direction where the lane curved around the corner of the pub and I realised suddenly that he was waiting for someone—someone who would probably be coming down the lane from the other direction. I knew the lane continued and opened out onto Oriel Square, which in turn led to Merton Street and the accesses to Christ Church Meadow. *Who could be coming from there?* I wondered.

I glanced quickly around. The wall I had crouched behind marked the boundary between the beer garden and the pavement in front of the shops. Behind me was a metal rack with several bicycles parked against it, and beyond that was another low wall. If someone came up the lane from the direction that Devlin was facing, they wouldn't be able to see me, but if someone came from behind me—which was the direction that I had come from myself—then they would see me skulking here against the wall and wonder what I was doing.

I peered back up the lane. I could see no one. Still,

just in case, I hastily untied one shoe, then picked up the ends of the laces and held them poised in my hands. If anyone saw me now, hopefully it would look like they had happened upon me just as I was crouching down to tie my shoelaces.

The sound of footsteps made me jerk my head up. Cautiously, I peered around the side of the low wall and looked towards the other end of the lane. A couple appeared around the corner, walking arm in arm, talking and laughing. They disappeared into the pub. Devlin turned his head slightly and I saw his face in profile. There was disappointment in his expression. He glanced at his watch.

Then I heard footsteps again. High heels. A tall woman came around the corner, with loose brown hair and beautiful dark eyes. She was wearing tight jeans tucked into leather boots and a figure-hugging sweater. She smiled as she stepped into the beer garden, heading straight for Devlin.

CHAPTER SEVENTEEN

I caught my breath, my heart pounding painfully in my chest. Then I felt my body go limp as the woman walked past Devlin and stopped at the table beyond his. I realised belatedly that there was a man sitting there. He was wearing a dark brown sweater that blended with the wood of the table and benches, and he had been hunched over his phone, which was why I had barely noticed him.

"Darling, have you been waiting long?" she asked him.

"A bit, but that's okay—I was catching up on some emails..."

I let out the breath I had been holding, feeling suddenly silly and ridiculous. What was I doing, skulking around like this? I should have just walked over to Devlin, said hello, and asked who he was waiting for. But just as I was about to stand up, a new figure came around the side of the pub: Damian Heath. Devlin put a hand up and the boy came rapidly towards him.

I felt a wave of relief mixed with shame. Of course! Devlin was meeting a suspect, not some woman. How could I even have thought that of him? I scooted along the wall until I was at the very end, which was right next to their table, and strained my ears to listen to their conversation.

Damian dropped into the seat next to Devlin and looked surprised as the latter pushed a pint of beer towards him.

"How come we're meeting here and not at the college or the police station?" he asked suspiciously.

Devlin's voice was warm, friendly. "I thought this would be nicer and, since you're helping me with enquiries, I thought the least I could do was buy you a drink."

"Don't know how else I can help you—I've told you everything I know," said Damian sullenly.

"Well, you know how these things are... We have to go over the details again. It's a pain but it's got to be done. Cheers." Devlin raised his glass.

The boy hesitated, then raised his own glass and drank. After a moment, he put the beer down and I saw him relax slightly. "So... what do you want to ask me?"

"Well, I just need to go over the details of the day

before May Day. You said in your statement that you were in your room all morning, working on an essay?"

"Yeah, that's right. That was when Tanya came barging in and started screeching at Charlie like a banshee."

"And then afterwards?"

"I told you—I was pretty much in my room all day. Charlie and Tanya were having this fancy dress party that night and there were loads of people coming in and out. Charlie had bought a bunch of party props and stuff like that and everyone was coming to help themselves."

"And then?"

"Well, I got sick of all the noise and stuff in the late afternoon, and I went out for a bit of a wander, you know, to get some fresh air. And then I went back, went to dinner in Hall, and then got into my costume and went to the party. It was in Tanya's room. I stayed there till around twelve-thirty and then came back to my own room and crashed."

"Where did you go when you went out for this 'wander'?"

The boy avoided Devlin's gaze. "I... um... just into town. I walked up to Carfax and then turned around and went back."

"Did you buy anything?"

"No, I just wanted to get some air."

"Are you sure you didn't walk in a different direction... like, say, down past Christ Church

Meadow to the college boathouses?" Devlin's voice was still friendly but there was a hint of steel in it now.

Damian jerked slightly. "I... no, no—I told you, I walked into town."

"And what time was that?"

"Uh... must have been around five-thirty, six o'clock."

Devlin didn't say anything for a moment, then he gave a sigh and leaned forwards slightly. "Damian... I'm trying to help you, mate. I'm giving you the chance to correct any... discrepancies in your previous statement. This is just a friendly chat, remember—we're not in a police interview room. If there's something you didn't like to mention before, now would be a good time to tell me."

Damian hesitated, then shook his head.

Devlin's voice hardened and he abandoned his friendly manner. "In that case, you can explain to me why you're lying. I have witnesses who say they saw you and Charlie down by the college boathouse at around six that evening—the same time when you insist that you were walking into town."

Damian swallowed and I saw his Adam's apple bobbing. "I... I..."

"The witnesses also say that you and Charlie were having a massive bust-up," Devlin continued relentlessly.

"Okay, yeah, we were there," Damian admitted. "Charlie texted me just as I was leaving the college for my walk. He said he wanted to speak to me about something. But he didn't want to do it in college, so we agreed to meet down by the boathouse. But the... the argument was nothing—"

"It didn't sound like nothing to the witnesses who overheard you," said Devlin. "Not when Charlie was threatening to report you to the police."

Damian shifted in his seat, looking like he wanted to jump up and run away.

"It was about Tanya, wasn't it?" Devlin pressed.

"Yeah, it was about that bloody cow," Damian burst out. "It was the only thing we ever argued about, okay? Things were great between Charlie and me until Tanya Koskov came along," he said bitterly.

"So what was the fight about? Why did Charlie say you were taking advantage of a vulnerable girl?"

Damian looked uneasy. "It was nothing, I tell you! Charlie just got his knickers in a twist, that's all. It had nothing to do with his murder."

"I'll be the judge of that," said Devlin. "I repeat, Damian, what were you fighting about?"

"It... It was..." Damian licked his lips several times, his eyes darting around. "I told you, it was nothing—I just... I just offered Tanya a spliff and Charlie found out about it and cut up rough."

"A spliff?"

"Yeah, you know—a joint, weed, hash..."

"You were trying to get Tanya into drugs?"

"Hey!" Damian held his hands up in the classic surrender position. "No, no! It wasn't heroin or cocaine or something—it was just a bit of marijuana. I don't do hard drugs, okay? Everyone smokes a bit of weed at university."

"Not everyone," said Devlin dryly. "And I take it that Charlie obviously didn't."

Damian shuffled his feet. "Yeah, well…"

Devlin leaned back, narrowing his eyes. "Charlie was your best friend. It seems an extreme reaction, threatening to report you to the police just for offering a bit of marijuana."

"Well, you didn't know Charlie. He was a bit of a stuffed shirt that way. I mean, he liked to party and he liked to drink but he was old-fashioned about some things, especially about girls. He had this idea that they had to be protected and all that…" He gave a scornful laugh. "Protect Tanya? You're more likely to need protection *from* her!"

"You really dislike Tanya Koskov, don't you?"

Damian gave a shrug. "She's a stuck-up cow with more money than she deserves."

"And what about your friend, Charlie? He was very wealthy too. Must have been tough for you, living next to him, seeing all the things that he could afford, always struggling to keep up… were you jealous of him?"

"No, I wasn't," snapped Damian. "Charlie was cool, okay? He never rubbed his money in your face and he wasn't stuck up like Tanya. He was really generous—he'd give me gifts all the time and… and lend me money if I needed it. He was a good mate."

His voice cracked slightly.

"But this 'good mate' was threatening to report you, which could have meant being expelled from the university, or even a criminal conviction. Didn't you feel betrayed? And all because of a girl that you despised? You must have been really bitter and angry—and scared. All very good motives to murder Charlie to prevent him exposing you and to get revenge..."

"No!" Damian cried. He gave Devlin a fierce look. "No, that's bollocks! I was angry, yes, but the person I was angry at was Tanya, not Charlie. And anyway, I knew him... he wouldn't have really reported me. He was my friend and he wouldn't have done that to me. And likewise—I would never have hurt him." He paused, then added earnestly, "Look, if you don't believe me, then look at it from a cold-blooded point of view. It would have been stupid of me to kill Charlie. Having him around was much better for me, whereas now he's gone... well, basically, I'm not going to have a rich friend to sponge off anymore. It's not like I get any money from his will or something!"

I winced slightly as I heard those words, suddenly reminded of Miriam Hopkins and the fact that she was still a suspect in this murder case too. Damian was right. He didn't stand to gain from Charlie's death—if anything, he'd be killing off the golden goose. Miriam Hopkins, on the other hand, gained a lot from Charlie's death...

A shrill ringing pierced the air. Devlin took out his

177

phone and answered it curtly. After a moment, he hung up.

"I've got to go," he said to Damian, rising from the table. "But I might want to speak to you again."

"Yeah, all right..." said Damian, jumping up also. He couldn't keep the relief and elation out of his voice and I saw Devlin narrow his blue eyes thoughtfully.

"You're still keeping something back from me, Damian," said Devlin suddenly. "You've got my card and you know how to contact me. I suggest you come forward and tell me what it is of your own accord before I discover it myself..."

With those ominous parting words, Devlin turned and walked away from the table. I jerked back and scurried behind a couple of parked bicycles. Crouching over my shoe, I pretended to tie my laces, keeping my face turned away as he strode past me, going back up the lane towards St Aldate's. But even so, Devlin would definitely have noticed me if his phone hadn't rung again just as he was walking past and he was distracted as he answered it. I could hear his voice getting fainter as he walked back out to the main street.

I breathed a sigh of relief and slowly stood up, stretching my cramped muscles. My thighs were protesting and one foot had gone slightly numb. I rotated my ankle, grimacing as feeling came back into the foot, then glanced quickly back towards the pub. Damian was just leaving the beer garden and thankfully was not looking my way. He was headed down the lane in the opposite direction, back the way he had come.

I hesitated for a moment. I could probably still catch up with Devlin if I ran. On the other hand... I looked back to where Damian's figure was just disappearing around the pub. Making a sudden decision, I turned and ran after him instead.

CHAPTER EIGHTEEN

I'd assumed that Damian would head back to Haverton College, taking the back route along Merton Street, which came out onto the High Street just by his college. However, to my surprise, he left Merton Street and took the narrow lane that led towards Christ Church Meadow and joined up with Dead Man's Walk. I frowned, confused at his actions. Dead Man's Walk led to Rose Lane, which came out onto the High Street much farther down. Down by Magdalen College and the bridge, in fact. Was that where Damian was headed?

I followed him as close as I dared—which wasn't very close, since Dead Man's Walk was fairly exposed and, if he turned around, he would definitely see me if I didn't keep my distance. And thank goodness I did keep my distance, because when Damian reached the end of Dead Man's Walk, he stopped and threw a furtive look around. I dropped down instantly and did my shoelace-tying trick again. When I dared to look up, I was surprised to see that he had taken the right fork, which led down towards the meadow.

Christ Church Meadow was shaped roughly like an upside-down triangle, with the tip at the bottom touching the River Thames. It was bordered on three sides by lovely walks, the widest being the Broad Walk, which ran horizontally across the north side of the meadow (or the "base" of the upside-down triangle) and also parallel to Dead Man's Walk. That was the route I had taken on May morning. On the east side, the River Cherwell bordered the meadow, a small tributary which started up in north Oxfordshire, ran under Magdalen Bridge, and meandered down to join the Thames. There was a narrow path that ran between the meadow and the Cherwell, known as the Christ Church Meadow Walk, and this was the path that Damian was making for now.

I knew that path—I'd often walked there as a student when I wanted a peaceful stroll on a Sunday morning. It was a beautiful route, with the serene Cherwell on one side and the open meadow on the other. Trees growing along the banks of the river arched their branches over the path and formed an elegant avenue. In the height of summer, the Cherwell was popular with punters steering the long, narrow wooden boats so iconic to Oxford and Cambridge, but today the river seemed empty, probably because of the grey weather and slight nip in the air. The path was unpaved and could be muddy in wet weather, particularly as Christ Church Meadow was a flood meadow and turned into a marshland during the wet months of winter. Thankfully the path ran along a raised strip of land, which sloped down to the Cherwell on one side and to a ditch alongside the meadow on the other.

I followed Damian discreetly, wondering why he had come to this secluded walk. Perhaps he simply fancied a stroll through some greenery, but somehow I felt that there was a purposeful air to his manner. I was proven right a few moments later when I saw him veering off towards the ditch which ran alongside the right side of the path. He paused and looked over his shoulder, and I just had time to duck around the side of a tree trunk.

I thought for a moment that he had seen me, but thankfully the winding path hid me from view. When I peeked around the trunk, he had turned around again and was taking a few steps off the path and down into the ditch. I frowned. *What is he doing?* I hesitated, then ran lightly forwards, trying to keep behind the line of trees, until I was level with him, but on the other side of the path, beside the river. I huddled as best I could behind a tree trunk. It was a pretty narrow one and Damian would have been sure to see me if he looked around properly, but he seemed to be too intent on what he was doing. He had crouched down in the ditch and looked like he was searching for something.

I craned my neck but couldn't see what he was doing. After a moment's hesitation, I decided to go closer. If he looked up and saw me, well, I would just pretend that I happened to be walking here too. After all, it was a public pathway.

Slowly, I crossed the path and crept towards the ditch, trying to peer over Damian's shoulder. He had his back to me and was crouched down next to the tall grasses and bushes that grew in the ditch. I couldn't see what he was doing, but, from his posture, it looked like one hand was tucked against his body and the other was reaching forwards, groping in the undergrowth.

Then something snapped under my foot and there was a loud *CRACK!*

Damian whipped around, then teetered on his heels and lost his balance. His arms splayed out and he fell backwards into the ditch, by a pool of muddy water. There was a loud splash.

He looked up and saw me, and I saw his eyes widen with dismay—and fear.

"Sorry!" I said, giving him an innocent smile. "I didn't mean to startle you. I was just wondering what you were doing?"

"Uh... nothing," he said, scrambling to his feet. He glanced quickly at the pool of muddy water, then dusted off the seat of his jeans and took a step away from me.

I pressed on. "Then why did you go down into the ditch? You looked like you were searching for something."

He scowled at me. "Nothing, I tell you! I wasn't searching for anything. I... I just thought I saw something shiny... I thought someone might have dropped something valuable so I went down to check it out."

Yeah, right, a likely story. "Did you find anything?" I asked.

"No, nothing," he mumbled. "Must have been a trick of the light. Anyway, I've got to go. Late for a lecture..." And without another word, he turned and hurried off.

I stood watching his retreating figure as it disappeared into the distance. Something was nagging me—something about the scene just now—but I couldn't put my finger on it. I felt like there was something staring me in the face, some important clue I was missing...

What had Damian really been doing? I looked thoughtfully back at the ditch and hunkered down myself to look in the undergrowth. I pushed aside the long grass, being careful not to step into the muddy pool of water. I could see nothing. If Damian had been searching for something, it wasn't here. I stood up again and dusted off my hands, then, with a sigh, turned and headed back towards town.

***

"Gemma? Did you hear what I said?"

I gave a guilty start and refocused on Cassie across the table. "Sorry, Cass—I missed the last bit. Do you mind repeating it?

My best friend rolled her eyes. "You haven't been listening to a thing I said, have you? You're miles away!"

"Sorry, sorry!" I reached across the table and pulled the pieces of paper towards me. They were various designs for the tearoom website which Cassie had been eager to show me. She had rung me just as I was starting towards home from Christ Church Meadow and suggested that we meet at a café in town. But once we'd got here, I found myself struggling to keep my mind on things like search engine optimisation and website meta data.

"What are you so preoccupied about?" demanded Cassie. "That thing with Devlin again?"

"Oh, no." I gave an embarrassed smile. "I think you were right—I was just being silly and paranoid."

"So what were you thinking about then?"

"About the May Day murder," I confessed. "I just can't get it out of my mind. I keep going over the suspects in my head and it all feels so... so convoluted!"

"Convoluted?" Cassie grinned. "Well, aren't all murder cases convoluted? Otherwise the police would have caught the killer already."

"Yes, but what I mean is... well, usually there's one suspect who seems stronger than the rest, who you feel *sure* is the killer and you've just got to find the evidence to prove it. But this time..." I spread my hands helplessly. "They *all* seem to be equally likely—and also equally unlikely!"

"Surely the police must have a number one suspect? Who does Devlin fancy as the murderer?"

"He hasn't said. I know Miriam Hopkins was originally top of the list, because the murder weapon belonged to her and she couldn't account for her movements on May morning."

"And she stands to gain a lot by the boy's death," Cassie reminded me.

"Yes, that's right. But still, I just can't believe... Oh, it's crazy! It can't be Miriam!"

"Well, who else do the police have as suspects?" asked Cassie reasonably. "The girlfriend?"

"Yes, she's a definite possibility. She's assaulted someone in the past with a knife... *and* she had a fight with Charlie the day before he was killed, where she threatened to make him sorry for cheating on her."

"He was cheating on her?"

I shrugged. "I don't know. I doubt it, but it seems that Tanya Koskov is the jealous type—"

"Aw, come on!" said Cassie. "This is real life, not a TV soap opera! People don't murder each other out of jealousy—that's such a lame motive."

"Not premeditated murder, perhaps," I said. "But

I can see someone losing their head in a jealous rage and lashing out. The French even have a phrase for it—*crime passionnel*—the crime of passion, right?"

"But this wasn't that," Cassie pointed out. "This had to be premeditated—unless you're telling me that the murderer happened to walk around with a barbecue skewer in his pocket all the time, just in case he needed to stab someone in a jealous rage and wanted something sharp handy."

I giggled at Cassie's facetious tone. "No, you're right—and that's why I say it doesn't fit. Tanya might have had the best *opportunity* of killing Charlie—she was standing right next to him—and I can imagine her being bold enough and clever enough to take the risk of murdering him in public like that, as a sort of double bluff, but the method of murder just doesn't fit with her potential motive."

"Okay, what about the roommate then? I thought the police had him in their sights too."

"Damian Heath? Yes, he's a strong possibility. He hasn't got an alibi for the time of the murder either; he had easy access to the murder weapon since the skewer was just sitting in the boys' living room, waiting to be returned to Miriam... and he had a motive."

Cassie raised her eyebrows. "What motive?"

"He had a big fight with Charlie the day before the murder as well, and some witnesses overheard Charlie threatening to report Damian to the police."

"Charlie was going to report Damian to the police?

What for?"

"Well, the witnesses said it was to do with Damian taking advantage of Tanya in some way. Charlie was really angry about that. When Devlin questioned Damian about it, he said it was no big deal—that he was just offering Tanya a bit of marijuana and Charlie overreacted."

Cassie looked at me curiously. "How do you know all this?"

I flushed slightly. I was too embarrassed to tell Cassie about my little stunt earlier today, following Devlin around Oxford and eavesdropping on his conversation with Damian. I squirmed at the memory. I was worse than those women who snooped in their boyfriends' mobile phone text messages!

"I... um... just happened to come across Devlin questioning Damian outside the Bear Inn earlier today."

Cassie eyed me suspiciously. "That was a bit of a lucky coincidence."

I gave her a bright smile. "Yes, wasn't it? Anyway, I didn't want to disturb their interview so I just sort of... um... hovered in the background."

"You mean you eavesdropped," said Cassie with a grin. "Don't worry, Gemma, you can just come out and say it. I've spent enough time with the Old Biddies and, you know, they consider eavesdropping a fine art."

I laughed. "Yeah, all right, perhaps I did eavesdrop

a bit." I leaned forwards excitedly. "And I'll tell you something else: I followed Damian after the interview and he did something weird. He went down to Christ Church Meadow, down to the path by the Cherwell, and started rooting around in the ditch on the meadow side."

"In the ditch? What was he doing there?"

I shrugged. "I couldn't really see. It looked like he was searching for something... he seemed to be feeling around in the undergrowth. But then he saw me and got a fright and, of course, denied that he was doing anything specific." I rolled my eyes. "He gave me some cock and bull story about seeing something shiny and thinking someone might have dropped something valuable by the side of the path."

"Did you get a chance to look yourself?"

I nodded. "Yeah, after he went off, I had a good look around in the ditch but there was nothing. If there was something hidden there, I couldn't see it."

"Weird," said Cassie, shaking her head.

"It's been bugging me ever since. I feel like there was something I saw or heard, when I was with Damian, that's important somehow... but I just can't figure out what it is! Argh!" I pounded my fist on the table in frustration.

"Maybe you should stop trying so hard," suggested Cassie. "You know what they say—if you let it go, then maybe your mind will just remember of its own accord. Anyway, all this seems to suggest that Damian is our man, don't you think? He's got a motive, he's got means and opportunity—after all, we only have his word that he couldn't find Charlie and Tanya in the crowd—and now he's acting in a suspicious way and is obviously hiding something."

"Yes, but his personality is all wrong!" I burst out.

"Personality?" Cassie looked at me quizzically.

I gave her a rueful smile. "I hate to say it but I think the Old Biddies are right in this case. You know how they're always going on about the Agatha Christie methods of psychology and personality being as useful to solving a murder as stuff like forensic evidence? Well, I think I have to agree with them this time. I just don't feel that Damian has the right personality to have committed this murder. I've met him a few times now and I can tell you—he's a weaselly sort of chap. You know, shifty and dishonest and a selfish coward. I can imagine him as a small-time crook—like a thief or a blackmailer—but as a murderer? And especially this kind of murder? I just can't see him having the strength of character and the nerve to plan and execute this whole thing—and then to actually stab someone in cold blood... in public..."

"I don't think you can make judgements based on the few times you met the boy," argued Cassie. "It's not like you've known him for years. Maybe he's only shown one side to you. People are good at presenting different images of themselves."

"I guess... But I still think he's the wrong type."

"Okay, so if it's not Damian, who else could it be?"

Cassie lowered her voice slightly. "I don't suppose there's any chance it could be Miriam Hopkins after all?"

I looked at Cassie in surprise. "You're not serious?"

Cassie shrugged. "We can't accept Miriam's innocence just because Dora says so—you know people are biased about their friends."

"Yes, but Miriam... Oh, there's another thing!"

"About Miriam?"

"No, something else. Actually, it might be totally irrelevant to the murder case, but during Muesli's therapy cat visit at the nursing home this morning, we met an old naval captain whose room overlooks the river and Magdalen Bridge and part of the High Street. He's also a bit of a nosy old fellow and he likes watching what goes on below with a pair of binoculars. Anyway, he told me that he was watching the bridge on May morning and saw Charlie going off the side of the bridge. But what was *really* interesting was that he also noticed someone rushing off in the *opposite* direction."

"What do you mean, the opposite direction?"

"As in, after Charlie went over, everybody in the crowd rushed to the side of the bridge to look at the river, but this person was pushing his way through the crowd in the opposite direction. Like he was rushing *away* from the scene, rather than towards it like everyone else."

"You think that was Charlie's killer?"

I shrugged. "Well, it definitely seemed like he was trying to remove himself from the scene as quickly as possible."

"Did your naval captain see what he looked like?"

I shook my head in frustration. "No. He said it was a back view—somebody wearing a dark grey hoodie—and he couldn't even tell if it was male or female, although he thinks it looked like a man." I sighed. "I'm not even sure if I should mention it to Devlin. I was really excited at first but, now that I think about it, it all seems a bit vague and stupid—I don't know how they're going to find this person based on such meagre clues. Still, I suppose I ought to report it to the police and let them follow it up."

Cassie glanced at her watch, then started shuffling the papers on the table together. "I've got to go. I'm teaching a class at the dance studio this evening."

I sprang up and helped her. "Sorry, Cass—we didn't really get to discuss the website. Do you want to bring the stuff into the tearoom tomorrow and we can go over it when we have a free moment?"

"Yeah, all right." Cassie gathered her things and headed for the door of the café.

I started to follow her, then froze as my gaze alighted on a girl sitting alone at a table in the far corner of the café. It was Tanya Koskov.

CHAPTER NINETEEN

Tanya was sitting at a small table tucked into the front corner of the café, against the windows. She was gazing moodily out through the glass, her fingers fiddling with an espresso cup on the table in front of her.

"What is it?" asked Cassie as she turned and came back to where I was standing.

"That's Tanya Koskov," I said in an undertone, nodding my head in the girl's direction.

Cassie eyed the girl thoughtfully. "I saw her picture in the papers... Funny, now that I'm seeing her in the flesh, she's not quite how I imagined her to be."

"How do you mean?" I looked at her in surprise.

"I don't know—from the way you were talking and

all the press reports about her, I sort of expected someone harder and more glamorous and arrogant." She looked again at the girl across the room. "She looks a lot younger and almost a bit... well... lonely."

I looked back at Tanya. Cassie was right. Perhaps it was because the girl didn't have her guard up. It was as if I was seeing a different side to her. She looked a bit lost and vulnerable, and, although the corners of her mouth were turned down, she didn't look sulky and spoilt—just sad and lonely.

On an impulse, I gave Cassie a nudge. "You go on—I'm going to speak to her."

I made my way slowly across the café and stopped by Tanya's table.

"Hi, Tanya..." I said softly.

She looked up, startled, and I caught the glitter of tears on her eyelashes. Quickly, she dashed a hand across her eyes and the familiar mask of cynical indifference came down over her face.

"Yes?" she said, her tone hostile.

"Do you mind if I join you?"

She looked for a moment as if she would refuse, then she gave a shrug and indicated the empty chair opposite her.

I sat down and said, "I wanted to say I'm sorry about last night. I didn't mean to cause trouble between you and Damian—"

She gave a contemptuous laugh. "The trouble is there already. Damian, he never liked me. And now he is telling police that I killed Charlie—because we fight." She tossed her head impatiently. "Yes, we fight; I was angry—I was *very* angry. I think Charlie is lying to me—but kill him? No, of course I don't kill him! I just dump him... like that!" She snapped her fingers. "He is not worth me to do murder. There are many boys; Charlie was not my first. He is just one of many. I would not waste my time and energy to kill him. I do not even mourn him!"

Her voice broke suddenly and she turned sharply away, staring blindly out of the window and blinking rapidly. I looked down and busied myself straightening a couple of coasters on the table, feeling uncomfortable. I was also surprised. Could it be that underneath that haughty exterior, Tanya was grieving for her boyfriend? Did she really care for Charlie? It was hard to imagine the spoilt Russian girl caring for anyone except herself... And yet...

Tanya turned back to me, her face wiped clean of all emotion, and said coolly, "Anyway, Damian will be sorry for what he has tried to do to me. I will make him pay."

"Do you think *Damian* might have killed Charlie?"

She narrowed her eyes. "Yes, I say this to the handsome inspector also. Damian is a snake. He would think nothing of betraying his best friend." Then she sat back, her expression becoming bored. "But I am tired of this business. Already the police ask me questions, questions, and more questions! Now, they cannot speak to me without lawyer—so they speak to everybody else. All the time, in the college—they never stop! Even Mikhail, he has to speak to them—"

"Ah yes, Mikhail…" I suddenly remembered the grumpy Russian scholar. "Is he a good friend of yours?"

She shrugged. "He is fellow countryman. We are both from Russia. In the college, there are no others like us. He is true patriot and he loves my country."

"He's also very protective of you. He seems to spend a lot of time hanging around and trying to take care of you. Every time I've seen you, he's hovering behind somewhere. In fact, I am surprised he's not here today." I glanced around.

Tanya looked amused. "He is not my guard dog, if that is what you think. Mikhail is old-fashioned and he has old-style ideas about girls, how they need protection. It amuses me to let him look after me."

"Yes, but perhaps…" I paused as a new idea struck me. "Perhaps Mikhail began taking the role too seriously! If he had feelings for you and was very protective of you… and he thought that Charlie was treating you badly… maybe he murdered Charlie as a… well, like an old-fashioned, chivalrous sort of thing… or maybe because he was jealous and wanted you for himself!"

"You think Mikhail killed Charlie because of love for me?" She tossed her head back and roared with laughter.

"What's so funny about that?" I asked, irritated.

She struggled to stop laughing. "I am sorry—it is

just you do not know how ridiculous your words are. You see..." She leaned forwards and gave me a meaningful look. "Mikhail does not like women. He is—how you English say—he bats for the other team."

I stared at her, confused for a moment, then understanding dawned. "Oh! You mean he's..."

Tanya nodded, a mocking smile on her lips. "So I can assure you Mikhail did not murder Charlie because he was jealous of my love." She chuckled softly.

Feeling slightly embarrassed, I sat back. "Oh, well... It was just an idea—"

"Do not waste time on these little ideas." She smiled without humour. "I am telling you that Damian is the one who betrayed Charlie."

***

Instead of going straight back to my cottage, I decided to pop in to see my parents. I arrived at their North Oxford townhouse to find that my mother had company: the Old Biddies were sitting having tea with her in the living room.

"Gemma, dear!" cried Mabel in delight. "Just the person we were hoping to see! We went to your cottage first but you weren't there. I was just about to ask your mother to give you a ring..."

Uh oh. I eyed Mabel warily, wondering what crazy scheme she wanted to drag me into now.

"I'm not doing anything that involves disguises," I said quickly.

"Oh, you don't need a disguise for this, dear," said Glenda. "Although I suppose one ought to take some bandages just in case."

"And ice packs," said Florence with a nod.

This was beginning to sound ominous. I sat down on the sofa next to them, accepted a cup of tea from my mother, and asked nervously, "What's this about?"

"Look!" Mabel thrust a piece of paper at me excitedly. It was a small poster which looked like it had been torn off a bulletin board. It seemed to be an invitation to some kind of martial arts workshop.

"I don't understand," I said. "Why are you showing me this?"

"Look!" said Mabel again, this time pointing a stubby finger at a logo in the top right-hand corner of the poster. It showed a circle with a stylised fist inside it, and arched over the top of the fist were four letters: OKMC.

I frowned. The letters were vaguely familiar...

"They're the same letters that were on that jumper in Charlie Foxton's room!" Ethel piped up excitedly.

Of course. She was right. How could I have forgotten? That hoodie slung across the back of Charlie's chair, with these same letters: OKMC. I looked further down the page and discovered that the letters stood for Oxford Krav Mag Club. Then I remembered something else: Captain Thomas at the nursing home talking about seeing the person running away from the bridge on May morning. The figure had been wearing a grey hoodie, he said, with letters across the back. Starting with an O, ending with a C, and possibly EM or KM in the middle. Well, I was pretty sure now that the letters on that hoodie were OKMC. Which meant that someone who could have been the murderer was also a member of the Oxford Krav Maga Club.

"Charlie must have been part of this club," said Florence eagerly. "If we can speak to some of the other members, we might be able to pick up some clues to his murder."

"And it couldn't be better timing!" added Glenda. She pointed to the poster. "There is an *Introductory Workshop on Krav Maga for Ladies* tonight, you see. It's a wonderful opportunity to get into the club and chat to the members. It doesn't start until 8 p.m. so we could get an early supper first and—"

"Whoa, whoa..." I looked at the Old Biddies incredulously. "You're not actually thinking of going to *join* the class?"

Mabel drew herself up. "And why not?"

"Because—" I broke off. I couldn't believe I was even having this conversation. "Um... you do realise that Krav Maga is a deadly self-defence technique developed by the Israeli Army for hand-to-hand combat. This isn't Seniors Yoga!"

Mabel bristled. "Do you think we can't handle ourselves in a fight, young lady?"

"I just don't want you to get hurt. I mean, martial arts isn't really the kind of activity for... um... more mature individuals—"

"Oh, but Krav Maga is different," said Florence, pointing to the poster eagerly. "You see what it says here? *'Suitable for any age, size, or gender. Anyone can use Krav Maga techniques successfully to overcome a stronger opponent. Simple, powerful, easy-to-learn tactics for real-life situations. Perfect for the old, the weak, and the small.'*"

"I've always wanted to learn self-defence," said Glenda, fluffing her hair. "Men love a woman who can... what do the Americans call it? Kick arse!" She covered her mouth and giggled.

"You can't really be serious about this," I said weakly. "What if you fall down and break a hip?"

Mabel stood up, her arms akimbo, and looked at me indignantly. "My hips are fine, young lady. You worry about your own hips."

"I think it's a marvellous idea, darling," my mother gushed. "In fact, I would come too if it weren't for the fact that I've got bridge this evening at Dorothy Clarke's house. Although maybe I could see if I could cancel—"

"No! No, Mother—you go to your bridge game," I said hastily. I turned back to the Old Biddies and said with a sigh, "All right. I suppose there's no harm in going along to observe a class."

"We're not going to just sit there and observe!" said Florence, pouting.

Glenda and Ethel nodded vehemently. "We want to take part!"

I sighed and hoped fervently that, when we turned up, the instructors would tell the Old Biddies that they were too old for the class.

CHAPTER TWENTY

That evening, as I followed the Old Biddies down some narrow steps to a dingy basement in a side street near Oxford bus station, I wondered uneasily what I had let myself in for. A smell of stale sweat mixed with the artificial fragrance of deodorant rose to meet us and I wrinkled my nose in distaste. I could hear faint grunts and cries, and the occasional thump—none of which helped to make me feel more at ease.

We emerged into a vast room with low ceilings, which took up the entire basement level. The centre of the room was divided into two training areas, obviously used for classes and mock fights, and the sides were lined with cubicles and shelves filled with cushioned pads, groin shields, head guards, and punching gloves, as well as several giant black punching bags hanging from the ceiling.

The training area nearest the door was empty, but several pairs of men were sparring and wrestling on the far side of the room, with more watching from a long bench alongside the wall. Judging by their rippling biceps and muscular bodies, they were obviously long-time members, and several looked like they had been in real fights—and often. A few sported tattoos, two had shaved heads, and one had a broken nose. I swallowed nervously. I thought we were supposed to learn how to defend ourselves against thugs, not walk into a nest of them!

A slim young man in track pants came towards us with a smile and a clipboard. He thrust a hand out to me.

"You must be here for the *Introductory Workshop on Krav Maga for Ladies*."

"Er, I..."

Mabel shoved me out of the way and grabbed his hand, pumping it up and down. "Yes, we are."

"I... I'm sorry?" The young man looked taken aback. "You, ma'am?"

"Me and my friends," said Mabel, pointing to herself and Glenda and Florence and Ethel. "Oh, and Gemma too," she added as an afterthought.

The young man licked his lips. "The thing is... well, this isn't really a seniors' class—"

"Young man, it says on your poster that Krav Maga is suitable for everyone, including the old, the weak, and the small. Are you saying that the poster was lying?"

"Oh, no, of course not!" he said. "It's just that... when we said old, we weren't thinking quite *so* old—uh, that is..." He hastily amended his words when he saw Mabel's glare: "What I mean is... well, things can get a bit rough in class, you know."

"That's quite all right, young man," said Florence. "We're not as fragile as we look."

Speak for yourself, I thought.

"Well..." The young man looked helplessly around, then gave a resigned shrug. "If you would like to join the class, you're very welcome. I just need you to fill out these forms and sign the waiver." He handed out some papers to the Old Biddies, then looked at me. "And you, miss?"

It was on the tip of my tongue to say, "No, I would just like to observe", but I felt a flash of shame. Here were four little old ladies who were game enough to try this—was I going to be a chicken?

"Uh... yeah, thanks," I said, taking the form from him.

As we were filling them out, several other women began to arrive for the class. There were a mix of different ages and types, although a few looked like they didn't need any training to beat the living daylights out of someone. One girl with a high ponytail bounced restlessly from foot to foot, her hands already up in fists, looking like she was ready to punch anyone who so much as glanced at her the wrong way. Another woman with big beefy arms kept cracking her knuckles while she eyed the rest of us malevolently.

"Are you joining the class?" came a sneering voice next to us.

I turned to see a girl with a shaved head and a nose ring looking down her nose at the Old Biddies, a disbelieving smile curling the corners of her mouth.

"Yes, we are," said Mabel.

The girl snorted. "You sure you're in the right place, Granny?"

Mabel bristled, but before she could reply, we were called into the centre of the room. I gulped as I saw the big man with the broken nose waiting for us. *Oh my God, he's probably going to be called Rambo or The Rock or something and he's going to kill us!* But to my surprise, he introduced himself in a soft voice as Trevor and gave us a sweet smile as he invited us to gather around him.

The Old Biddies went eagerly forwards and I followed reluctantly. Trevor explained that he would show us how to disarm and escape from an attacker.

"But first, we're going to get you warmed up and in the right frame of mind," he said. "I want you all to start walking in a big circle around me."

I fell into step with the Old Biddies as we began circling the room.

"Right, first, I want you to walk with your shoulders hunched, your eyes down, and take small, hesitant, shuffling steps..."

I tried to do as he bid, feeling silly and self-conscious.

"And now I want you to stand up straight, with your shoulders back, lift your chin, look straight ahead, and take confident strides."

I altered my stance and changed the way I walked as directed. To my surprise, I did suddenly feel much more empowered.

"You see? Just adopting the right posture and changing the way you move makes you feel more in control of the situation, right? It's important to know that criminals are always looking for weaker victims. If you seem like someone who's nervous and uncertain or if you've got your head down, texting on your phone, and you're not observing your environment, then you make yourself an easy target. But if you just walk looking purposeful and confident, you will already reduce your chances of being attacked." Trevor clapped his hands together once. "Good! Turn around and circle the room in the opposite direction."

I spun around and found myself next to Glenda.

"Isn't this exciting?" she whispered.

Hmm... "exciting" wasn't the word I would have used, but I had to admit, so far, the class was turning out better than I had thought. If it was just posture and attitude, I could learn to swagger with the best of them! My confidence went out the window a second later, however, when Trevor began going around handing out large cushioned pads with arm straps attached.

"Okay, now I'm going to show you an easy way to both defend yourself against an attacker and push into their space, to scare them off. Raise your arms with your elbows bent, so that they're held in front of your face—almost as if you're hiding your eyes with your hands." He demonstrated. "Good, now if someone comes at you, this is the immediate defensive position you assume, so that you protect your face. But at the same time, I want you to charge into your attacker, holding your elbows out in front of you—they make a very effective weapon. This way you push into *their* space and scare them back."

He looked around with approval as we all tried to copy him. "Good, good... and make sure you yell out as you're charging into your attacker. Let's have some aggression!" he urged. "Scream, yell, curse—let it all out! Women tend to 'freeze up' and go very quiet when attacked, so you've got to learn to make some noise. That in itself will put off your attacker. So come on! LET ME HEAR YOU!"

I looked around in embarrassment and let out a half-hearted squeak, feeling extremely silly. I nearly jumped out of my skin when a bloodcurdling screech came from next to me, and I turned to see the Old Biddies standing with their bony elbows jutting out and their spindly legs splayed in different directions, their wrinkled faces scrunched up in ferocious scowls.

"Ninnyhammer!" yelled Glenda.

"Dunderhead!" shouted Florence.

"Scoundrel!" squeaked Ethel.

"Nincompoop!" boomed Mabel.

"Brilliant! Fantastic!" Trevor clapped his hands. "Now, I want you to get into pairs—one of you with a pad—and practise attacking each other."

The group began breaking up. Trevor glanced at the Old Biddies uncertainly.

"I'll do it with them," I said quickly, worried that Mabel and her friends might be paired with one of those women who was sneering at them earlier.

"But we're too many!" Glenda protested, looking around the room. "The others are all in pairs whereas there are four of us against Gemma."

"Oh, I'm sure this young lady can manage the four of you," said Trevor with a smile.

I laughed as I lifted the cushioned pad and faced the Old Biddies.

"Okay, who's first?" I said, grinning. "Don't worry, I'll be very gentle and I won't—"

"AAAAAAAAAAGGHHH!"

The Old Biddies charged. I gasped as Mabel rammed into the pad with the force of a battering ram, just as Glenda hooked an arm around my neck, Ethel pummelled my stomach with her fists, and Florence kicked avidly at my knees.

"Wait...! You're not... Hang on...! *Ow!* Hey, that's not—!"

I choked and spluttered, scrambling backwards as they punched and kicked and wrenched and shoved. It was like a geriatric tornado had been unleashed in the room. I caught sight of Trevor and the rest of the class watching open-mouthed before something smacked against my shins, causing me to lurch sideways.

"*OWWW!*"

I tripped, stumbled, and went down with a yelp, feeling my ankle twist sharply beneath me. The Old Biddies piled on top of me, still pummelling and yelling.

"Whoa! Okay! Timeout! Timeout!" cried Trevor, hurrying over to my rescue.

The Old Biddies slowly lifted themselves up, their wrinkled cheeks flushed and their white woolly hair dishevelled. Trevor reached down to help me to my feet. I glared at the four old ladies, who looked slightly shamefaced now.

"Are you all right, Gemma, dear?" asked Ethel.

I coughed and wheezed. "I...I think you've broken my ribs."

"Really, young people are so fragile these days," said Mabel, clucking her tongue.

Slowly, I stood up with Trevor's help, my head spinning slightly. I winced as pain shot through my ankle and hastily took my weight off that leg.

Trevor looked at me in concern. "Are you all right? Have you hurt yourself?"

I saw the rest of the class gawking at me and felt my face going red. "Er... no, no, I'm fine. It's... I think I just twisted my ankle a bit..." It was embarrassing enough being floored by four little old ladies without having to admit that I'd been injured too.

I waved a hand. "You guys carry on—I think I'll just sit out for a few moments," I said, groping at the remnants of my tattered pride. I staggered to the side of the room and leaned against the wall for support.

"All right, class," said Trevor, clapping his hands. "Let's get on to the next thing. We're going to learn about the chokehold."

"Ooh! The chokehold! I can't wait," squealed Glenda, rubbing her hands.

Trevor smiled at the rest of the class. "Right... who would like to partner with these lovely old ladies then?"

The rest of the room all recoiled from the Old Biddies.

"I'll go with *her*," said Mabel, pointing at the girl with the shaved head and nose ring who had sneered at her earlier.

The girl went pale and swallowed nervously, and I had to stifle a laugh. It looked like someone was getting her first lesson tonight in never underestimating senior citizens!

CHAPTER TWENTY-ONE

As the class started battering each other again, I hobbled over to the long bench alongside the far wall and lowered myself down gratefully. The young man sitting next to me gave me a smile and I realised that despite the scary-looking skull tattoos on his arms, he was actually quite friendly. Besides... I glanced back towards the class, at Trevor with his rippling biceps and smashed nose—and then at Mabel, with her wrinkled chicken legs and fluffy white hair—and I knew which one I'd be more terrified of. Appearances could be very deceiving.

"They're quite something, those friends of yours," said the tattooed young man with a laugh. "We've had all sorts come into the club but none like them!"

"Yeah," I said wryly. "I didn't think they'd take to

Krav Maga so... er... enthusiastically."

The young man laughed again. "Well, funnily enough, being older does help sometimes. They're not so bothered about what other people think so they can really get stuck into it. Younger people get all self-conscious and worry about looking like a plonker and then they make half-arsed attempts... and you know, in fighting, you've got to *mean it*—if you want to win."

"You're probably right," I said with a rueful smile. "I spent so much time worried about looking like a twit, I ended up looking like a huge twit anyway."

"Hey, don't be too hard on yourself. Even the most advanced Krav Maga practitioner gets his arse kicked every once in a while—like Pete here, right?" said the young man with a chuckle, elbowing the man next to him.

The other man didn't respond in kind. He was an older, thickset man with a dark, swarthy face and eyebrows that almost joined up in the middle. I noticed that he had a faint black eye.

"Piss off!" he snarled. "That sodding tosser cheated! Otherwise I would have beat him, fair and square. But what do you expect from these university knobheads? Prissy mummy's boys, that's what they are. They don't really know how to fight—"

"Hah! Well, that prissy mummy's boy walloped you good an' proper, Morrow!" scoffed another man, coming over to join us. He was winding some white boxing tape around his hands. "Reckon that boy would've made a good tryout for the club team—"

"If any uni student comes on the team, then I go!" growled Pete Morrow, springing up. "Bloody tossers! They should never come here in the first place. They should stay in their fancy colleges where they belong!" He turned and stalked away.

There was an awkward silence for a moment, then the young man gave me an embarrassed smile.

"Don't mind Pete. He always goes around like a bear with a sore head. And he's got a bit of thing about the University."

I nodded understandingly. The "town vs. gown" rivalry was well known in Oxford and stretched back centuries, with some pretty gory incidents in the past that had resulted in many casualties on both sides. But even though there was still a bit of lingering tension between the two factions, I always thought that any serious vendetta had long since died out.

As if reading my thoughts, the young man added: "Most of us don't mind University students coming to join us. You get a bit of good-natured bantering and insults, but none of it is usually serious."

"S'good to get a bit o' fresh blood sometimes," said the man with the boxing tape. "Good to have some sparrin' partners who think differently. And some o' the University kids aren't half bad." He grinned. "Pete's just sore because that boy gave him a good wallopin'."

"We have these friendly matches," the young man explained to me. "Trevor sets them up so that we can

H.Y. HANNA

practice our moves in a 'real-life' situation. Krav
Maga isn't like most martial arts with their strict
rituals and etiquette—it's more like dirty street
fighting, using every trick in the book to disable your
opponent. And Pete's one of the best at the club—but
Charlie had a few tricks that Pete didn't think of."

My ears perked up. "Charlie? Charlie Foxton?"

The young man frowned. "Not sure. Could be. We
don't pay much attention to last names here at the
club."

"So Charlie beat Pete?"

The man with the boxing tape laughed. "He didn't
just beat him—he walloped him! It was pretty
embarrassin' to watch. Especially with Pete always
goin' on about the University boys bein' pansies."

The young man nodded. "Yeah, Pete took it real
hard. In fact, he wouldn't admit that he'd lost—kept
insisting that Charlie had cheated. Even after the
match was all over, he went over to Charlie and
started getting in his face. And then the next thing
we knew, the two of them were at it again! Only this
time they were doing it for real and it was pretty
vicious. Trevor was livid. It's one of the club rules
that there's no fighting off the floor, and once a match
is done, the loser has to accept the score."

"What happened?" I asked.

"We had to get in an' separate them," said the man
with the boxing tape. He shook his head. "'Twas a
bad night, that."

"When was this?" I asked.

"Last week... think it was Wednesday?" He looked at the young man, who nodded his head in agreement.

Two days before May morning, I thought. "Did you hear that Charlie was the boy who was killed at Madgalen Bridge on May morning?" I asked.

"Bloody hell, really?" said the man with the boxing tape. "I read about it in the papers but I wasn't payin' much attention. Thought it was another o' these stupid stunts that the University students get up to."

"*I* knew," said the young man, his face sobering. "Trevor told me that the police were here yesterday—a detective sergeant—asking some questions."

"Did you tell him about Charlie and Pete's fight?"

"I wasn't here," said the young man. "And neither was Pete. But I suppose Trevor must have mentioned it." He turned wide eyes to me. "Hey... you don't think Pete had anything to do with the boy's death, do you? He's a bit of a grumpy old git but he's not a murderer!"

I shifted uncomfortably. I could see that both men's friendly manner had changed and there was now hostility in their gaze. Whatever they might say about the "town vs. gown" rivalry being over, they didn't take kindly to the suggestion that one of "their own" was being made a scapegoat for a university student's murder.

Thankfully, at that point I heard Trevor announcing the end of class and I got up from the bench to rejoin the Old Biddies. They ambled towards me, glowing with exercise and elation, and I noticed several of the other women—especially the one with the shaved head and nose ring—giving them a wide berth.

"Gemma, dear—you missed most of the class!" cried Ethel.

"Such a shame! It was so enlightening. I can now do an Eye Strike and a Spinning Slap Kick, you know," announced Glenda with great pride.

"How's your ankle, dear?" asked Florence.

I looked down and my heart sank. My ankle seemed to have swollen to twice its normal size. I tried to put my weight on it, gasped in pain, and lifted my foot up again.

"Oh dear, that doesn't look very good," said Ethel.

"I...I'm sure it'll be fine," I said, grimacing as I hobbled on the spot. "I just need to put some ice on it when I get home."

"You need to get that looked at properly," declared Mabel. "But don't worry, dear, I've just rung your mother and she's coming to pick you up."

"My mother?" I looked at her in dismay. "No, I tell you, I'm fine..."

My protests fell on deaf ears and fifteen minutes later—after a long, painful hobble up the stairs from the basement—I found myself standing at the side of the road, propped up by the Old Biddies, as my mother's car pulled up next to the curb.

My mother got out. "Oh my goodness, darling! What happened?"

"It's nothing, Mother—don't worry. I've twisted my ankle, that's all. I just need to get back to the cottage and put some ice on it—"

"Back to the cottage? Oh, no, we must get you to the hospital and have that ankle X-rayed."

"What? No, Mother— there's no need for that. I'm sure it's fine," I said desperately.

"Nonsense, darling, it could be broken for all you know! You might never walk again!"

Gee, thanks for the vote of confidence.

My mother continued blithely, "In fact, I think I will ring Lincoln and ask him to come and meet us in A&E. Isn't it lucky that he's on call tonight?"

I groaned inwardly. I might have known. Any excuse to bring Lincoln Green on the scene. Lincoln was the son of my mother's closest friend, Helen Green, and it was their lifelong ambition to see the two of us engaged. When I'd first returned to Oxford, my mother had been thrilled to find that Lincoln had moved back too, and she had done everything she could to throw us together. And okay, I had to admit, Lincoln was a nice guy. He was kind, good-looking, and an eminent doctor to boot. Perhaps if Devlin hadn't been around, things might have been different...

But in my heart, I'd always known that Devlin was the man for me. I had known it eight years ago when he had proposed after our passionate student affair, but I'd listened to the wrong advice and made the wrong decision. This time, I wasn't going to make the same mistake again. We'd been given a second chance—Devlin and me—and I wasn't going to lose it.

Still, even after I'd made it clear that I had chosen Devlin, my mother wasn't giving up. She simply acted like our relationship was a temporary blip and that I would come to my senses soon. And she didn't stop trying to throw me and Lincoln together at every opportunity.

"Mother, Lincoln is an intensive care consultant. You can't call him for a stupid little case like a twisted ankle," I said in exasperation.

My mother waved my protests away and, before I knew what had happened, I'd been hustled into the car and we were on our way to the hospital.

CHAPTER TWENTY-TWO

By the time we got to the hospital, my ankle was throbbing so badly that I was beginning to think it might be a good idea to get some professional medical attention after all. Supported by my mother, I hobbled painfully into Accident & Emergency, and sat down in one of the plastic chairs in the waiting area, while my mother went off to register. It was a Monday evening and things were quieter than they would have been on a weekend, but the A&E was still fairly busy. I resigned myself to a long wait. I knew enough about triage to know that someone like me would rank very low down on the list of emergency priorities.

To my surprise, however, a tall, good-looking man with neat brown hair and dark brown eyes strode into the A&E waiting area barely ten minutes later.

"Lincoln!" my mother cried, waving madly. "I'm so glad to see you! Gemma has been distraught waiting for you."

"What?" I spluttered. "Mother, that's a complete—"

"Hallo, Gemma," said Lincoln, the corners of his brown eyes crinkling in amusement as he came over and crouched down beside me.

"Hi," I said, giving him a sheepish look. "Sorry about this. I did tell my mother not to call you—"

"Oh, I don't mind, Gemma. You know I'm always happy to see you." Lincoln smiled at me. "I'm on call anyway and it's fairly quiet on the ICU ward tonight. Now, let's have a look at this..." He bent and examined my foot, eliciting a gasp of pain from me as he probed my ankle.

"Hmm... looks like you've been in the wars a bit," he commented. "Might be a good idea to have it X-rayed after all. It's probably just a sprain, but you don't want to be messing around if there are any fractures. I'll go and speak to the nurses and get your X-ray sorted."

He went off and a few minutes later, as I was being wheeled to Radiology, I had to grudgingly admit that perhaps my mother's idea to call Lincoln had been a good one. Without him, I would probably have been sitting in the A&E until the early hours of the morning. Instead, I was out again and having my foot strapped in less than an hour.

"No broken bones," said Lincoln cheerfully as he stood by my bedside whilst the nurse finished wrapping my ankle in a supportive brace. "Hopefully it's just a mild sprain but you'll need to stay off that ankle for a few days. I'm giving you some anti-inflammatory tablets and painkillers as well."

"But... but the tearoom re-opens tomorrow," I said. "I've got to get back to work—"

Lincoln shook his head firmly. "I'm sorry, but you have to take time off. You've got to rest that ankle to let the ligaments have a chance to heal. The swelling might go down quickly and it might heal faster than expected, but for tomorrow, at least, I want you to stay home and keep the weight off that ankle."

"Oh, but—"

"Doctor's orders, Gemma," Lincoln said sternly. Then he smiled. "Surely one day won't matter? Cassie will be there, won't she?"

"Yes, and the Old Bi—I mean, Mabel Cooke and her friends will be helping out too... But you don't understand—I haven't missed a day of work since I started the tearoom!"

"Well, I'm sure they'll manage without you. And if you're feeling much better tomorrow evening, you can think about going to the tearoom the next day— just to sit at the counter, mind you. No running around, serving customers." Lincoln wagged his finger at me. "Now, I'll go and fetch your mother. Devlin's probably in the waiting area too. Maybe he can take you for a drive tomorrow afternoon..." He trailed off as he saw my puzzled look.

"Devlin?" I said. "He's here in the hospital?"

"Yes, just now when you were having your X-ray... I saw him around the corner. I assumed that he'd come to see you."

"No..." I said slowly. "I haven't had a chance to let him know what's happened yet."

Lincoln frowned. "Oh. Perhaps I made a mistake— although I was sure it was him..."

"What was he doing?" I asked. "Was he questioning someone?"

"No, actually, he... he seemed to be escorting a woman."

"Oh." I swallowed. "What did she look like?"

"Well, she was slim, blonde, very attractive... er, I mean..." Lincoln stammered, flushing slightly. He gave me a sideways look. "Er... well... as I said, I might have been mistaken and it wasn't him."

At that moment, we heard my mother's voice outside the cubicle. A minute later, she sailed in brandishing a pair of crutches. "Darling! Look what I've got for you."

Lincoln looked relieved by the interruption. "That's a great idea, Aunt Evelyn. It'll help Gemma keep her weight off her ankle."

"Yes, but it *is* such a distance to the car," said my mother coyly. "And really, Gemma shouldn't be walking..."

"Oh, I'll be fine—especially now that I've got those..." I said, reaching for the crutches, but my mother slapped my hand away.

"Oh, no, no, these are for tomorrow. You really must stay off your feet as much as possible tonight, don't you agree, Lincoln?" My mother gave him a coquettish smile. "You're so big and strong—I was thinking, perhaps you could carry Gemma out to the car?"

I looked at my mother in horrified disbelief.

"Oh... of course. It would be a pleasure," said Lincoln gallantly.

"No," I gasped. "I don't need to be carried! This is ridiculous—"

Once again, my protests fell on deaf ears and I found myself being scooped up by Lincoln and carried out of the hospital in his arms, while my mother trailed behind us, beaming. My face was so red, everyone probably thought I had scarlet fever. I mumbled a "thank you" as Lincoln deposited me gently in the front passenger seat, and then I spent the rest of the drive home fuming, trying not to think evil thoughts about my mother.

It had been decided that I would stay with my parents for a few days until my ankle healed, and the Old Biddies had thoughtfully fetched Muesli from my cottage. She came trotting up to inspect my bandaged foot as I hobbled into my parents' foyer.

"Right. A hot drink, darling, and then off to bed with you," said my mother briskly.

I felt like I was nine again as my mother settled me in my old bed, brought me a hot drink, fussed over me, and then finally, after kissing me goodnight, left me with Muesli curled up against my hurt ankle. The medication they'd given me at the hospital was starting to kick in and I pulled the blankets up drowsily. As I drifted off to sleep, I thought suddenly of Devlin again. I had sent him a text, telling him what had happened, after we'd got back, but I hadn't heard from him. I frowned, feeling hurt and disappointed. Okay, I had downplayed my injury in my message, but still, I thought that he would have called to see how I was.

Unless he was busy...

I remembered what Lincoln had said. *Had Devlin really been at the hospital? What had he been doing there? And who was that blonde woman he had been with?*

With these thoughts tumbling through my mind, I sank at last into a troubled sleep.

CHAPTER TWENTY-THREE

"Oh, Muesli, go away..." I muttered, giving the little tabby cat a gentle shove as she attempted to climb onto my lap yet again.

Shifting restlessly, I tried to find a more comfortable position. After a day of sitting around doing nothing, I was not in the best of moods. And although Cassie had already rung once and told me that everything was going fine, I was worried about my tearoom. I sighed. I'd never been good with inactivity, especially in the working week when it felt like everybody else in the world was busy planning, working, learning, discussing... and here I was, sitting on my parents' sofa, with nothing more to look forward to than more daytime TV.

Still, at least I'm having a bit of peace and quiet, I

thought. My mother had gone out to meet some friends for lunch and it was nice to have a break from her gushing abut Lincoln's masterly doctoring last night. I leaned back against the cushions and glanced at the clock on the mantelpiece. It was still only 2:30 p.m. Cassie had said that she would pop in after work but the tearoom wouldn't close for several hours yet...

I sighed and looked back at the laptop on my lap. I might not have been able to do proper work at the tearoom but there was something else I could work on: the mystery of Charlie Foxton's murder. I flexed my fingers over the keyboard. After all, we were in the internet age and they did say that there was nothing you couldn't find online...

"*Meorrw!*" said Muesli from the cushion next to me. She reached out a paw and prodded my stomach.

"Not now, Muesli..." I muttered distractedly as I typed some keywords into the search engine. *Damian Heath.*

A list of results came up. There were several Damian Heaths, mostly Facebook profiles. I clicked on a couple of the entries, scanning the photos... *Aha!* That was him. The picture showed a grinning Damian with a rainbow-coloured knitted beanie cap on his head. His arm was slung around the shoulders of someone just out of the picture. I wondered if it was Charlie. I scrolled down the page. Since I wasn't Damian's "friend" on Facebook, I couldn't see most of his posts—only the occasional public joke or funny video that he had shared. Nothing helpful. Anyway, I doubted that Damian would have posted about the planned murder of his best friend on social media.

Next, I tried *Miriam Hopkins*. I hadn't really expected to find her and I was right. There were a few Miriam Hopkinses on Facebook, but, from their profile photos, they were all much younger. Like many of the older generation, it was unlikely that Miriam had much of a presence online.

"*Meorrw...*" said Muesli peevishly, as she pawed my abdomen again. I knew what she wanted: to climb into my lap and curl up for her afternoon sleep.

"Not now, Muesli..." I said absently, my eyes still on the screen.

"*Meorrw!*" insisted Muesli and she climbed into my lap, wedging herself somehow into the space between the laptop and my abdomen.

"Muesli!" I said in exasperation.

The little tabby took no notice, shoving the laptop away to make room for herself. She began kneading my thighs, purring loudly, her bum in my face. I leaned around her and tried to continue working. I typed *Tanya Koskov* and didn't get very much. Hmm... I remembered that "Tanya" was short for her full name, "Tatiana". I tried *Tatiana Koskov* and, again, got a few hits but nothing interesting. *Oh wait...of course.* I remembered the importance of the patronymic in Russian names. In fact, now that I thought about it, I remembered Mikhail calling the Russian girl "Tatiana Vladimirovna" rather than "Tanya". Chances were, the media might use that, especially in Russia. I tried again, curving my arms awkwardly around Muesli to reach the keyboard. She was blocking my view of the laptop and it was almost impossible to see what I was typing.

"Muesli! I can't see anything!" I said irritably, trying to look around her furry bum.

The little cat turned around, padding on the spot, trying to make herself comfortable. My laptop beeped as she stepped on the keyboard.

"*MUESLI!*"

I started to lose my temper, then paused, my eyes on the screen. Somehow, Muesli's antics combined with my jostled typing and the auto-complete feature had brought up a set of search results which looked very interesting. I lifted my laptop up and propped it on the arm of the sofa, leaving Muesli happily snuggling on my lap, having got her own way. It meant that I had to twist in a really awkward fashion to read the screen, but hey, anything for a quiet life. Besides, it seemed that I might have to thank Muesli for helping me flush out a clue.

My eyes scanned the screen eagerly as I scrolled down the page of results, clicking on several articles. Many were in Russian but, although I couldn't understand the text, I could guess from the accompanying photos what they were about. They showed Tanya at various clubs and parties, her slim figure draped with expensive designer outfits, her expression haughty and brooding as she stared into the camera. She was surrounded by various other young people—handsome men and beautiful girls— all obviously from Russia's celebrity circles and "high society". There was one shot of her getting out of a limousine and entering a ballroom, accompanied by a much older man with grey hair and a shrewd, clever face. Again, I couldn't read the Cyrillic script, but I guessed that this was Vladimir Ivanovich Koskov escorting his daughter to a function, with a host of bodyguards in the background behind them, looking exactly like the Hollywood stereotype of KGB agents with their dark shades, toothbrush moustaches, and black leather gloves.

I opened up Google Translate in a separate window, randomly selected a few sections of text from various articles, and pasted them into the translation box. I knew it wasn't very accurate, but it was better than nothing. Most of the stories were the usual stuff of celebrity gossip mags: *Has Tatiana Vladimirovna had plastic surgery? Surely her bottom lip has been looking swollen and strange in recent photos... Was Tatiana Vladimirovna pregnant? (Gasp!) That outfit she wore to the premier must be hiding a baby bump... Such a scandal! How embarrassing for Vladimir Ivanovich Koskov—those photos of his daughter leaving the nightclub drunk and practically unconscious... Oh my God, how much did Tatiana Vladimirovna's customised Chanel handbag cost?... Have you heard about the Caviar Diet that Tatiana Vladimirovna is on? But really, she's looking so thin and haggard... Have you seen how fat Tatiana Vladimirovna is looking lately? That dress she wore to the awards ceremony just didn't flatter her at all. Unless... (Gasp!) do you think she might be pregnant?*

Round and round the stories went, ending with a recent one—only a few weeks ago—about a scandal regarding nude photos of Tanya which had mysteriously appeared online and then disappeared again. I rolled my eyes. No doubt Papa Koskov had paid someone off again. I heaved a sigh of frustration and shut the browser down. Nothing of much interest there. I hadn't really expected there to be—after all, I knew the police had far more sophisticated databases and resources they could search—but still, I was disappointed. I had been hoping that somehow I would spot a clue in the general media that the police might have missed.

By the time Cassie arrived to visit me that evening, I was nearly crying with boredom.

"I don't care what Lincoln or my mother says, I'm going back to work tomorrow!" I said fiercely. "I can't face the thought of another day like today, sitting here like a vegetable on the sofa."

Cassie chuckled and handed me a cardboard box. I recognised it as similar to the boxes we used to pack takeaways for customers at the tearoom.

"Here," she said. "To cheer you up a bit. Dora

sends her love."

I opened the box and my face lit up. "Cassie! You're a star!"

Cassie smiled and went into the kitchen where she made us each a cup of tea while I climbed onto a stool at the kitchen counter and helped myself to the selection of goodies that she had brought. They were obviously leftovers from the day's baking at the tearoom: a couple of scones, a wedge of blueberry and vanilla bean cheesecake, three lemon curd tarts, a few muffins, and a heavenly slice of banoffee pie. I pounced on the last and had eaten half of it before Cassie handed me a fork and a plate.

"Dora's outdone herself today," I said as I licked the fresh whipped cream off my fingers.

Cassie had placed two of the muffins into the sandwich toaster to warm them up and now watched as they turned golden brown. "Yeah, the muffins are particularly good. We had so many customers ask for them that Dora had to make a third batch. That's why there's some left." She took the muffins out of the toaster and tossed one onto my plate, keeping the other for herself.

I cut the muffin in half horizontally and spread some fresh butter into the signature "nooks and crannies" of the interior, watching as it melted into a golden circle.

Cassie chuckled. "I had to do a lot of explaining, though, to American tourists who ordered 'muffins' from the menu and then couldn't understand why they got a flat round of bread instead of something resembling a big cupcake!"

"Hey—not just any flat round of bread," I protested. "A soft, chewy, delicious round of bread, toasted to brown perfection and topped with oozing butter…"

"Maybe we should re-name them 'English muffins' to avoid confusing the tourists?"

"Mmm…" I picked up my muffin and bit into it, savouring the wonderful combination of warm, moist interior and crispy toasted outer crust, all fragrant with melted butter. "I think if people taste this, they won't care what we call it."

Cassie laughed. "Gemma, you're acting like you haven't eaten any decent baking in weeks! You've only been away for a day."

"It feels like a year. Anyway, how was it?" I swallowed the last mouthful of muffin and looked at my best friend anxiously. "Did it go okay today? Were there a lot of customers? Big tour groups? Did the new supply of tea leaves come in? What about that catering order for the village committee?"

Cassie grinned. "Relax, Gemma! Much as I hate to say it, we managed fine without you. In fact, I think the Old Biddies were secretly delighted that you were away because Mabel could rule the roost. You should have seen her: she was standing behind the counter, giving commands like a brigadier general, while we all meekly ran around obeying her orders…"

Cassie rambled on and I let her talk, smiling

contentedly. There was something soothing about listening to all the gossip of village life, from the scandal of Mrs Ellis putting her lacy knickers out to dry on her washing line to the tragedy of Mr Peters discovering that his prize roses had been infected by aphids... I hadn't realised how much I'd miss it, even just being away for a day. Although I didn't live in Meadowford, I spent so much time there at work, and so many local residents came into my tearoom, that I felt like I was very much part of the community there.

"So, what about you?" said Cassie at last. "What have you been doing all day, aside from watching reruns of *Neighbours*?"

I made a face. "Feeling sorry for myself, mostly. My mother was fussing over me all morning, which drove me a bit bonkers. Thank goodness she was meeting friends for lunch and she's been out all afternoon—in fact, she still hasn't come back yet. Probably out shopping in Oxford somewhere. And... and Devlin hasn't called," I added in a small voice.

Cassie looked surprised. "What—you mean Devlin hasn't spoken to you since yesterday?"

I shook my head. "I sent him a text after we got back from the hospital to let him know what had happened but I haven't heard from him since. Oh, there was a missed call from him last night—I went to bed early and I must not have heard my phone. But I thought he'd call again today..."

"Well, I'm sure there's some explanation," said

Cassie. "It's not like Devlin."

"I don't know—he's been acting so weird lately..." I trailed off.

Cassie rolled her eyes. "Not this again! I thought you said it was all sorted—that you were just being paranoid—"

"Yeah, that's what I thought... But now I'm not so sure."

"Why not?"

"Oh, just... a couple of things have come up..." I said evasively, not really wanting to repeat the story about Lincoln seeing Devlin at the hospital with the mysterious blonde. It sounded so clichéd and sordid.

Cassie gave me a look. "You know, you don't have to wait for him to call. *You* could just ring *him*."

I raised my chin. "If Devlin's not interested in finding out how I am, I'm not going to beg for his attention. He knows where I am. He's got my number. He can give me a ring—if he can be bothered."

Cassie sighed. "Okay, listen, I'd better go. But I'll give you a ring tomorrow and see how you are. Oh, and I'll email some website design stuff over to you. Good chance for you to look through things while you're still stuck at home."

"What do you mean? I'm planning to be back at the tearoom tomorrow!"

Cassie gave me a severe look. "Don't be stupid, Gemma. It won't kill you to rest for another few days. You don't want to twist your ankle again. I've heard that if you don't let the ligaments heal properly, you'll end up with all sorts of problems in the future."

"I've got my crutches. I don't see why I can't come and—"

"How are you going to hobble around on your crutches and carry a heavy tray filled with tea and scones? You won't be any good to us at the tearoom and you'll just get in the way," she said bluntly. "You're much better staying home and resting that ankle. The faster it heals, the faster you'll be back at work."

I heaved an impatient sigh. "Oh, all right!"

***

Cassie left soon afterwards and I was just about to settle down and try to read a novel when my phone rang. I saw Devlin's name on the screen. I snatched it up eagerly, then had to compose myself before I answered

"Gemma?"

"Oh, hi, Devlin." My voice was decidedly cool.

"Gemma, are you all right? What happened yesterday? I've been thinking about you all day."

"Nice of you to finally call," I said.

Devlin sounded puzzled. "What do you mean? I told your mother that I'd be tied up in meetings all day. We've had a team from Scotland Yard come to visit and I've been in an all-day conference with them. Didn't she give you the message?"

"No," I said, surprised and mollified. "She never told me you rang."

"I didn't just ring; I came to see you. Last night—but you'd already gone to bed."

"Oh, you did?" I said, softening even further.

"I saw your mother," said Devlin, a note of reserve in his voice. "She told me that you were sleeping and not to be disturbed. So I left, but I asked her to let you know that I had come, and that I'd be stuck in a conference all day today but that I would call you as soon as I got out."

"She never told me anything..." I said in a chastened voice, feeling suddenly bad for being angry at him. I also felt a flash of annoyance at my mother. Why hadn't she told me?

"Anyway, how are you, Gemma? How's the foot? Is it serious?"

"No, it's just a sprained ankle. But I have to stay off it for a few days."

"Well, can you stay off it while sitting in my car?" said Devlin with a smile in his voice. "It's only six now. We've got a couple of hours of light still. The only good thing about this conference today is that I'm getting off early so I intend to make the most of it. Fancy going for a drive?"

I felt a rush of happiness. "I'd love to. I'm going a bit crazy sitting here in the house."

"Great—I'll be over in twenty minutes. See you then."

CHAPTER TWENTY-FOUR

Twenty minutes later, I was settling into the front passenger seat of Devlin's Jaguar while he gently tucked a rug around my legs. Then he got into the driver's seat and we slid smoothly away from my parents' house.

"Where are we going?" I asked.

"You'll see… it's a surprise," said Devlin, a smile hovering at the corners of his mouth.

I gazed out of the window curiously as we drove through the streets of central Oxford and then turned into the High Street and cruised down towards Magdalen Bridge. I looked at Devlin quizzically. Surely he wasn't taking me to the site of the murder? Then understanding dawned as we turned off the High Street at the bottom, just before the bridge, and into the small car park in front of the Oxford University Botanic Garden, which sat across the street from Magdalen Tower.

Devlin killed the engine and jerked his head towards the back seat. "Fancy a picnic?"

I turned around and realised that there was a large wicker picnic hamper and a couple of folded blankets on the back seat.

"Oh!" I said, smiling with delight and anticipation. "What a brilliant idea!"

It was slow going but, with the help of my crutches, I made my way through the arched main gateway of the Botanic Garden, past the Conservatory and the luxuriant beds of the Walled Garden, to the open grassy bank beside the river. I looked around with a sigh of pleasure.

I used to love coming here as a student but I hadn't had a chance to visit since returning to Oxford. Not that I was much of a botanist, but it was always fascinating to walk around and see the huge variety of plants and trees and flowers, even if I didn't understand half the Latin names (my favourites were the gigantic lily pads in the Tropical Lily House). As the oldest botanic garden in Great Britain, it had such a sense of history too; they say that J.R.R. Tolkien used to come and sit under his favourite tree here: an enormous Austrian pine, which was possibly the inspiration for the Ents, the walking, talking tree people of Middle Earth in his famous *Lord of the Rings* trilogy.

I sank gratefully down on the soft blanket that Devlin had spread out on the grass and leaned back on my hands, enjoying the balmy evening weather. Despite being cool and grey yesterday, today it felt very summery, with the warmth of the sun still lingering in the air. The River Cherwell flowed past in front of me, dark and serene, heading south towards Christ Church Meadow and then on to join the Thames. I glanced to the left, upriver, where a fleet of punts were moored next to the bank, just underneath Magdalen Bridge. It was where most tourists hired the long, wooden boats for cruising on the river; it was also—I remembered with a shiver—next to the spot where Tanya had rushed screaming that fateful morning and waded into the water to pull in Charlie's lifeless body.

I turned hurriedly away and focused on the more pleasant prospect of the contents of the picnic hamper. Devlin was unpacking this now, laying out the plates and cutlery which had been strapped to the underside of the lid, and then lifting out an assortment of delectable picnic treats: gourmet oat crackers paired with vintage cheddar, creamy brie and dense, buttery Shropshire blue cheese, miniature pork pies still warm from the oven, caramelised onion chutney, a loaf of fresh bread, a lovely watercress and pomegranate salad, and even a couple of Scotch eggs, golden and crispy in their breadcrumb coating. For dessert, there was a huge bag of caramel popcorn, slices of rich, traditional fruitcake, and a bowl of fresh strawberries, luscious and red and gleaming.

"Where did you find such amazing strawberries?" I marvelled as I popped a juicy red fruit into my mouth. "I didn't think the season had even started yet."

"I've got my sources," said Devlin with a grin as he reached into the basket again and pulled out a bottle of champagne and two glasses.

I raised my eyebrows. "What are we celebrating?"

"Nothing," said Devlin as he popped the cork. "I just thought we deserved to treat ourselves a bit." He filled my glass with sparkling liquid and handed it to me with a smile.

I sipped the golden champagne and looked out over the river again. It was so calm and peaceful here and I felt a sense of contentment settle over me. I also felt a sense of shame for doubting Devlin; it was so sweet of him to arrange this surprise, and he had been nothing but solicitous and tender since he had come to pick me up.

"Penny for your thoughts?" he asked.

I gave a guilty start and peeked at Devlin from under my eyelashes. The last thing I wanted to do was ruin the romantic mood by confessing that I had been harbouring suspicions about him.

"I... um... I was just thinking about the May Day murder," I said quickly. "I don't suppose there have been any developments? I know you were in a conference all day."

"Yes, there have been some developments, actually," said Devlin. He glanced sideways at me. "I'm afraid Dora isn't going to like this very much."

"What do you mean?"

"We've had fresh evidence come to light—evidence which shows that Miriam Hopkins was in the vicinity of Magdalen Bridge on May morning."

I sat upright. "Miriam? Are you certain?"

Devlin nodded. "She was seen on CCTV footage. I've been getting one of my detective constables to go through all the security footage collected from various stores on the High Street. It's a long, tedious process, which most of the time doesn't yield much, but this time he's come up with a result: one of the shops at the very bottom of the High Street, just before Magdalen College and the tower, has got a security camera fixed above the front door with a good view of the street. And according to the time stamp on the video, Miriam Hopkins was walking along the pavement on the opposite side, heading towards the bridge, at 5:23 a.m. that morning."

"But are you sure it's her?"

"Yes, there's no doubt. She's wearing a raincoat with a distinctive Middle Eastern paisley pattern. In any case, you can see her face quite clearly. She was obviously heading for Magdalen Bridge at a time when she told us that she was nowhere near the place. I intend to question her again first thing tomorrow morning." He leaned forwards slightly. "But I'm sure I don't need to tell you, Gemma, that this doesn't look good. The fact that she lied to the police already makes her look guilty, and combined with the other things stacked against her..."

I sighed and thought of Dora's friend: that kind, careworn face, her gentle, motherly manner... Could I have been wrong about her? Could Miriam Hopkins really have been the murderer?

"I just can't believe it..." I murmured. "It seems so out of character!"

"Well, what do you really know about her character?"

"Not much, that's true," I admitted. "But Dora does! They've been friends and colleagues for years."

"But can you trust Dora's judgement?"

"I—" I hesitated.

The honest answer was, I didn't know. In fact, you could argue that I barely knew Dora that well myself. I had only met her earlier this year and she had only been working at the tearoom for a few months.

"I suppose not," I said with a sigh. "I imagine that Dora would be fiercely loyal to her friends.

"Yes, and because of that, possibly blind to her friends' faults," said Devlin.

"Yeah... and I'm probably a bit biased myself. It just seems like there are so many people more likely to be the murderer. Oh! Speaking of which, I almost forgot! Has your sergeant mentioned a guy called Pete Morrow at the Oxford Krav Maga Club? You know, Charlie Foxton was a member there."

"Hmm... not that I recall. Why?"

Quickly, I told him about my Krav Maga experience with the Old Biddies. I could see Devlin trying not to laugh as he listened to my account.

"It's not that funny," I said sourly.

"Aw, come on, Gemma, the whole thing is hilarious! The thought of these four little eighty-year-old grannies battering you to a pulp and sending you to hospital... and you were afraid to hurt them!" Devlin gave up and roared with laughter.

"Well, who would have known that they had such an aggressive streak in them?" I muttered. "And Ethel was the worst! She looks like a puff of wind could blow her away... and she was punching better than Rocky Balboa! Anyway," I said, keen not to dwell on my humiliation, "the only good thing was that I had to sit out most of the class and I got chatting to some of the members there. Most of them were quite nice, but there was one chap called Pete—Pete Morrow—he had a real chip on his shoulder about Oxford university students. And apparently he'd lost a match to Charlie last week—lost very badly. It sounded like a big loss of face in front of the club and he's still really bitter about it."

"You think he killed Charlie in revenge?" said Devlin sceptically.

"Well, he was angry enough to go after Charlie again after the match was over. They had to pull them apart."

"That still doesn't connect him to May morning."

"No... but somebody from the Krav Maga Club was

there on the bridge when Charlie was killed and Pete Morrow seems the most likely candidate! I haven't told you all my news yet," I said as I saw his puzzled look. "There was someone wearing a hoodie, with the Oxford Krav Maga Club logo on the back, running away from the scene just after Charlie went over the bridge."

I recounted my meeting with Captain Thomas at the nursing home and what he told me he had seen through his binoculars.

Devlin whistled. "It's all highly circumstantial, of course, but it does seem very suggestive. Certainly enough for us to bring Pete Morrow in for questioning. It's a shame I didn't manage to speak to you yesterday—aside from the fact that I wanted to know how you were, it would have been good if I had known this because I could have got my sergeant to look into this today while I was tied up in the conference."

"Yeah, I probably should have texted you when I got to the hospital. I got side-tracked by my mother and Lincoln... although if I'd known that you were just around the corner—"

Devlin looked startled. "Me?"

"Yes, Lincoln saw you at the hospital... with a blonde woman," I said, trying to keep my voice neutral.

"Oh... oh, yes... right..." Devlin looked down and made a great show of cutting up a piece of cheese and laying it on a cracker. He put it in his mouth and chewed slowly, looking away before he answered. I couldn't shake off the feeling that he was playing for time.

He swallowed and said casually, "Yeah, that's right—I had to meet someone there."

"In relation to the case?"

"No, not this case," he prevaricated.

"You mean, one of your other cases?"

"Yes... you could say that."

I looked at him searchingly but he was busy fiddling with the bottle of champagne, not meeting my eyes.

"Would you like a top up?" he asked.

"Uh... No, thanks. I've had enough."

"In that case..." Devlin looked around us. "Maybe we'd better get going. The light's fading and it might start to get cold. Your mother would never forgive me if you caught a chill."

I glanced around. He was right. Twilight was falling and the garden was empty. I helped to gather the remainder of the food and place it back in the hamper. Devlin started speaking rapidly, telling me about a colleague who was thinking of leaving London and transferring to the Cotswolds area. I listened half-heartedly and made suitable replies, but my mind wasn't really on what he was saying.

Suddenly my happy contentment evaporated and all my doubts came flooding back. I wasn't imagining it. Devlin was being evasive—I was certain of it. Why hadn't he mentioned being at the hospital last night?

Who was the blonde woman he had been with and why wouldn't he talk about it?

I followed him silently as we walked back to the car. We didn't speak as we loaded the picnic paraphernalia into the back seat, then got into the front. Devlin seemed lost in his own thoughts and I was brooding with mine. However, as the car turned out of the lane and back onto the High Street, I was suddenly jarred out of my preoccupation by the sight of a figure on the other side of the road.

It was Damian Heath, I realised, standing on the corner of Haverton College. He was deep in conversation with someone—a short, stocky figure who stood with hands shoved into his pockets, his head bowed and shoulders hunched beneath the dark hoodie he wore.

As the car turned onto the High Street and started gliding smoothly away, I looked back and craned my neck to keep them in sight. The stocky man shifted slightly and light from a streetlamp fell on his dark, swarthy face. For a moment, I thought I recognised him.

"What is it, Gemma?" asked Devlin, flicking his eyes to the rear-view mirror.

I turned around in the seat even more, straining to see, but we were moving too fast and the curve of the High Street obscured the view.

I turned back to face forwards. "I... It's probably nothing," I said. "I thought I saw... but I'm probably wrong."

CHAPTER TWENTY-FIVE

My ankle felt a lot better the next morning—so much so that I decided I would go in to work after all. My mother, however, wouldn't hear of it and, when I tried to argue, she called Cassie at the tearoom and I got a smart telling-off from my best friend.

"Don't be silly, Gemma! One more day won't make a difference and we're managing fine without you. Honestly, you're not as indispensable as you think," she said teasingly.

"Well, if you're sure..." I said. "I feel bad that you're all working so hard and I'm just lounging around at home."

Cassie laughed. "Working so hard? I've barely been allowed to do anything. The Old Biddies have taken over the tearoom! Mabel is running the place like a military drill sergeant—I think the customers are practically eating and drinking on command."

"Oh no, you're not serious? What if she upsets the customers—"

"Relax, Gemma, the tourists are loving it! It seems to fit perfectly with their idea of a traditional English tearoom—having these little white-haired old ladies going around serving tea, being bossy and asking nosy questions about their private lives. So stop worrying and get it into your head that you're not needed here! In fact, I don't want to see your face until you're walking normally on that ankle again."

I hung up feeling a lot better. Cassie always cheered me up with her blunt, earthy attitude and irreverent take on things—courtesy of her liberal upbringing in a rowdy, chaotic household with artist parents who prized creativity and free expression. It was so different to my own repressed upbringing in a stereotypical British upper-middle-class household with its focus on correct etiquette and "proper" behaviour. Despite eight years in the more relaxed culture of Australia, I probably still took life a bit too seriously and Cassie's teasing was good for me.

Settling myself in my parents' sitting room again, I resolved to enjoy my second day of enforced holiday. Perhaps I'd tackle one of those books I'd been meaning to read for months. But as I picked up a thriller novel and began turning the pages, I found my mind wandering—in particular, wandering back to the murder of Charlie Foxton.

I wondered again about what I had seen last night just as we were turning into the High Street. Had that been Pete Morrow standing on that street corner talking to Damian Heath? Why? As far as I knew, Damian wasn't a member of the Krav Maga Club, so what had he been speaking to Pete Morrow so earnestly about?

My mother came into the sitting room, dressed to go out. "I'm just popping into town, darling—would you like me to pick up anything for you?"

"Where are you going, Mother?"

"Just to the High Street. There's a lovely new women's clothing store that I want to have a look at. Eliza Whitfield told me that they've got wonderful Liberty print blouses. She bought two last week and they seem to be running a special sale at the moment."

"Do you mind if I come with you?" I asked impulsively. "There's something I'd like to check out at Haverton College—that's near the bottom of the High Street. Maybe you could drop me there and I can meet you somewhere later?"

"Well, of course, darling, but are you sure you should be walking on that ankle?"

I extended my left leg and rotated my foot. "It's a lot better, Mother. Honestly. And I've got my crutches…"

Fifteen minutes later, I found myself being deposited outside Haverton College. I waved my mother off, then hobbled through the main gate into the Front Quad. I'd half-expected one of the college porters to stop me and ask my business but the only porter I saw was busy talking to a group of students and barely gave me a passing glance. I suppose someone hobbling on crutches didn't look like much of a security risk!

I made my way across the Front Quad, through the archway, and then across the Rear Quad until I reached Staircase 5, where Damian and Charlie's room was. When I got there, I suddenly remembered the four flights of stairs up to the top level and my heart sank. *Maybe I should abandon the idea...* Then I straightened my shoulders. No. I'd come all the way into town—I didn't want to give up now.

I took a deep breath and began to climb. It was pretty hard work, especially manoeuvring the crutches, and I had to stop frequently to rest. Once I thought of giving up, but by then I was already halfway up and it would have been just as much effort to go back down as it was to continue. When I finally reached the top landing, I was breathing hard and sweating profusely, and my ankle had started to throb again.

As I hobbled towards the boys' door, I suddenly thought of something else. What an idiot I was! I didn't even know if Damian was in his room—it was the middle of the morning and chances were that he was at a lecture or something. I might have climbed four flights of stairs for nothing!

Annoyed with myself, I leaned forwards to knock

on the door. That's when I noticed that it was slightly ajar. Frowning, I pushed it gently. It creaked as it swung open and I stared in shock. The place was in a shambles! Someone had gone around and emptied every drawer, pulled all the books off the shelves, opened all the cupboards. Even the contents of the fridge were tossed on the floor. The place had been completely ransacked. I took a few steps in—then I saw something which made my heart kick in my chest.

There was someone sprawled on the floor in the centre of the room. I couldn't see his face from where I was standing—the couch was in the way—but his legs were sticking out. I recognised those drainpipe jeans. My heart pounding uncomfortably, I hobbled forwards and peered over the back of the couch.

It was Damian Heath.

I didn't need to go any closer to see that he was dead. His face was a hideous purple colour, blotchy and swollen, and his tongue was hanging slightly out of his mouth.

I gulped and looked quickly away, taking a few hasty steps backwards. This wasn't the first time I had seen a dead body, but it always came as a horrible shock. Besides, I had never seen anyone killed this way before.

Damian Heath had been strangled to death.

CHAPTER TWENTY-SIX

It was also not the first time I'd called the police after discovering a murder, but things still felt very surreal as I sat on a stone ledge outside the staircase and watched the police photographer and members of the SOCO team hurrying to and fro. The CID had arrived too—not Devlin, but his detective sergeant. I noticed that the young man lost a bit of his usual cocky swagger after he'd been up to the room and seen the body; in fact, he looked slightly green. He had a quick chat with one of the crime scene investigators, then came over to question me.

"The inspector's held up—he's down in Blackbird Leys working that other homicide, but he's on his way." The young sergeant made a face. "It's a pretty vicious murder. And the killer was obviously searching for something too. The whole place's been turned upside down." He hesitated, looking at me. "I... I guess I should really let the guv'nor question you—you being his girlfriend an' all," he said, embarrassed.

"Actually, that's probably exactly why Devlin shouldn't question me," I said cynically. "Go ahead, just interview me like a normal witness—forget that I have any special connection to the Force."

He nodded and started taking me through the questions. When we'd finished going through how I'd discovered Damian, he asked why I had come to see the boy in the first place.

"Well, I was following a sort of hunch, really," I said. "I thought I saw Damian last night talking to a man I'd seen at the Oxford Krav Maga Club—"

The sergeant's head jerked up. "Pete Morrow?"

I stared at him. "Yeah, how did you know?"

"I was just checking up on him. That's why I got here so quickly—I was already in town. I was on my way to the Club, actually. The inspector told me about your experience there..." He started grinning, then quickly schooled his features into a more sombre expression. "And he told me to check out this Pete Morrow character. Well, I ran a couple of background checks on him this morning and found that Morrow's got a record. A couple of assault incidents—drunken brawls—and he's done a bit of time for petty theft. Nothing too serious, but he's in the system."

"Oh." I digested this. I wasn't that surprised. I know they say you shouldn't judge someone on appearances, but Pete Morrow looked like he would have a record. Still, could someone who had been involved in petty crime plan an elaborate stunt like the murder on May morning? Somehow, I felt like Pete Morrow would be more likely to attack you with a knife in a dark alley.

"Morrow isn't his real name, you know," the sergeant added.

I looked at him sharply. "What do you mean?"

"Well, he's actually not English—he's a Russian immigrant. Came to this country in his late teens. His real name is Morozov but he decided to call himself Morrow when he started work. He works as a butcher in one of the shops in the Covered Market."

"He's Russian?" My mind was whirling. Was this just a strange coincidence? Or was there some connection between Pete Morrow—Morozov—and Tanya Koskov?

"You'd better find Pete immediately and see if he had an alibi for Damian's murder," I said.

"Oh, don't worry—he's top of the list," said the sergeant. "But first we need an accurate time of death from the forensic pathologist... Ah! Here she is..."

The sergeant's face lit up and I saw a gleam of appreciation in his eyes. I glanced across the quad and saw a slim Asian girl coming towards us. Although she was dressed in the unflattering white bodysuit and hood of the forensic team, she still radiated beauty and charm. Dr Jo Ling, the new forensic pathologist on the CID team. I'd met her recently and I had to admit, although she was the kind of girl you'd love to hate, you couldn't help but warm to her. She caught my eye as she crossed the quad and gave me a cheery wave, then continued on her way to the staircase.

"And here's the guv'nor now," said the sergeant, making an unconscious effort to stand up straighter.

I turned and saw Devlin stride into the quad, dark and handsome in his tailored charcoal-grey suit, his piercing blue eyes narrowing as he scanned the area and sized up the situation. But what really caught my eye was the woman at his side. She was slim, blonde, and, despite being slightly older, was still very attractive, with a thin, heart-shaped face that reminded me slightly of a fox. She was dressed in a simple Lycra top and black leggings, which nevertheless showed off her great figure. My heart gave an unsteady lurch.

"Who's... who's that?" I asked the sergeant.

"That?" He grinned lasciviously. "That's Mel. Mel Buckley." He dropped his voice. "She's one of our singing canaries. The prettiest one, I reckon."

I stared at the sergeant. "Canary? You mean she's an informant?"

"Shh!" He glanced quickly around. "Yeah, Mel's been helping the inspector on the Blackbird Leys homicide. Lucky sod—what I wouldn't give to work with her," he added with another grin.

"So... where would you normally meet up with an informant like her?"

He shrugged. "Depends. They usually pick and choose, tell us a time and place, and we meet 'em there. Usually somewhere very public, where lots of people go regularly and where they can have a good excuse for being there."

"Like a hospital?"

He looked puzzled. "Dunno if I've ever met anyone at the hospital. But yeah, I suppose."

I felt a rush of relief. So that was the explanation. It was as simple as that. Devlin had been meeting Mel—his informant—at the hospital. I felt like an enormous weight had been lifted off my shoulders. Again, I felt ashamed at having doubted him. *I have to stop giving in to these ridiculous suspicions!* I told myself. It was all Tanya Koskov's fault—all the silly stuff she had said about the signs of Charlie cheating had corrupted my mind and put ideas into my head.

As if conjured up by my thoughts, the beautiful Russian girl walked into the quad at that moment, followed as usual by the faithful Mikhail. She stopped short when she saw the police activity around Staircase 5. They were just bringing the stretcher out of the staircase with the body covered by a sheet.

"What has happened?" asked Tanya harshly, going towards the stretcher.

Devlin had been talking with Jo Ling but now he

moved quickly to intercept her. "Miss Koskov—I was wondering if I might ask you a few questions?"

Tanya turned to him and I thought she was going to tell Devlin that she wouldn't speak to him without a lawyer, but, to my surprise, she gave a curt nod.

Devlin flicked his eyes towards Mikhail, then back to Tanya. "Have you just come back to the college? Where have you been?"

"Lectures," she said. "What has happened?"

"Damian Heath has been murdered."

Her eyes widened. "Murdered?"

"Can I ask you where you were between the hours of ten and twelve last night?"

"I... I was here in college—in J.C.R.," said Tanya.

"Are you sure?"

Tanya furrowed her brow. "Yes, after dinner, I went to my room to work on essay. And then I decided to go to J.C.R. to sit and read magazines."

"And you were there from ten o'clock until midnight?"

"Yes, she was," a thick, accented voice spoke up. Mikhail stepped forwards. "I was in Junior Common Room also. I saw Tatiana Vladimirovna—she was there during that whole time."

I saw Tanya glance at him quickly, and her lips parted slightly as if she was about to say something, then she changed her mind and pressed them together.

"And what were you doing there?" Devlin asked Mikhail.

"Me, I play the pool."

"Were you playing with anyone?"

The Russian scholar gave him a contemptuous look. "No. I play myself." His implication was obvious—that nobody would be good enough to play with him. I found his pompous, superior manner incredibly irritating, as usual.

Devlin turned back to Tanya. "Was there anyone else in the J.C.R.?"

Tanya looked bored. "A few people came in, yes. Earlier, around ten o'clock. They sit and watch news. And then two girls come and sit beside me. They talked very loudly. But after that, it was just Mikhail and me. He was beside pool table and I was on sofa by window."

"And after that?"

"I go back to my room. You ask that girl, Nicola—she lives on my staircase. I pass her as I am going in. Anyway..." Tanya tossed her head. "These are stupid questions! You think I kill Damian? Why? He is nothing to me."

"That's not what you said to me last time," I spoke up, hobbling forwards on my crutches.

Tanya turned to me, her eyes narrowing. "What do you mean?"

"When I saw you at the café in town," I reminded her. "You told me that you were angry at Damian for trying to get you in trouble with the police. You said: *'Damian will be sorry for what he has tried to do to me. I will make him pay'*—remember?"

Mikhail made a sudden, irritable movement towards me, like a dog bristling at someone insulting his master, but I ignored him. All my attention was on Tanya. Was I imagining it or did the girl look slightly uneasy underneath her haughty demeanour?

"I did not say that!" she snarled. "You are daughter of bitch! You are just like everybody else, trying to attack me. *Da ti yebanulsa!* I am not talking anymore without lawyer. Out of my way!"

She shoved me violently aside and stormed out of the quad. I gasped in surprise as her shove sent me reeling backwards. Staggering, I lost hold of my crutches, fell over, and collapsed in a heap on the ground.

"Gemma!" cried Devlin, rushing to my side, his blue eyes filled with concern. He lifted me tenderly and helped me to my feet. "Are you all right?"

"Yes, fine..." I said, catching my breath. I wriggled my ankle experimentally and was relieved when I felt no pain. "Just lost my balance."

Devlin looked at the empty archway through which Tanya and Mikhail had disappeared, and his face hardened. "I'd like to haul that girl in for assault right now!"

"It's okay, Devlin," I said. "Don't get upset on my account. If you bring her in and don't have enough to hold her, you might never get another chance, given the lawyers she's got around her. I'd rather you waited until the right moment, when you have enough evidence to arrest her—assuming that she's guilty, of course." I gave a wry laugh. "She might just be a really bad-tempered spoilt cow, that's all... that doesn't make her a murderer."

"Still doesn't excuse her for what she did to you just now," said Devlin angrily.

"So it's confirmed that Damian was killed between ten and midnight last night?" I asked.

"That's what Jo reckons. We still have to find the murder weapon, though. He was strangled, but not with a rope or a wire. From the lack of abrasion marks around his neck, Jo thinks it was probably something very soft—like a silk cloth or scarf." Devlin looked at the empty archway again thoughtfully. "I'm going to get a warrant to search Tanya Koskov's room and confiscate any silk scarves she has; get Forensics to test them—see if there are any fibres or even DNA linked to Damian. It might take a while but if the evidence is there, we'll find it," he said grimly.

Then his eyes softened as he looked back at me. "You should get back home, Gemma, and rest that ankle. My sergeant says he's questioned you formally already. If I have any further questions, I'll give you a ring later." He glanced around the quad and sighed. "I wish I could take you home myself but—"

"No, it's fine, don't worry," I said. "I know you've got a lot to do here at the crime scene. And anyway, I've promised my mother to meet her at the Queen's Lane Coffee House—she's probably waiting there for me already."

"I'll get a squad car to drop you off there."

"No, don't be silly! It's only five minutes' walk up the High Street from here. I'll be fine—I'll just go slowly." I reached up and gave him a kiss. "I'll speak to you later."

CHAPTER TWENTY-SEVEN

Almost as surreal as discovering Damian Heath's dead body was finding myself back in my parents' house that afternoon, listening to my mother fuss over arrangements for dinner, as if nothing had happened.

"... and I thought I'd start with split-pea soup. Professor Obruchev says pea soup is very popular in Russia—they make it with dried beans and smoked meat—so I'm interested to see what he thinks of our English version and how it differs. Of course, I could have made mushroom soup—that's apparently very popular too—or maybe broccoli soup... I don't think they've got that, although they do have their famous Russian cabbage soup, of course... What do you think, darling?"

"Er..." My head was spinning with all the soup variations. "Why don't we start with melon?"

My mother gave me a reproachful look. "One must start with a soup, darling, for a proper dinner! Oh, and don't forget—I will need you to keep Professor Obruchev entertained while I check on the roast. I'm doing a rack of lamb with rosemary and garlic, and it will be in the oven already when he arrives, but I'll have to make up the gravy from the juices and cook the root vegetables for the mash... And your father had to go to an unexpected meeting for the University Examinations Board this afternoon, so he might be home late. You'll have to sit and chat with the professor."

"Okay," I said without much enthusiasm.

I had completely forgotten that today was the day the visiting Russian professor was coming to dinner. To be honest, after everything that had happened, the last thing I felt like doing was being sociable. But I knew there was no way I could get out of it, and a few hours later I found myself waiting for our guest after I had changed into a "nice dress" to please my mother.

When he arrived, Professor Obruchev seemed as jolly as ever, bouncing into the house in the same ancient brown suit, even more ancient shoes, and faded silk neckerchief, and pumping my hand enthusiastically when he saw me.

"Ah, Gemma Philipovna! I cannot tell you how much I have been thinking about wonderful food I had at your tearoom!"

"Oh... er, thank you," I said. "I'm glad you enjoyed it."

"It was exquisite! Delicious! I must inform my wife when I return to Russia. Perhaps you can let me have some recipes and she can attempt to bake your British creations?"

"Oh... sure, I'll ask my chef, Dora. She's the one who produces all those delicious cakes and scones. I have to confess, I'm not much of a baker myself."

"Ah, but you have talents in other directions, no? Your father has been telling me about murders in the village and in Oxford also, which you help police to solve. You have—what the English call it—a keen nose for truth?"

I gave an embarrassed laugh. "Well, a lot of it was luck, I think. I just happened to be in the right place at the right time."

"Ah, you are modest! That is very English. Always, you Englishmen talk less than it is. But now I hear that you are involved in new murder? Death of student on May morning?" He leaned closer and waggled his eyebrows. "Do you have idea already for identity of murderer?"

"Well, I..." I hesitated. His face was creased in his usual jovial smile and yet his eyes seemed to be watching me keenly.

"You are very interested in the murder," I commented.

"Ah! But of course—murder is always fascinating!

Especially when it is one as dramatic as this... like from pages of novel, no? I enjoy the detective story very much."

"You should meet certain friends of mine," I said with a wry smile. "They enjoy detective stories very much too. In fact, half the time, they seem to think that they *are* in a detective story! And they always think they know better than the police."

"But yes, I believe also that sometimes the amateur can see things police cannot," said Professor Obruchev earnestly. "Although in your case, you have special advantage, hmm? Your young man—he is detective in Criminal Investigation Department, your father tells me."

"Yes, Devlin is a detective inspector with the Oxfordshire CID," I admitted. "But he doesn't talk about work much."

"Ah, but he must tell you more than what is revealed to the public, no? For example, if they have suspect and are close to making arrest?"

I looked at him thoughtfully. "Professor—may I ask, why are you so interested in this case?"

He laughed easily. "Perhaps it is because it happens on day I arrive in Oxford. *Oy!* To think it should have been happening at same time, on other side of town!"

I looked at him in surprise. "You arrived in Oxford on May morning? I thought my mother said you arrived the day after."

He looked flustered for a moment and said, "Yes,

yes, there was mistake in dates. I came earlier but I did not want to trouble your parents so I did not contact them. I decide to see Oxford myself for one day first."

"Oh darling, you're not making Professor Obruchev discuss that dreadful murder business, are you?" said my mother, coming out of the kitchen to join us.

"It is my apologies, Mrs Rose!" cried the Russian professor, springing up. "It is I who invited Gemma to speak of this topic. You see, for me, it is exciting opportunity to come so close to murder. It is like famous mysteries that you British are so fond of reading and writing, is it not?"

"Well, murder and mayhem are certainly not fit subjects for the dinner table," said my mother firmly. "We'll go in and sit down now. Philip has rung and said that he is on his way, so he should be joining us any moment."

We followed her meekly into the dining room and took our places at the table, just as my father came hurrying through the front door. However, as Professor Obruchev made to sit down at the dining table, there was a mournful yowl and he sprang up again in shock. We all peered around to see Muesli stretched out on his chair, looking up at him reproachfully.

"Muesli!" cried my mother. "You naughty kitty! What are you doing there? Come off Professor Obruchev's chair."

"*Meorrw!*" said Muesli defiantly. She rolled on her back and twisted so that she was looking at us upside down, her head tilted in an adorable fashion, her green eyes unblinking.

"It is okay," said the professor with a chuckle. "I have cats myself at home also; the Russian Blue— you know this cat? It has great green eyes, with black circle around, just like yours."

"Yes, I've heard of Russian Blues. They're beautiful," I said. "Is it a boy or a girl?"

"I have two: one boy, one girl. They are brother and sister. The girl is Lilia—it is Russian for Lily; the boy is Rasputin. And this one?" He smiled as Muesli continued to stare up at him, upside down. "You call her by name for breakfast food?"

I laughed. "Yes, her name is Muesli, like the Swiss cereal with the rolled oats and dried fruits and nuts. It's a bit similar to what Americans call 'granola', I think."

"It is an unusual name, this, for cat."

"I suppose so. She used to belong to someone who was a keen baker before I adopted her, so perhaps that explains it."

"Come on, Muesli, you must get off now," said my mother, trying to shove the little cat gently off the chair.

Muesli, however, was having none of it. She batted my mother's hands away and gave a petulant, "*Meorrw!*"

"It is all right," said Professor Obruchev. "I shall

sit on this chair here next to her."

So a new place setting had to be set up for the professor and everyone had to shift over one place, so that Muesli wasn't disturbed. I rolled my eyes. *How do cats always manage to get their own way in everything?* The little tabby spent the rest of dinner watching Professor Obruchev, her big green eyes following his every movement as he drank the soup, then helped himself to the roast lamb, mint sauce, mash, and gravy. Finally, after a delicious dessert of sticky toffee pudding, we moved to the sitting room for tea and coffee, and Muesli followed us, once more settling herself next to the Russian professor and regarding him curiously.

"She seems to have taken to you," said my father with a chuckle.

My mother made a flustered gesture. "If she is bothering you, Professor, we can always—"

"No, no, it is fine. As I say, I like cats. It seems that she would like to play?" he said with a laugh as Muesli reached up suddenly and swiped one of the dangling ends of the neckerchief tied around his throat.

"Muesli!" cried my mother in mortification. "I'm so sorry—"

"No, it is fine," the professor assured her. "All cats are like this. Mine also."

He sat back and tried to smooth his neckerchief flat against his chest, but the more he tried to tuck it away, the more Muesli seemed interested in the silky fabric. She reached up again and caught it with her paw. My mother took a sharp intake of breath as we saw Muesli's sharp little claws dig into the fragile fabric.

I looked around and picked up a fishing rod toy lying on a side table. "Here, would you like to use this, Professor?" I said hastily.

Professor Obruchev took the toy and gave it a flick. Muesli's head jerked and I saw her pupils dilate, her eyes growing dark and enormous. She turned, the neckerchief forgotten, and pounced on the feather bait at the end of the string.

"Oho! She is fast, this one!" laughed Professor Obruchev as he waved the rod around and Muesli chased after it.

I had to admit, I was pretty impressed by my little cat's reflexes: no matter how quickly the professor flicked and jerked the string, she always seemed to be one step ahead of him, pouncing and twisting through the air. Her prowess seemed to egg the professor on, getting him worked up in a fever of excitement as he attempted to outwit Muesli.

"Aaah! No... no... *Oy!* You see, I am faster!" He laughed and yanked the rod sideways, jerking the bait out of Muesli's claws just in the nick of time. The little cat sprang after it, grabbing the string and rolling over, kicking and clawing with her back legs. "*Ozornik!* That is good... But you shall not win... aaah... no! I have new trick for you... I do this! And this! Ah, but you are clever... oh! *Ne etot—*"

"Professor!" I grabbed his arm. "What was that you said just now?"

He looked at me in puzzlement. "I... I am not sure...?"

"The last thing you just said," I said urgently.

"I said *'ne etot'*. It means: 'not this one'."

I leaned forwards eagerly. "Is there another phrase in Russian that sounds similar?"

They were all looking at me in bemusement now, my mother and father in particular.

"What do you mean, 'similar'?" said the professor. "There are many phrases that are similar, using these words—"

"I was thinking of something that sounded like... *'NATO joy evict'*?"

"*NATO joy evict*?" The professor frowned. "But that makes no sense."

"No, not in English, but I just realised... perhaps it's a phrase in Russian? I'm probably pronouncing it wrong. I'm actually repeating what someone else said, but does it sound like any phrase in Russian to you?"

"*NATO joy evict... nato joy evict...*" the professor mumbled, looking down and stroking his beard. Then he brightened. "Perhaps you refer to *'ne tot chelovek'*?"

"Yes!" I said excitedly. "Yes, that could be it! What does it mean?" I looked at him eagerly.

"It means 'not this man'—or perhaps in English you would say 'wrong man'."

"Wrong man?" I stared at him, my mind spinning.

"Where did you hear it—these words?" asked the professor.

"I—" I stopped short, remembering his eager prying into the progress of the investigation, and the fact that he had actually arrived in Oxford on the day of the murder, not *after* the murder as I had thought... Maybe I was just being paranoid again, but what did I really know about Professor Obruchev? He wasn't a close colleague of my father's. Was it just a coincidence that a Russian scholar— who happened to know the Koskovs personally— should arrive in Oxford at around the same time as Charlie's murder?

"Oh, um... it was nothing important," I said, giving him a nonchalant smile. "It was just a phrase I heard some tourists say in my tearoom and I wondered what it meant. There was a large group of young men and they got very loud and excitable, shouting this phrase at each other. They must have been discussing a story about mistaken identity or something."

Professor Obruchev seemed satisfied and didn't question me further. By this time, Muesli seemed to have calmed down and had settled next to our guest to give herself a wash. My mother hastened to pour the tea and coffee, and pass around the box of Belgian chocolates. Conversation wandered to the state of British politics and I tuned out, leaning back on the sofa instead and brooding over what I had just learned.

It was all still guesswork, of course, but if that phrase had been heard next to Charlie, just before he went over the bridge, there was a chance that it had been uttered by the murderer. Which meant that the murderer was Russian and, in the heat of the moment, he had blurted out the words in his native tongue.

It also suggests that the murderer made a mistake, I thought with sudden excitement. The Australian backpacker had reported that he heard someone cry "*Aagh!*" and then this phrase: "*Ne tot chelovek!*"— which could have been the murderer crying: "*Aagh! Wrong man!*"

So did that mean that Charlie Foxton hadn't been the intended victim after all?

CHAPTER TWENTY-EIGHT

It was a wonderful feeling to be able to walk—okay, hobble—into my tearoom the next morning and get back into the thick of things. My ankle felt so much better that I was able to put a bit of weight on it and I was down to using just one crutch. Although I knew I still couldn't do active waitressing duty, I had convinced Cassie that I would be useful behind the counter—in particular, ringing up all the bills for customers who had finished and were leaving.

As the "morning tea" rush started and customers began filling the tables, I stood behind the counter and looked happily around: the spring sunshine streaming in through the thick glass of the mullioned windows, gleaming on the silver cutlery and fine china teapots at the tables; a young couple laughing as their two-year-old bit into a slice of Victoria sponge cake and got jam all over her chin; two elderly ladies—village residents by the look of it—huddled together over their tea and scones, busily sharing some gossip; a group of American tourists *oohing* and *aahing* as Cassie laid out a selection of cakes on their table; another group of tourists eagerly posing for photos with the tearoom's inglenook fireplace and chattering away excitedly in Japanese... I gave a sigh of contentment. I hadn't realised how much I had missed my little kingdom.

The Old Biddies had come in to help as usual, although Mabel looked slightly miffed at having been "dethroned" as queen of the tearoom. I soothed her ruffled feathers, however, by sharing all the new things I'd learned about the murder case since that fateful Krav Maga class three nights ago.

"Hmm... this Pete Morrow—he sounds exactly like the type of man to be a murderer," declared Mabel. "Yes, I remember seeing him at the club. Short stocky fellow, with a swarthy complexion—isn't that right, dear? Yes, yes, swarthy men can't be trusted. They always turn out to be the bad ones in books. And he has such thick eyebrows too," she added, as if this decided the case.

I rolled my eyes. "This isn't a novel. You can't take against a man just because of the way he looks!"

"But villains are always swarthy," insisted Glenda. "Although I must say, I do like a swarthy man myself. There is something so attractive about hairy men, don't you think?"

"I... er..."

To my relief, Florence interrupted: "But he must be the villain! I'm sure Swarthy Pete killed Damian."

"He certainly has no alibi for the time of Damian's murder," I agreed. "And he was definitely in the vicinity just a few hours before."

"Oh, you mean when you saw him with Damian on the street, dear?"

"Yeah, I thought I saw them talking to each other on the corner just outside Haverton College the night Damian was strangled. And I spoke to Devlin briefly this morning before coming in to work—he told me he questioned Pete Morrow yesterday afternoon and the man confirmed that it *was* him talking to Damian on the street."

Mabel pounced on me. "Well, there you have it! Isn't that an admission of guilt?"

"Not really. Pete said that it was Damian who stopped him in the street—Damian recognised the hoodie—and asked about the Krav Maga Club because he was anxious to learn some self-defence."

"Ooh, it sounds like Damian was worried for his own safety," said Glenda.

I glanced at her. "You know, I hadn't thought of it like that... but you're right. Maybe Damian had some inkling that he was in danger, or perhaps he had even been threatened."

"But by whom? It can't have been Swarthy Pete because then Damian wouldn't have approached *him* for help—"

"Unless he didn't realise the threat came from

Swarthy Pe—" I caught myself and scowled at the Old Biddies. "Er... I mean, from Pete Morrow. The threats could have been anonymous."

"But why would anyone threaten Damian anyway?" asked Florence.

"He knew something about Charlie's murder," said Mabel emphatically. "Maybe he saw something on May morning which could incriminate the killer—so he had to be silenced."

"So... you mean it was Swarthy Pete who killed Charlie as well?" asked Ethel.

I frowned. "Well, right now, he does look like the top suspect. There are a lot of things adding up against him." I held up my fingers and counted them off. "One: he had a strong motive for wanting revenge after Charlie humiliated him at the Krav Maga Club. Two: he was seen running away from the bridge on May morning—and he admitted to Devlin that he was there; he said he had gone to watch the celebrations, but after the choir finished singing, he suddenly needed the toilet, which was why he ran off (although that seems a bit of a lame excuse to me). Three: he works as a butcher in the Covered Market, so he would have a good idea of where to stab someone to cause a fatal injury, and he would also be used to handling metal meat skewers. Four: he was one of the last people seen with Damian just before the latter was killed and he doesn't have an alibi for the time of that murder. Oh! And... and..." I added excitedly, holding up the last finger. "Five: he's

Russian—his real name is Morozov—and that phrase that the Aussie backpacker overheard, which was possibly the murderer crying out just after stabbing Charlie, was in Russian."

The Old Biddies were watching me, goggle-eyed.

"But... he's the murderer then!" cried Glenda. "Why haven't the police arrested him?"

"A lot of that is circumstantial. It wouldn't stand up in court. Devlin says he needs more concrete evidence. Also, Pete Morrow isn't the only suspect. We mustn't forget Tanya Koskov. She had motives for killing both Charlie and Damian—although I admit, they're weaker. She certainly had the best opportunity to stab Charlie, plus she's a medical student, so she would know where and how to inflict a lethal wound. And she had easy access to the murder weapon."

"But didn't you say, dear, that she has an alibi for Damian's murder?"

"Well... she *says* she was in the J.C.R. the whole time, but the only person who can vouch for that is Mikhail Petrovsky, and I wouldn't put it past him to lie for her. He's so patriotic and loyal to his fellow countrymen—I think he would see it as his duty to 'protect' another Russian from suspicion. In fact, I think he would do it just to spite the British police, if nothing else!"

"What about Miriam Hopkins?" asked Mabel suddenly. "Are the police still considering her a suspect as well?"

"Oh, no, there's some good news there," I said, smiling. "Devlin questioned Miriam again to ask her about the CCTV footage, which showed that she *had* been near Magdalen Bridge on May morning, when she had told the police that she hadn't. And she admitted that she had lied previously."

Ethel gasped. "Why did she lie?"

"It was because of her son. He contacted her the night before, saying he needed money—and asking her to meet him by Magdalen Bridge. Apparently he's in a bit of trouble and on the run from the police himself, so he wanted to meet in a busy, public place where he could disappear easily in the crowd. And he made her promise that she wouldn't tell anyone she had been to meet him, especially not the police. Spun her some story that he was being persecuted unfairly and that he just needed more time to prove his innocence." I rolled my eyes. "So Miriam lied to protect him."

"Do the police believe her?"

"Devlin says he does. He's checked up on the son—Jeremy Hopkins—and the story fits. Jeremy is wanted for fraud and theft, and escaped arrest a couple of days ago. They think he might have gone across on the ferry to Ireland now, but they've alerted the Garda—the Irish Police—and Devlin is sure they'll catch him soon. So it seems that the only thing Miriam was guilty of was a mother's soft heart."

Mabel made a clucking sound with her tongue. "It's always the way. Mothers can never see the faults in their own children."

Nor fathers, I thought, considering the numerous times Vladimir Koskov had bailed his daughter out of trouble. Still, if Tanya was guilty of murder—possibly double murder—I didn't think Koskov would be able to protect her this time...

***

It was a busy day and, despite spending most of it perched on a stool behind the counter, I was exhausted by the time the end rolled around. Still, I decided it would be good to stay a bit later and catch up on some paperwork and accounting. Dora and Cassie left just before six, but the Old Biddies seemed happy to linger, helping themselves to leftovers from the kitchen and settling down to a late "tea"—or perhaps early supper—at one of the tables. They were just making a fresh pot and asking me if I'd like a cup when the front door of the tearoom opened with a tinkle of bells.

"I'm sorry, we're closed—" I started to say, then I paused in surprise as I saw who was standing in the doorway.

It was Tanya Koskov.

CHAPTER TWENTY-NINE

"Hello, Tanya," I said warily, remembering the violent way she had pushed me the last time I saw her.

The Russian girl hesitated in the doorway, fiddling with the zipper of her Gucci handbag, and I noticed that she didn't seem her usual haughty, sardonic self. Instead, she looked uneasy and embarrassed.

"I asked Detective O'Connor where to find you," she said at last. "He told me this address."

"Oh. Um... yes?"

She glanced at the Old Biddies, who were regarding her with avid curiosity. I followed her gaze, then said, "Do you want to come into the kitchen? We can talk in there."

She nodded and followed me inside. I knew the

Old Biddies would probably be glued to the door, eavesdropping, but at least this gave the illusion of privacy. Gesturing to a chair by the big wooden table in the centre of the room, I invited Tanya to sit down.

She shook her head and stood stiffly. The silence stretched between us. Then she made an awkward movement. "I...I come to apologise," she muttered.

"To apologise?" I stared at her. This was the last thing I expected.

"For way I treated you yesterday," she rushed on. "I should not push you like that or... or call you daughter of bitch. I was angry... but... it was wrong thing to do. I am sorry. I hope... I hope you are not hurt." She looked down again quickly.

I was touched in spite of myself. It had obviously cost Tanya a lot of pride to come here today and apologise to me. I wondered if perhaps it was the first time she had ever apologised for her behaviour in her life. I felt myself softening towards her.

"Thanks... It's all right—I wasn't really hurt." I paused, then added, "It was very nice of you to make a special trip here to apologise. I appreciate it."

She scowled and kept her head down, twisting the zipper some more. "I know when I am wrong. I am not afraid to admit it."

I hesitated, then decided to seize the chance. "Tanya... can I ask you something?"

"What?" She looked back up at me.

"It's about Damian's murder." I looked her straight in the eye. "Yesterday, when Inspector

O'Connor was asking about your movements between ten and midnight, you said you were in the J.C.R. the whole time."

"Yes, so?"

"That's not true, though, is it? I saw your face when Mikhail spoke up and said that he could vouch for you being there the whole time. He was covering for you, wasn't he?"

For a moment, Tanya looked as if she wouldn't reply, then she gave a lazy shrug and said, "And if he was?"

"So he *was* lying!" I exclaimed. "What was the truth, Tanya? Where were you really?"

She gave an impatient sigh. "I was in J.C.R. like I say. But I left earlier—maybe around 11:40 p.m. What does it matter?"

"It matters because it makes all the difference in a murder investigation! Where did you go?"

She raised her chin. "I went for walk."

"Where?"

She shrugged. "Just around college. I want fresh air before I go back to my room."

"Did you meet anyone? Anyone see you?"

"No, it was very late and it was dark," she said irritably. "Nobody was there."

"So no one could confirm your story—that you were out walking—as opposed to going to Damian's room? This means there's about twenty minutes unaccounted for... enough time for you to have committed the murder."

Her eyes flashed furiously and a wave of red colour swept over her face. For a moment, I thought she was going to strike me again. I took a hasty step backwards. The action seemed to recall Tanya to herself and she took a deep breath. Then she gave me a disdainful look.

"It is the truth. I go for walk. I did not go to Damian's room. I don't need anybody to confirm this. I know I am innocent."

"If that's the case, why did you lie to the police? Why claim that you were in the J.C.R. the whole time?"

"I did not lie," she snapped. "It is Mikhail who said that. I simply let him speak for me."

"Well, you certainly didn't speak up to correct him."

She looked at me like I was an imbecile. "Of course I do not correct him. I know I did not kill Damian. So it is not important if I leave J.C.R. early or not. Otherwise, police will think just like you—they will ask me where I go and who saw me during that twenty minutes—and it is all unnecessary. It is wasting police time."

"It's not wasting police time—it's telling them the truth," I said in exasperation. "Giving the police the wrong information could seriously affect their investigation. You've got to tell Devlin—Inspector O'Connor, I mean, about this. You've got to revise your statement."

She rolled her eyes. "Fine. I will call him and tell

him later." She gave me a searching look. "Why you care so much? Why are you so keen to help police?"

"Why aren't you?" I retorted. "Your boyfriend was murdered. I would have thought that you'd want to bring his killer to justice."

Tanya blinked and, for a moment, I saw the flash of pain in her beautiful grey eyes. Then the cold mask came back down over her face. "This is not about Charlie. This is about Damian—and for him, I feel nothing."

"But the murders are connected!" I insisted. "Damian must have been killed by the same person who murdered Charlie. It's too much of a coincidence otherwise. Come on, Tanya... you knew them both very well. You spent so much time together. Can't you think of any reason why they would both have been killed? Was there something that they were involved in together?"

She shook her head slowly, for once seeming to make the effort to consider my question seriously. "No, there is nothing," she said at last. "Yes, they do many things together; the parties, the—how you say—the pranks, but nothing to do with crime."

"And what about the few days before May morning—can you remember anything special happening in those days? I know the police have already asked you this," I said quickly as I saw her make an impatient movement. "But you've had more time to think. Has anything new occurred to you? Anything strange that might have happened?"

"No, nothing. We go to lectures... and practical classes in laboratories... and tutorials..."

"Yes, and what about the evenings? May Day was on Friday. What did you do on the Thursday evening before? I remember Damian mentioning a party in your room—"

"Yes, Charlie and me—we decided to have party together. But not in his room—in my room. I had idea for fancy dress party," she said with a hint of a smile as the memory came back to her. "Charlie liked this very much. He wanted to be Sinbad the Sailor. Me, I thought I would like to be Xena Warrior Princess."

"Yes, I remember. That was the reason you borrowed the barbecue skewer from Miriam, right? But then you didn't use it?"

"Yes. I wanted Arabian sword to go with Xena costume but I could not find good one in costume shop. Then Charlie told me Miriam has collection of Arabic things and he will ask her. She said yes, she has barbecue skewer which looks like Arabian sword. She brought to college for me to borrow. But then I changed my mind—I decided to dress like genie instead so I don't need sword. So I did not use skewer. I left it in Charlie's sitting room to return to Miriam."

"And who else knew about this skewer? I mean, aside from you and Charlie... and Damian, I suppose, because he shared Charlie's room."

Tanya shrugged. "Many people. Charlie had many, many friends. They were always coming to his room—the door is never locked. Everybody was there on Thursday, before the party. Charlie bought many things from costume shop for anybody to use, and many things for the party also. Drinks and food and fun things for party."

I remembered Damian mentioning Charlie's generous tendencies. It sounded like it was open house and I could just imagine what it must have been like, with party supplies and costume props scattered everywhere, balloons, packs of beer, plastic glasses, bottles of wine... Any number of people could have been in the boys' room that Thursday and nicked the skewer without anyone noticing in the general chaos. I sighed. This was looking like a dead end. Still, I couldn't resist trying one last time:

"And are you *sure* you don't remember anyone acting strangely at the party?"

Tanya threw her hands up. "How do you expect me to remember? It is so many people! Here—" She reached into her handbag and pulled out an expensive smartphone in a gold case. She swiped the screen, bringing up her photo gallery, and shoved it in front of me. "You can see yourself. Look—see how many people at party!"

I took the phone and scrolled through the photos. She was right—it looked like a typical raucous student party, the room packed to bursting and everyone having a great time. People posing in their costumes. Couples kissing for the camera. Friends pulling faces at each other. Every picture showed flushed faces and slightly drunk grins. I saw a picture of Damian and Charlie, their arms around each other's shoulders, leering at the camera. They were dressed in identical Sinbad outfits, except that Charlie was wearing a satin turban on his head, which went well with his costume, whereas Damian was wearing a rainbow-coloured knitted beanie cap, which looked slightly ridiculous.

Tanya saw me pausing on that photo. "You think Damian looks stupid, yes? Always, he wears that hat. All the time. Everywhere. He said it is his 'lucky beanie' but I think it is ugly and stupid—and so dirty! He never washed it." She curled her lips back in disgust.

I continued scrolling through the photos, noting that Tanya was right. Damian was wearing his beanie cap in every photo... and I remembered his Facebook profile photo, also with the same beanie cap.

Then I realised that the photos on Tanya's phone had changed. Instead of a rowdy party, the last few pictures showed a misty dawn sky, darkened figures walking along a street, and a tall structure I recognised, silhouetted against a pale sunrise. The great bell tower of Magdalen College.

"Oh..." I said.

Tanya's face changed. "Those are photos from May morning," she said, her voice going flat.

I looked down silently at the last photo on the phone. It was obviously a selfie and showed Tanya and Charlie standing together on Magdalen Bridge, with Magdalen Tower partly in view behind them, and crowds of people milling around them. I stared hard at the picture but there was no one I could recognise in the crowd. I had had a sudden hope, of course, that I would see Pete Morrow, perhaps, lurking in a sinister fashion in the background of the picture. But it would have been too good to be true.

"That... that is last photograph I have with Charlie," said Tanya gruffly.

I cleared my throat and hastily began to scroll back—then I froze.

I stared at the photo.

"Tanya," I said urgently, "you said that the beanie cap was Damian's special thing, right? You said he was always wearing it... so why is Charlie wearing it in this picture?"

She looked at the picture in surprise, as if noticing the cap for the first time. "Oh... that. It was because Damian left it in my room after party. Maybe it fell off. He was drunk and he went back to his own room to sleep, and he forgot it. Charlie stayed with me that night and in the morning, when we were going out for May morning celebration, it was very cold. Charlie had no hat so he decided to wear beanie cap to keep his head warm. Then he can return to Damian later when we meet him on bridge."

"Oh my God—that's it!" I cried, clutching her arm. "Don't you see? That was the reason Charlie got killed! It *was* a case of mistaken identity!"

Tanya stared at me in puzzlement. "Mistaken identity?"

"Yes! Charlie was never supposed to be the victim—the killer was looking for *Damian* but in the crowd and in the dim light just before dawn, it was hard to see—all you can see is a sea of heads... The two boys were similar in height and build—and since Damian was well known for always wearing his 'lucky beanie'—it was like his trademark—of course, anyone would assume that it was him when they saw the rainbow-coloured cap in the crowd. That would also explain why the murderer cried out 'Wrong man!'—he realised after he stabbed Charlie that he had made a mistake!"

Tanya looked even more bewildered now. "Wrong man? Who cried wrong man?"

I didn't bother to explain. My mind was feverishly working, fitting the pieces of the case together. Yes, it all made sense now. And *that* also explained the second murder: Damian hadn't been killed because he knew something about Charlie's murder, but because *he* was the original victim all along. The murderer had simply finished his job.

But why did someone want Damian dead in the first place? Was it something that Damian had seen or heard? Some sensitive information that he knew and had been silenced for? He had been scared, I was sure of that. I remembered his nervous manner and his sudden desire to learn self-defence, and I thought back to the day I had followed him down that secluded path between the Cherwell River and Christ Church Meadow... In my mind's eye, I played the whole scene again: Damian skulking in the ditch next to the meadow, groping around in the undergrowth... then whirling around, startled, and falling over backwards into the puddle with a splash... and then getting up, dusting off his jeans and hurrying off... his figure retreating into the distance...

I frowned. There was something... something that had bothered me at the time and been nagging me ever since. Something I had seen? Something which hadn't seemed right...

I gasped out loud. I realised what it was: Damian's jeans. As he walked away, I'd had a clear view of them and they had not been wet. And yet... if he had fallen into the puddle, they should have been soaking. So he hadn't actually fallen into the water at the bottom of the ditch. But there had been a loud splash. I was sure of it. So what had caused that splash?

It came to me suddenly: *something had dropped into the water.*

Damian hadn't been *looking* for something in the undergrowth—he had been trying to *hide* something that he already possessed! I remembered now the way he had held his left hand against his body—the way you would if you were clutching something. He had been wearing a short jacket that day and might have had something in an inner pocket. Something that had fallen out when he'd taken a tumble in the ditch. He had probably been hunting around for a good spot to hide it when I came across him. I remembered the way he had glanced quickly at the puddle after falling down—he must have been checking to see if any sign of the packet was visible and been relieved that it was completely covered by the water.

With me standing there watching him, he had obviously decided that it was best to leave the packet submerged for the time being rather than call attention to it. So he had made some excuse and hurried off. In any case, if he was looking for a safe place to hide something, a puddle at the bottom of a ditch was as good a place as any.

I have to get my hands on that packet and see what's inside! I thought. But would it still be there, hidden in the puddle? Or would Damian have had a chance to return and move it?

There was only one way to find out.

CHAPTER THIRTY

I became aware of my name being called and came back to myself to find Tanya looking at me with a mixture of confusion and impatience. I realised I must have been standing there, lost in thought for several minutes, while she waited for me to answer her question.

"I'm sorry, Tanya!" I glanced at my watch. It was just past seven. There would still be at least an hour of light. "I haven't got time to explain but I've got to get to Christ Church Meadow and find something! It could be the answer to the whole mystery!"

I rushed out of the kitchen door—only to collide with the Old Biddies, who had been huddled together on the other side with their ears pressed to the door.

"Oomph!" I staggered sideways, leaning on my crutch to steady myself.

"Gemma—what on earth—?"

"I can't talk now!" I gasped as I saw a bus through the tearoom windows. It was the bus for Oxford and it was pulling up at the stop on the opposite side of the street.

Leaving the Old Biddies staring after me, I hobbled like mad out of the tearoom and across the road, getting on the bus just in time. As I settled down in a seat at the back, I thought suddenly of Devlin. I should really let him know about the latest twist: that Charlie had been killed by mistake and that Damian had probably been killed for something he knew—maybe something he had—which he had hidden. But as I groped in my pockets, I realised that I didn't have my phone with me. *Argh.* I remembered now; I had taken it out to use the calculator function when I was doing the accounts and must have left it on the counter in the tearoom in my rush to leave.

I sighed with annoyance. Never mind. There would be more than enough time to fill Devlin in on all the details later. The important thing now was to get to Christ Church Meadow and find that packet.

The journey into town seemed interminably slow—the bus seemed to stop every ten minutes—and I was twitching with impatience by the time it finally set me down at the top of the High Street. I took the shortcut down past Merton Street to the lane which led to Dead Man's Walk and the access to Christ Church Meadow. A sense of déjà vu swept over me. I felt like I had been hurrying through this route over and over again the past few days...

It was a quarter to eight now and the light was starting to fade. I hobbled faster, not wanting to be stuck out on the Christ Church Meadow Walk when the sun finally went down. There were no lights along the path or by the meadow or the river, and it would soon be pitch dark. In the distance, I could hear faintly the sounds of cars and the hum of the city, but here, by the meadow, it was quiet—almost eerily so. There was only the whisper of the breeze through the tall grass and the occasional low rumble from the herd of English Longhorn cattle in the distance.

At last, I came to the turn in the path that I remembered, where the river curved around a jutting section of the bank. It was just past here, I recalled, that Damian had veered off the path and down into the ditch at the edge of the meadow. I followed in his footsteps, straining my eyes in the failing light for any sign of that large puddle... *Aha! Yes, there!* I saw the glimmer of water and hobbled closer, sinking to my knees by the water's edge. I peered at the surface but could see nothing in the muddy water. Pushing my sleeve up, I reached into the puddle, making a face as the cold water swirled against my skin.

"Ugh..." I muttered, groping around in the puddle and stirring up mud everywhere. It was deeper than it looked—there must have been a hollow in the ground, which was probably why rain had collected here and formed this stagnant pool.

Then I felt it: the edge of a slim, smooth object. I pulled it out, water dripping off the edges as I held it up to the light. It was small, flat, and rectangular, wrapped in several layers of plastic. I stood up and, leaning against my crutch, carefully began unwrapping the packet. It had been sealed very securely with duct tape, which required quite a bit of effort to rip off, although this meant that it had also been protected from the damp. I peeled off several layers of plastic to find a brown manila envelope, still completely dry. The paper rustled as I pulled the flap open and shook the contents out.

They were photographs, I realised. Then, as the fading light caught the gleaming contours of a bare arm, a long smooth leg, the shadowy curve of a naked breast, I felt my face flushing as I realised what kind of photographs they were. Oh, they were very artfully done in black and white, with clever lighting so as never to show *too* much, but nevertheless, they were not the kind of erotic nude images that you wanted plastered over the tabloid newspapers. Especially if you were the daughter of a prominent Russian billionaire.

I stared down at Tanya Koskov's wide grey eyes as she looked out at me from the topmost picture, wearing nothing but a black choker around her neck. And something came back to me... something I had read that day I had been stuck at home and doing "internet investigation". Amongst the newspaper and magazine articles about Tanya's latest designer handbag and Tanya's possible pregnancies was one about Tanya's nude photo scandal. Pictures of the

Russian girl had appeared suddenly on the internet—and then disappeared just as mysteriously. I remembered the article because it had been recent; in fact, maybe only a month old.

I looked down again at the photographs in my hands. Surely it was too much of a coincidence? There couldn't be two sets of nude photos… which meant that Damian had probably been involved—maybe even responsible—for that scandal. I remembered Kate, the sweet blonde girl I had chatted with in the Haverton College J.C.R., saying: *"…I think he liked to live the rich life and, you know, being around Charlie… well, I suppose he felt like he had to keep up with his friend…"*—and I wondered suddenly if Damian had somehow got hold of these photos and tried to use them as blackmail fodder. After all, Tanya was wealthy and Damian would have seen her as fair game. Had he tried to get money out of her by threatening to expose these photos? Maybe he had even put one online as proof of what he was capable of—which would have explained why a photo had appeared briefly and then disappeared.

And it would also explain something else! I thought back to that fight between Charlie and Damian: Charlie had been furious and accused Damian of "taking advantage of a vulnerable girl". That wasn't because Tanya had been offered a bit of marijuana, as Damian claimed—it was because Charlie had found out that his best friend was trying to blackmail his girlfriend!

And it also gave Tanya Koskov the best reason to murder Damian, I realised. Perhaps these photos had been a youthful indiscretion in her teens—they looked like the kind of thing an aspiring model might be tempted to do if seduced by a smooth-talking photographer—and now she regretted them. Or perhaps she didn't regret them; perhaps she was proud of them and had kept them, maybe even shared them with Charlie. What she hadn't planned on, however, was Damian finding out about them and, even worse, getting hold of them. So by killing him, not only did she remove the threat of the photos, but also his power to blackmail her. Someone as proud as Tanya Koskov would never have submitted to blackmail. In fact, I could see her taking revenge on Damian just for daring to think that he could control her. Was this what she had meant when she said she would "make him pay"?

But... if Tanya was the killer, why had she murdered Charlie? Surely she couldn't have mistaken him for Damian, because she knew Charlie was wearing the beanie cap and, anyway, he was standing right next to her. I frowned. It didn't make sense...

I stuffed the photos back into the envelope. It didn't matter—the important thing now was to get back, find a phone, and tell Devlin what I'd discovered. Clutching the envelope to my chest, I began to hobble back towards the lights of the city. I realised suddenly that I had a more urgent problem:

to get out of Christ Church Meadow before I was locked in. Its several gated entrances were always shut at sundown. I had scaled them once when I was student and sneaked into the Meadow after dark with some friends, but it was a precarious climb over spiked metal railings and I didn't fancy trying it again, especially with a crutch.

I glanced worriedly at the sky: the sun was just visible on the edge of the horizon. I doubled my pace, hobbling faster. The kissing gates leading into Rose Lane at the east end of Dead Man's Walk were the closest. Twilight was falling and it was getting so dim now that it was hard to make out the shapes around me. Trees and buildings blurred into dark forms in the distance and the path became a hazy band stretching in front of me.

With some relief, I saw the junction up ahead where Christ Church Meadow Walk joined up with Dead Man's Walk and merged into the path that led to the kissing gates. At this distance, I couldn't see if they were still open... but they looked open. In fact, it looked like there was a figure standing by them. My spirits lifted. It was probably the Meadows groundsman locking up. I'd made it just in time.

"Hey! Wait!" I called, trying to hobble faster.

A few moments later, I arrived breathlessly at the gates and tumbled through them.

"Oh, thank goodness! Thanks for waiting for me— I thought I was going to get locked in for the night— " I gasped.

Then I stopped as I recognised the figure.

"Oh! It's you. I thought you were... What are you doing here?"

"Waiting for you," said Mikhail Petrovsky, whipping something out of a coat pocket and stepping close to me.

I looked down and caught my breath as I saw the sudden, sharp gleam of a knife.

CHAPTER THIRTY-ONE

"I have been waiting for you a long time," said Mikhail in a conversational tone. "I did not want to reveal myself by following you down to the river—it is too exposed there—but I knew you were likely to come out via this gate so it was a simple matter of waiting here. Like a spider waiting for a fly." He laughed softly. It was not a pleasant sound.

I stared at him, noticing that he was no longer speaking with a thick Russian accent. Oh, the accent was still there, but it was much fainter and overlaid with an "American" tone. It gave him a totally different persona—younger, smoother, less the dry, pompous Russian academic... which I realised now must have been a disguise.

"Who *are* you?" I asked hoarsely.

"You can still call me Mikhail," he said with a smile. "That name is as good as any."

"What do you want?" I demanded.

He nodded towards the packet still clutched against my chest. "Ah... I want what you found. I suspect it is what I have been searching for—what that *kozyol*, Damian, tried to hide from me."

"Tanya's photos? But why should you wan—?"

Understanding dawned and I stared at him with new horror. "It was *you*, wasn't it? It wasn't Tanya—it was *you* who stabbed Charlie on the bridge. And it was you who strangled Damian, probably with that neckerchief you're wearing now! That's why you jumped to confirm that Tanya was in the J.C.R. the whole time between ten and midnight—not to give *her* an alibi but to give *yourself* one! You were pretending to protect Tanya but actually using her to protect yourself—by saying you saw her in the J.C.R., you were telling the police that you were with her during that time and therefore couldn't have been going up to Damian's room. But actually, that was exactly what you did, wasn't it? As soon as Tanya left the J.C.R. at 11:40 p.m., you slipped up to Damian's room and murdered him."

He gave me a mocking look. "*Bravo*. You have brains—more brains than the English police, it seems."

"And that also explains Charlie's murder. Tanya wouldn't have made that mistake between the two boys—but *you* did! Because you were in a hurry, you only saw Charlie from the back—and you knew that Damian was meeting them—so when you saw his rainbow beanie cap, you assumed that it was Damian. You stabbed him, then realised your mistake. That's why you cried out."

"Yes, that was a mistake," he said with no emotion. "But it did not matter in the end. Charlie Foxton was not worthy of the daughter of Vladimir Ivanovich Koskov. It is a good chance for Tatiana Vladimirovna to finish with him."

I drew a breath. "So I was right? You did all this out of love for Tanya?"

"Love?" He laughed outright. "What is love? It is an emotion for the weak. No, I don't waste time on love. I do my duty for my country, for the great men of my country—the men that will make Russia stronger." He paused, then added bitterly, "But even he is weak because of love. It is terrible to see a man—a great man, powerful, ruthless, feared by all in business—bend to the will of a spoilt girl."

"You're talking about Vladimir Koskov, aren't you? You work for him! I was right in my impression that you were like a faithful hound hanging around Tanya... You *are* a guard dog! Or a bodyguard, rather. Vladimir Koskov sent you to Oxford with his daughter, didn't he? To watch over her and protect her unobtrusively. That's the reason your Russian scholar disguise. Somehow he wrangled it so that you got accepted for a graduate degree at the same college that Tanya was in. And then what...?

Did you catch Damian trying to blackmail Tanya with those photos?"

"I intercepted the message," said Mikhail coldly. "Tatiana Vladimirovna does not know, but I check all her emails, all correspondence that comes into her pigeonhole in the college Porter's Lodge, all messages and notes that come to her room. I saw the message from Damian asking for money. And I heard from Mr Koskov about the photo on the internet. He wanted me to pay the money—just like before, to buy the silence. Anything to keep his Tatiana safe." His lips curled in disgust. "But me—I don't pay. No, I don't pay *kozyol* like Damian Heath! I have experience of blackmail—it is never finished. Always, they come back... and always, they want more and more money. I will not allow a great man like Vladimir Ivanovich Koskov to be controlled by a stupid English boy!" He flushed angrily. "So I decided to kill him. It is easy— I have killed before. And then it will be over. No more danger to Tatiana Vladimirovna, no more messages asking for money."

"Did Tanya know this?"

He gave a humourless laugh. "No. She knows nothing. Why should I tell her? It is not her business to know. She thinks only that I am boring nanny sent by her *papa* to look after her. She does not realise how I keep her safe."

"You mean, she wouldn't have kept silent if she knew that you murdered Charlie."

"No, she would not understand the sacrifice

necessary. She would make trouble. Already she talks too much to you and police. But what do you expect?" He gave a contemptuous shrug. "She is a woman. They are weak."

I felt a flash of irritation at his male chauvinist attitude and had to bite my tongue on a retort. I'm not much of a feminist but the man's patronising superiority was intensely annoying. Still, I was uncomfortably aware that in this situation, he definitely had the upper hand. For one thing, he had the knife and I could feel the sharp prick of the blade against my right side, where he was holding it against my abdomen. His other hand was clamped around my left arm, pinning me against him. I didn't dare struggle for fear of the knife going into my side.

I glanced desperately around. In front of us, the lane stretched lonely and empty. Behind us, back through the kissing gates, was the wide expanse of the Meadow and dark walkways around it... but even if I managed to get free, how far would I get hobbling? He'd catch me within a few yards here in the lane. And if I escaped back into the Meadow, I would be effectively trapped in there. All the other gates would be locked now and the only other way to escape was to cross the river bordering the other side— something I didn't fancy doing in the dark, when I was unable to swim properly with my weak ankle...

"Do not waste time trying to think of escape," said Mikhail, his voice amused as he read my thoughts. "There is no way. I would catch you in two seconds."

He was right. I took a shaky breath. My only hope lay in stalling, on the slim chance that someone might come down this lane and rescue me. It wasn't completely impossible. True, few people tended to come down here after dark, especially once the Meadow gates were locked. But you never know...

In fact...

I peered at the dark lane ahead of me. Was I dreaming or were there four small figures coming slowly towards us? They were moving furtively, hugging the stone wall which ran alongside the lane, and it was hard to see in the dark... but could it be...?

My heart leapt in hope and I almost called out for help. Then I caught myself just in time. I glanced at Mikhail out of the corner of my eye. He had taken the packet of photos from me and was now busy opening it, checking the contents. His head was down and he hadn't noticed the four elderly figures creeping towards us.

Nonchalantly, I shifted my position and angled my body around, turning on the spot. Mikhail shifted absently with me, keeping his knife at my side with one hand, but with his attention still on the photos in his other hand. Slowly, I managed to move him around so that he was facing the kissing gates, with his back to the lane. But just as I was congratulating myself, he tucked the photos into an inner jacket pocket and looked up with a brisk air.

"Okay, now we go," he said, jabbing me with the knife tip.

I felt a moment of panic. My eyes flicked to the dark figures coming furtively up behind him. The only advantage they had was the element of surprise. I had to keep him talking.

"How did you know I was coming here?" I asked quickly. "What made you think of coming to Christ Church Meadow?"

"I followed you," he said with a careless laugh. "You did not see me, no? I was on the bus from Meadowford-on-Smythe."

"What on earth were you doing there?"

"I went with Tatiana Vladimirovna. She did not know that I followed her. I saw her go into your tearoom and I suspected that she will talk to you—that she will tell you too much. Then I see you run out and I have—what do Americans say—a hunch? So I follow you. I got off the bus after you and I followed you here to the Meadow. But when I saw you go to the path beside the river, I came back to wait here. I know you will have to come back out this way." He made an impatient movement. "And now, enough talking. We will leave here. I must—"

He broke off suddenly, cocked his ear, and spun around, just as the Old Biddies covered the last few yards to reach us.

"Let her go!" shouted Mabel.

"Yes! Let Gemma go or you'll be sorry!" cried Glenda, holding her arms up, elbows jutting out in a familiar Krav Maga stance.

"What is this?" Mikhail looked startled for a

moment, then he burst out laughing. "Is it four *baboushkas* I see in front of me?"

"Baboushka yourself!" snapped Florence. "We're warning you—"

"*You* are warning *me*? HA! HA! HA! HA!" Mikhail laughed so hard that he had to let go of me to clutch his sides. He snorted and gasped, tears coming out of his eyes. "HA! HA! HA! H—"

He broke off as, with a yell, the Old Biddies piled into him. Screaming, shoving, punching, kicking, they attacked him from all sides. For a moment, I felt a wave of triumph and smiled in delight. *Let's see how superior Mikhail feels now!* I couldn't wait for the Old Biddies to demolish him with their new Krav Maga skills.

Then my smile slipped.

Wait... what's happening?

Belatedly, I realised how silly I had been to think four little old ladies could overpower the Russian bodyguard. This was no polite, simulated Krav Maga class. This was the real thing. And while Mikhail might have been temporarily surprised, he had recovered quickly. He was also a trained bodyguard, not any old Joe Bloggs on the street. The Old Biddies suddenly found themselves pitted against a deadly opponent with expert skill.

My heart lurched as I saw Mikhail block a punch from Mabel and give her a shove which sent her reeling; he caught Glenda's arm just as she tried to jab him in the eyes and twisted it, making her cry out in pain; he dodged a kick from Florence and hooked his leg around her ankle, making her trip and crash to the ground.

"No!" I cried, hobbling forwards to help.

Then there was a blood-curdling screech, followed by a high-pitched, quavering: "*You nincompoop!*"

I looked up to see Ethel swinging her handbag at Mikhail's head. The Russian didn't even flinch. He stood and laughed at her while she swung the lavender handbag up in an arc, then brought it down with a loud *thunk* on the side of his head.

Mikhail stopped laughing.

Noiselessly, he dropped to his knees and toppled over on the ground. I stared disbelievingly at him. He was out cold. Then I turned incredulous eyes on Ethel who was standing next to me, gazing down at her handiwork.

She glanced up, clutching her lavender handbag to her chest, and gave me a smile, looking the epitome of a sweet old lady.

"Well, we did warn him, dear. We told him that he would be sorry!"

CHAPTER THIRTY-TWO

"The *Old Biddies* knocked him out?" said Devlin incredulously. He glanced over at where the paramedics were loading Mikhail onto a stretcher, then across to the ambulance where another paramedic was checking four little old ladies over for injuries.

I nodded. "I wouldn't have believed it if I hadn't seen the whole thing with my own eyes! I thought he was going to kill them—and then Ethel just sort of shrieked and clobbered him with her handbag." I shook my head in admiration. "Honestly, I thought all this Krav Maga stuff was a lot of nonsense but maybe there's something in it after all. I mean, how else can you explain how a frail little old lady managed to wallop a trained bodyguard double her size?"

"Hmm..." said Devlin, looking sceptical. He narrowed his blue eyes thoughtfully as Mabel, Glenda, Ethel, and Florence trundled over to join us, followed by the paramedic who had been examining them.

"How are they?" he asked the paramedic.

"Nothing too serious. A couple of scrapes and bruises—oh, except Miss Webb here has strained her shoulder. Must have been when she gave the Russian the killer punch with her handbag," he said, looking at the little old lady admiringly.

Ethel blushed. "Oh, it was nothing really. Just a little move I picked up in Krav Maga class, you know," she twittered, clasping her lavender handbag to her chest.

Devlin raised an eyebrow and eyed Ethel speculatively. "It must have been a powerful move, taking down a grown man with nothing more than a leather handbag..."

As he spoke, he reached out and plucked the handbag out of Ethel's hands. It lurched in his grasp and he nearly dropped it. He lifted it up again with some effort.

"Bloody hell! What have you got in this?" he asked.

He reached down and unzipped the vintage leather bag. There, nestled amongst the tissues and gum drops and hand creams and loose change, was an enormous red brick. We all stared at it in awe.

"Krav Maga technique, eh?" said Devlin dryly, taking the brick out. "I think perhaps Mikhail Petrovsky owes his present condition more to the fact that he was smacked on the head by a very large brick."

He looked at the Old Biddies sternly, waiting for an explanation.

"Well, they did tell us in class to use anything handy we could find for weapons," said Mabel with great dignity. "And to always have things ready on our person that we could use to protect ourselves."

Glenda nodded. "That's part of the Krav Maga philosophy."

"Where on earth did you get it from?" I asked, still staring at the monster brick.

"Oh, from up there," said Ethel, nodding towards the start of the lane. "I think someone has been doing some repairs or renovation, and the builders left a pile of unused bricks at the side of the path. I picked one up as we were creeping here and put it in my handbag—I thought it might come in handy." She giggled and the other Old Biddies smirked.

"Miss Webb," said Devlin, sounding exasperated, "I won't be taking it further this time but just so you know for the future: regardless of what your Krav Maga class tells you, you do realise that it is an offence in the U.K. to carry a concealed weapon, even in self-defence?"

Ethel opened her eyes very wide and looked up at him innocently. "Oh, but I didn't pick up the brick to use as a *weapon*, Inspector. I meant that it might be handy in my *garden*—you know, I saw this programme on the telly where they showed you how to use unused bricks as markers for your herb garden. You can write the names of the herbs on the side using stencils and it adds a lovely personal touch to your borders. Ever so clever, really!"

Devlin sighed. "Just... please leave unused bricks where they are and don't carry them around in your handbag."

As the Old Biddies trotted off, escorted by a constable, Devlin turned to me and said in exasperation, "It's a wonder she didn't dislocate her shoulder, swinging that brick around. It weighed a tonne!"

I stifled a laugh. "You can't expect me to criticise them. The Old Biddies probably saved my life."

"Which wouldn't have been necessary if you hadn't got involved in the investigation in the first place," growled Devlin. "I told you not to meddle, Gemma. You were all very lucky. If things had been different, Mikhail Petrovsky could have hurt you badly. All of you. He'd murdered two people recently and he wouldn't have hesitated to kill again."

I sobered, chastised. "Yes, you're right, of course. It's no laughing matter."

Devlin's face softened. He slid an arm around me and pulled me close. "But I'm very, very relieved that the Old Biddies' Krav Maga technique was so good," he said with a wry smile. He dropped a tender kiss on my forehead. "Thank God you weren't hurt, Gemma."

"Mmm..." I slid my arms around his waist and snuggled closer to his chest, savouring the reassuring, solid warmth of his body. I felt Devlin pull me closer and then his head came down and his lips captured mine in a kiss. *This* was the kiss I had been waiting for. Soft and tender, then deepening into an urgent, hungry demand that felt as if it would consume me. The world around us ceased to exist. It was just Devlin... the hardness of his body... the possessive weight of his hands around my waist... the touch of his mouth on mine...

Slowly, I became aware of wolf whistles and catcalls around us. Someone—it sounded like Devlin's sergeant—yelled out: "Should I book a room, guv'nor?"

We broke apart. There was a flush on Devlin's cheeks as he saw his colleagues smirking at him.

"All right, all right... Get back to work!" he said, a sheepish grin on his face.

My own cheeks burning, I stepped away from Devlin and straightened my clothes. Clearing my throat, I said, "I never got a chance to ask them—how did the Old Biddies know that I was here? For that matter, how did you? I couldn't believe it when I heard the sirens—we hadn't even had time to call the police."

"You can thank Tanya Koskov for that," Devlin said. "She rang me when she got back to her college and told me that she had been to see you at your tearoom—and that she had promised to let me know about her previous false alibi for Damian's murder. When I asked her where you were, she told me that you'd rushed off to Christ Church Meadow. I got the impression that something was wrong, so I dropped what I was working on in Blackbird Leys and came here as fast as I could. Of course..." He smiled. "I wasn't as fast as the Old Biddies. They followed you from Meadowford."

"Seems like everybody followed me from Meadowford today," I said dryly.

"They were eavesdropping through the kitchen door and heard most of your conversation with Tanya. So after she left, they discussed things amongst themselves and started to get worried about you. They called a taxi and got the driver to bring them down to Christ Church Meadow. On the way, they rang and told me everything they had overheard. I was on my way here myself—we weren't sure which gate you'd gone in at, or which one you'd be coming out of, but I took a punt and told them to head for Rose Lane, as it's the closest one to Haverton College." He blew out a breath. "Thank God my punt paid off."

There was a commotion farther up the lane and I saw headlights approaching, then a dark green Land Rover pulled to a stop as police constables prevented it from driving any closer. My eyes widened as Lincoln got out of the driver's seat. He went around to the front passenger seat and opened the door. My mother stepped out and hurried towards me. Behind her, my father and Professor Obruchev got slowly out of the rear of the car, the latter looking slightly bewildered and still clutching a dinner napkin.

"Darling! Mabel Cooke rang and told me what happened!" cried my mother, rushing over. "We left the restaurant straight away. Such a nightmare trying to get a taxi on a Friday night! Thank goodness Lincoln was home and could come to get us and drive us here." She fussed over me, patting my arms, smoothing my hair. "Are you all right?" She gasped and lowered her voice to a dramatic whisper: "Did that animal assault you?"

"I'm fine, Mother, I'm fine. He barely touched me. It was all over really quickly."

"Yes, well, Mabel did say that the Russian was a bit of a limp rag. Nevertheless, I still think it's a good idea to let Lincoln examine you," said my mother blithely, reaching over, grabbing Lincoln's arm, and hauling him next to me. "Nothing like an expert doctor's opinion!"

I flushed and glanced at Devlin, who was still standing on my other side, then at Lincoln, who looked intensely embarrassed.

"*Mother!* The paramedics have already examined me and I'm fine, I tell you," I hissed through clenched teeth.

Devlin cleared his throat. "I think I might go and have a word with my team. Excuse me." He turned and strode away.

I started to call him back but was interrupted by my father and Professor Obruchev coming over to join us. My father asked in his gentle, quiet voice how I was, then the Russian professor thrust himself forwards and grasped both my hands in his.

"Oh! Gemma Philipovna! I am very distressed to hear—it is one of my countrymen who has been responsible for murders!" He looked at me earnestly. "I hope this will not give you bad association with Russia—"

"Oh no, not at all. There are evil men everywhere, in every culture and every country." I smiled at him. "I'm looking forward to visiting Russia someday and enjoying tea from a samovar."

"*Davai!* I will have great pleasure in sharing Russian tea culture with you!"

"That's lovely... but I really think we need to let Lincoln examine Gemma now," said my mother, hustling my father and Professor Obruchev away. She gave us a coy smile over her shoulder. "Take your time, Lincoln—make sure you give Gemma a thorough check-up!"

As the three of them hurried back to the car, I gave Lincoln an apologetic look. "I'm really sorr—"

"It's okay," he said with a chuckle. "There was nothing good on TV tonight anyway. Seriously, though, Gemma, I'm glad you weren't hurt. Wouldn't have wanted to see you back at the hospital."

"No, I was really lucky that the Old Biddies

showed up when they did. Although... you know it was *them* who put me in hospital last time?"

"No, really?" Lincoln laughed.

"Yes, they were practising their Krav Maga techniques on me and got a bit too enthusiastic," I said.

Lincoln laughed even harder. "Maybe Devlin should consider hiring them as Senior Consultants for the CID," he suggested, glancing farther up the lane where Devlin's black Jaguar was parked in front of a police car.

I followed his gaze and saw a familiar attractive blonde woman standing near Devlin's car. Mel Buckley. She was looking at her watch and saying something to Devlin. He nodded and gestured to the police car, and Mel gave him a wave, then began walking to the car. I realised that she must have been with Devlin in Blackbird Leys, working the other case, and had ended up being dragged along when Devlin rushed here. Now she was obviously keen not to hang around any more than necessary and was asking for a patrol car to take her home.

I saw Lincoln notice me watching her and felt compelled to explain. "That's one of the informants who helps the CID," I said. "Devlin is working with her on a homicide case in Blackbird Leys. She's the woman you saw him with that day at the hospital."

Lincoln glanced across and looked confused for a moment. "No... actually, she wasn't."

"What do you mean?"

He hesitated. "I mean, it was a different woman I saw Devlin with."

I frowned. "Are you sure?"

"Yes. She was similar in some ways... blonde and... you know, attractive..." Lincoln flushed slightly. "But it was definitely a different woman."

I turned back and stared at Mel Buckley, who was getting into the police car. Then I looked at Devlin, who was talking to his sergeant. Could there be *two* informants who worked with the CID, who were both blonde and attractive? It seemed incredibly unlikely. In that case, who was the woman that Devlin had been with at the hospital? I felt that familiar prickle of unease and, quickly, I squashed it. *No, I said I wasn't going to do that anymore.*

I took a deep breath and plastered a smile on my face. "Oh... well, maybe I got it wrong. Anyway, it's not important. Listen, I think Devlin is going to be stuck here for a while longer. Would you mind giving me a lift back, along with my parents?"

"Of course not. It would be a pleasure." Lincoln put a solicitous hand under my elbow and turned towards his car.

Devlin glanced up and saw us. He gave me an understanding nod and a smile, and raised his hand in a wave. I hesitated, then waved back. Then, with a last troubled look at him, I turned and followed Lincoln to his car.

***

"And what's banoffee pie? I've never heard of that but it sounds very interesting!" said the American lady, looking up from the tearoom menu.

I smiled her, feeling a strange sense of déjà vu. Barely a week ago, I had been standing here in my tearoom answering this very question. That had been last Friday—the morning of the May Day celebrations and Charlie Foxton's murder. And now it was Friday again; I couldn't believe that only a week had passed since then. In a way, it felt like a whole lifetime...

When I finally got back to the counter, I found Cassie laughing and talking with Seth, who had returned from his academic conference yesterday and had popped in to say hello.

"Gemma—Cassie's just been filling me in on what's happened." Seth pushed his glasses up his nose, his usually serious brown eyes bright with interest. "I can't believe that I go away for a week and you manage to get yourself involved in another murder!"

"Not just involved... she solved it!" came a voice behind us.

We turned around to see Dora sticking her head out of the kitchen door. Her face was wreathed in smiles. "Gemma, I've just been talking to Miriam on the phone and she asked me to give you a personal thank you. She is really, really grateful to you for—"

"Oh no, I hardly did anything for her," I protested.

"You found the real killer," said Dora with an

emphatic nod. "That was the best thing you could have done for Miriam. If you hadn't made all the connections, the police might still be—" She broke off suddenly and sniffed the air. A rich buttery smell of baking was wafting out of the kitchen but it was also tinged with the faint scent of burning. "Oh my God— the scones!" cried Dora, disappearing back into the kitchen.

"I'm glad Miriam wasn't involved in the murders," Cassie said as the kitchen door swung shut. "For a while there, it was looking a bit iffy."

"Yeah, me too," I said. "I don't know what I would have done if I'd had to break the news to Dora that her friend was actually guilty. I think I would have chickened out and left it to Devlin to tell her."

"Speaking of Devlin, are things okay now between you guys?" asked Cassie in an undertone.

I hesitated, then said brightly, "Um... yes, of course. We're going out to dinner tomorrow night, actually. Devlin told me he's booked a table at the Cherwell Boathouse."

"Ooh... the Cherwell Boathouse—the most romantic restaurant in Oxford!" said Cassie with a wink.

I smiled weakly. "Yes, it should be nice. Devlin has just wrapped up his Blackbird Leys case as well, so things should hopefully be quieter for the next few days. Maybe even the next few weeks if I'm lucky."

"Well, that's what you get for falling for a handsome detective," said Cassie with a grin. "Talk about being married to the job! Still, you lucky cow—I haven't been to the Cherwell Boathouse in forever! I need to find a chap to take me..."

Seth cleared his throat next to us. "Um... uh... Cassie? I was wondering if you... I mean, you probably wouldn't... but I just thought I'd ask... er... on the off-chance, you know... that... er... maybe you'd like to... like to... uh... go with me to—"

"Oh, cripes! I forgot to take the forks to that Indian family!"

Cassie sprang up from the counter, hurried to the sideboard, grabbed some cutlery, and rushed over to a table by the fireplace, leaving Seth looking chagrined after her. I gave him a sympathetic smile.

"Maybe you can try and ask her again later."

"Oh... er..." Seth blushed furiously and looked down, fiddling with his bicycle helmet. "Actually... er... I'd better get going. I'm giving a tutorial tomorrow and I've got to do some preparation, mark some essays..."

I sighed as I watched him beat a hasty retreat. I wished there was some way I could help Seth, but this was a battle he was going to have to fight himself. Not so much the battle for Cassie's affections, actually, but the battle with his own shyness and lack of confidence. Every time I thought he was making some headway, things would take two steps back again.

A girl was coming into the tearoom just as Seth was leaving and I realised with some surprise that it was Tanya Koskov. She caught my eye and gave me a hesitant smile, then came over to the counter.

"Hi, Tanya," I said, feeling slightly uncomfortable. After all, the murderer had turned out to be her bodyguard and, although I knew she hadn't been involved, she was still connected.

"Hello..." She cleared her throat, looking uncharacteristically unsure of herself. "I... I hope you are recovered now from..." She cleared her throat again. "Mikhail, he was my... my protector but I did not... It was not my..."

"It's okay, I know you weren't involved," I said quickly. "Mikhail told me that he was acting independently and that you didn't know what he was doing."

She looked relieved. "Yes. I did not know anything... It is wrong, what he did. I am... I am sorry."

I gave her a smile. "You don't have to apologise for him, Tanya."

"Yes, I do," she said fiercely. "And my *papa* apologises also. I spoke to him last night. He is coming out of hospital tomorrow. He is very angry. They are sending Mikhail back to Russia and... my *papa* will deal with him." She took a deep breath and added, "I told him also that I don't need *nyanya* anymore. I am not baby. I can take care of myself."

I raised my eyebrows. "Did your father agree?"

She lifted her chin slightly. "He did not want to. But in the end, he followed my thinking. He must let me become a woman—and grown woman does not need nanny." She smiled. "So... no more *nyanya* for me while I am at Oxford."

I smiled too, feeling suddenly that this was a different girl from the one I had first met a week ago. More mature, wiser, and... thoughtful to others.

Tanya gave a sudden laugh. "You know what my *papa* cannot believe? The story of your friends—the old ladies—attacking Mikhail. Still, he cannot understand how they defeat him."

I chuckled and looked across the tearoom to where the Old Biddies were ambling around the tables in their sturdy orthotic shoes and woolly cardigans, nodding, smiling, and gossiping with the customers.

Tanya followed my gaze and said, "That is them, yes?"

"Yes, they look like such sweet, harmless old ladies, don't they?"

"Ah..." Tanya grinned at me. "In Russia, we know always to be careful of the *baboushkas*. They are old but they are powerful."

I looked at the Old Biddies again and grinned as well. "Yes, I think in England too."

EPILOGUE

"Muesli! Stop it—what are you doing?"

I watched in exasperation as my little tabby cat attacked the pile of tissue paper that I had just painstakingly smoothed out and folded. It was Saturday morning and I had a couple of hours before I had to be at the tearoom, so I was taking the opportunity to finally do a bit of unpacking.

So far, though, the place was looking even more of a chaotic mess, with mountains of emptied cardboard boxes, used bubble wrap, and wrinkled butcher paper everywhere. And my little cat was certainly not helping. Muesli was delighted with all the new "toys" on offer and had spent the last half an hour diving in and out of boxes, shredding cardboard, and rolling around, pouncing on anything that moved.

She was clutching a scrunched-up piece of newspaper to her tummy now, rolling on her back and kicking enthusiastically to "disembowel" her prey. I tried to pull it out of her grasp and she dug her claws in.

"*Meorrw*!" she protested.

"Muesli, stop it… you're making a mess! I need—"

The sound of the doorbell made me look up. I leaned over and caught a glimpse of a vehicle through the kitchen windows, parked in front of the cottage. It looked like a delivery van. My heart sank.

Oh no. Please. Not more plants.

I glanced over to the corner of the sitting room where—along with the Taiwanese rubber tree, the Jurassic sago palm, and the spiky bromeliad—there were now two sprouting spider plants, a Mexican yucca, and a Weeping Fig, courtesy of another visit from my mother last night. At this rate, I was going to have to hire a full-time gardener.

I sighed and got up. As I walked to the front door, I wondered with a shudder what it was going to be this time. *A Madagascan Dragon Tree? A West African Snake Plant?*

But when the door swung open, I was met with an enormous bouquet of two dozen red roses.

"Miss Gemma Rose?" the delivery boy asked, looking up from a clipboard.

"Yes, that's me," I said, still staring at the bouquet in wonderment.

He smiled and handed the roses to me. "These are for you." He doffed his cap, then turned and went back to the van.

I shut the front door and walked slowly back into the sitting room, inhaling the gorgeous fragrance of the roses. They were absolutely beautiful—deep red, with velvety soft petals just unfurling, elegantly wrapped in black tissue paper with an ivory ribbon. There was a small card tied to the ribbon and I turned this over. My heart skipped a beat as I recognised the bold, dark handwriting.

Can't wait to see you tonight.
D

A rush of love and happiness filled me. I took a deep breath and let it out slowly. Everything was going to be fine. I would ask Devlin about that blonde woman at dinner tonight and I was sure there would be a good explanation…

Next to me, Muesli hopped up on a chair and stretched her neck towards the roses.

"*Meorrw?*" she said, her little pink nose twitching as she sniffed the bouquet and looked up at me inquiringly.

I laughed. "Yes, Muesli, I'm sure some of these are for you."

FINIS

For other books by H.Y. Hanna,
please visit her website:
www.hyhanna.com

AUTHOR'S NOTE

This book follows British English spelling and usage. For a glossary of British slang and expressions used in the story, as well as special terms used in Oxford University, please visit:
www.hyhanna.com/british-slang-other-terms

BANOFFEE PIE RECIPE

<u>INGREDIENTS:</u>

(U.S. measurements are in brackets but be aware that results may vary since the recipe will not be as accurate as weighing the ingredients.)

For the base:
- 100g butter, melted (7 tablespoons)
- 250g digestive biscuits (2-1/4 cups graham cracker crumbs in the U.S. can be substituted)

For the topping:
- 1 tin of sweetened condensed milk (14 ounces) eg. Nestlé Carnation or Eagle Brand
- 100g butter, melted (7 tablespoons)
- 100g dark brown soft sugar (1/3 cup plus 2 tablespoons)
- 3 tablespoons water

- 300ml whipping cream (1-1/4 cups)
- 4 small bananas (this can be increased or decreased according to taste)
- Grated chocolate
- + Approx 9 inch loose-bottomed cake tin, greased

INSTRUCTIONS:

1) Crumble the digestive biscuits (or graham crackers) in a food processor until they become fine crumbs. Pour in the melted butter and combine well, until the crumbs stick together when pressed.

2) Press the crumbs into the bottom and sides of your cake tin. This is the base of the pie. Chill in the refrigerator for at least 10 minutes.

3) Melt the dark brown sugar and 3 tablespoons of water in a non-stick pan, over a low heat, stirring continuously until the sugar has completely dissolved. Add the remaining butter and condensed milk and bring to rapid boil, for at least 1 minute. Stir continuously until the mixture forms a thick, golden toffee sauce. (This step is important for creating a delicious, thick caramel / toffee)

4) Remove the toffee sauce from the heat and spread most of it over the pie base (reserve a small amount to keep at room temperature for drizzling over the pie at the end). Refrigerate for at least an hour – until the toffee is semi-firm. (It can be kept in

the fridge until ready to serve)

5)   Beat the whipping cream using an electric mixer, until it is very thick and forms soft peaks.

6)   Carefully remove the pie base from the cake tin and place it on a serving plate.

7)   Slice the bananas thinly. Arrange them on top of the toffee sauce in the pie, followed by a layer of the whipped cream (alternatively, you can fold them gently into the soft whipped cream, then spoon the mixture over the toffee sauce). Keep a few slices back for decoration on top.

8)   Decorate the top of the pie with the last few slices of banana and sprinkle with grated chocolate. You can also drizzle some more toffee sauce on top (you may need to rewarm it slightly if it has thickened too much to drizzle)

Tips

- Thoroughly chill the mixing bowl and beaters before whipping the cream.
- Use a vegetable peeler to make chocolate curls. Drag the peeler across the edge of a chocolate bar.

Enjoy!

ABOUT THE AUTHOR

USA Today bestselling author H.Y. Hanna writes fun mysteries filled with suspense, humour, and unexpected twists, as well as quirky characters and cats with big personalities! She is known for bringing wonderful settings to life, whether it's the historic city of Oxford, the beautiful English Cotswolds or other exciting places around the world.

After graduating from Oxford University, Hsin-Yi tried her hand at a variety of jobs, including advertising, modelling, teaching English and dog training... before returning to her first love: writing. She worked as a freelance writer for several years and has won awards for her poetry, short stories and journalism.

Hsin-Yi was born in Taiwan and has been a globe-trotter all her life, living in a variety of cultures from the UK to the Middle East, the USA to New Zealand... but is now happily settled in Perth, Western Australia, with her husband and a rescue kitty named Muesli. You can learn more about her and her books at: **www.hyhanna.com**

Sign up to her newsletter to get updates on new releases, exclusive giveaways and other book news!

https://www.hyhanna.com/newsletter

ACKNOWLEDGMENTS

Thank you as always to my wonderful beta readers: Basma Alwesh, and Rebecca Wilkinson for their tireless enthusiasm and for always finding time to squeeze me into their busy lives. Special thanks also to my proofreaders, Connie Leap and Jenn Roseton, for their eagle eyes in checking the manuscript and their helpful suggestions.

A special thank you to Olga Devitskaya for helping me check the Russian phrases and words used in the story. I am also very grateful to the talented Kim McMahan Davis of *Cinnamon and Sugar... and a Little Bit of Murder* blog, for acting as my "baking consulant" and helping me test the Banoffee Pie recipe, and providing the U.S. measurement equivalents.

And last but not least, to my wonderful husband for his patient encouragement, tireless support, and for always believing in me—I couldn't do it without him.

Made in the USA
Middletown, DE
28 September 2023